SINFUL OATH

KIRA COLE
CALLIE STEVENS

Copyright © 2024 by Kira Cole

All rights reserved.

No part of this book may be reproduced in any form or by any electronic or mechanical means, including information storage and retrieval systems, without written permission from the author, except for the use of brief quotations in a book review.

1

BIANCA

"Fuckity fuck *fuck*!" I cry as I yank my hairbrush through my tangled hair.

Wedding days are meant to be a cause for celebration. But so far, all this day has done is make me want to lock myself in the bathroom with a bottle of tequila.

It's my own stupid fault for not double-checking my alarm last night before I passed out.

I wish someone had told me how much work is involved when you're a bridesmaid. I thought all I had to do was put on the dress that my cousin Rosanna picked out and walk down the aisle and be done with it.

Oh, how wrong I was.

It was past midnight by the time I finished double-checking the RSVP list for all two hundred guests and confirming it against the seating chart and catering choices.

I don't think Rosanna even *knows* two hundred people, but we're from a big Italian family so everyone who's somewhat related to us automatically has a spot on the guest list.

The last thing I remember before my head hit the pillow was silently promising myself that I would get up early to steam my dress and wash my hair before heading to the Waldorf for the ceremony.

If only future Bianca had a time machine...

I glare at myself in the bathroom mirror, noting the dark under eye circles. I should be leaving for the venue in thirty minutes but looking at the state of my hair and face, it's going to take a miracle to transform myself into a somewhat presentable human in such a short amount of time.

I am so *fucked*.

Thankfully, Rosanna is pretty relaxed in terms of the bridesmaids' hair and makeup so I tame my long brown hair into a slick back bun, hoping it looks chic rather than greasy and apply more natural makeup that makes the blue of my eyes pop, as that's all I have time for.

As I slap on some mascara and call it a day, I head back out into the main living space of my Manhattan studio, cursing at the state of the room.

It's not a very large space so it doesn't take much for it to get out of control, but the empty pizza boxes littering the coffee table along with discarded seating charts and clothes on every surface, make me cringe.

I'm better than this, but I put it down to wedding stress.

"I'm eloping when my time comes," I mutter as I wade through the countless lists of guests and registry items, searching for my dress which I eventually find slung over the back of the couch.

"Shit, I completely forgot to steam it," I groan.

The material is fairly forgiving but it would look better if I could get out the huge crease down the center of the dress before I walk down the aisle.

"I'm going to murder past Bianca," I mutter under my breath as I toss the dress over my arm.

By the time I've collected my heels and packed my

dress into a garment bag and sorted another bag with overnight things, my makeup, and my trusted pair of Converse to change into later, I only have two minutes to get into my car and start driving across to the venue.

Muttering yet more curse words in a mixture of English and Italian as I search for my keys, eventually finding them tucked under an old Chinese takeout container on the countertop, I dart out of my apartment and start taking the stairs two at a time.

I can already feel a thin film of sweat building on my top lip and the back of my neck as I throw open the front door to the building and dart around the side to where my Mercedes is parked.

Throwing my bag onto the passenger seat, I slide behind the wheel and press the *start* button.

Nothing happens.

"Oh, please. Don't do this to me," I moan, pressing it again.

The dashboard remains dark, and the engine is yet to roar to life as I continue to press the ignition.

"No, no, no!" I cry out, slamming my hands against the steering wheel.

Pulling my phone out of my back pocket, I check the time.

I am officially running behind schedule, and by the time I call for an Uber and get to the Waldorf, Rosanna will already be walking down the aisle, and I'll be on my way to the burning pits of hell for being so disorganized on the biggest day of my cousin's life.

Opening up my Uber app, I quickly order a car while praying that my cousin has chosen today of all days to not be on time.

"I'm going to have to change in the backseat." I sigh, looking over at the green garment bag.

My app says the car is six minutes away, so I climb out of my Mercedes, grab my things and head around the corner to wait for my ride.

The sight of the silver Prius pulling up to the curb has me sagging with relief, and I quickly climb into the back and shove a handful of twenties into the center console.

The driver tries to catch them and hand them back. "Ma'am, you've already paid—"

"I'm running late to a wedding and need to change. This is to make sure you don't creep on me in the mirror, got it?" I look into the rearview mirror, letting my fiery Italian side show, the side which often makes men run for the hills.

The driver's eyes widen, but he nods.

"Eyes on the road, and we won't have a problem." I open up my garment bag and get to work.

As we pull up outside the Waldorf, I'm slipping on my gold sandals and scrambling to get out of the Uber before it's even come to a complete stop.

"Thanks for not being a creep!" I call over my shoulder as I dart across the sidewalk and head inside the hotel.

The wedding is being held on the private rooftop, so I make my way across the bustling lobby toward the elevators at the far end.

Throwing my bag over my shoulder, I glance up to notice the elevator doors on the left are open.

"Wait!" I cry as I note a tall man in a black suit step into the elevator. I bend down and slip off my gold heels, grabbing them in my right hand before breaking out into a run. "Hold it!"

The carpet is scratchy against my bare feet, and I'm suddenly aware that I'm in a backless dress with no bra, meaning my boobs are threatening to make an appearance, but I don't care. I need to get on the elevator.

I throw my hand out and manage to stop the doors from completely closing.

They spring open, and I step inside, nothing short of fuming as I glance at the dark haired stranger leaning against the back wall.

"What the hell?" My breathing is coming in heavy pants as I bend down to slip my shoes back on.

Even in my heels, he still towers over me and is just as broad, his arms practically bursting out of his jacket sleeves.

If I wasn't so exhausted or pissed off, I might have taken a second to admire him.

"Sorry, I'm in a hurry." He shrugs those delicious shoulders.

His voice is gruff like sandpaper, and a shiver runs down my spine as he finally looks down at me with an eyebrow lifted. His perfectly styled hair is a deep rich brown, a perfect mirror to the eyes that are boring into me with such intensity that, for a moment, I forget why I'm annoyed.

"Obviously, so am I," I huff, folding my arms across my chest and looking away before my cheeks have a chance to turn beetroot.

I lean forward and press the button for the rooftop terrace, despite it already being lit.

"You're here for the wedding, I assume?"

I nod, keeping my eyes forward, though I can feel his stare burning into my skin.

"Bride or groom?"

"Bride," I mutter, still annoyed. "You?"

"Groom." I can't help but glance back up at him, and he

grins, a dimple appearing in his right cheek, softening his stone-like features.

He leans against the wall of the elevator and looks at me with a smirk. "Maybe later you'll let me buy you a drink?"

"It's an open bar."

He chuckles. "Ouch."

"Besides, I'll likely be busy with all my bridesmaid duties."

His eyebrows lift again as he glances down at my dress.

This time, I can't stop my cheeks from burning as he eyes the gold silk gown that clings to every curve of my body, and compliments my tanned skin and mahogany hair.

"You're a bridesmaid?"

"The bride is my cousin."

"Is that so..." He rolls his lower lip between his teeth.

My eyes fall to his full lips, and the air leaves my lungs as I watch as his tongue darts out to moisten them.

I swallow, my throat feeling thick.

"Are you family or..." I let my question trail off, partly due to the fact that my brain seems to be malfunctioning from being in such close quarters with a man of his size and looks.

"Yes. The groom and I are very...*close*." There's a certain hint of amusement in his eyes as he speaks.

It must be a joke I'm missing, perhaps from past college days spent in a frat house on Greek Row.

As the doors slide open revealing the packed rooftop terrace where the ceremony is being held, he offers me a last wink before stepping out. "Well, enjoy the wedding."

As he disappears into the crowd of guests, I roll my eyes, but I'm soon distracted by the sight of the terrace.

It's almost midday, and the sun is beaming down over the guests, casting the space in a warm glow. Arches of soft pink peonies and white roses line the aisle, with rows of white chairs on either side, with gold ribbons tied to the back.

I take a moment to look around at all the guests, many already holding glasses of champagne that are being carried around on trays by waiters.

"It's breathtaking, isn't it?"

I jump at the sound of my father's voice as he appears beside me, wrapping a comforting arm around my shoulder.

"Ah, *Papino*," I sigh, glancing up at my father.

His salt and pepper hair is styled neatly, and he's wearing a crisp linen suit that I had picked out for him. "You look very dashing," I tease. "I'm glad I didn't miss anything! It's been one thing after another, what with my alarm not going off, then my car wouldn't start "

"*Bambina...*" My father takes my hand, squeezing tightly.

I turn toward him. A deep crease forms between his eyebrows, and his mouth is pulled down into a frown.

"Something's troubling you." I scan his face for any indication of what's wrong.

Emilio Bellucci is not a man who shows much feeling, but his blue eyes are filled with nothing but sadness as he looks around at the bustling terrace.

"Yes." He avoids my eyes.

"What is it, *Papino*? Is it Rosanna? Is she okay?" I glance around, my heart sinking in my chest.

Has she had second thoughts? Has the groom?

"No, it's nothing to do with Rosanna."

I let out a breath, relaxing just a little. If the bride and groom are still going through with the wedding, any other issue will be trivial.

"Then what is it? I really need to go and check on

Rosanna before the ceremony starts. We are already a few minutes late."

"Come with me, we shouldn't discuss this so publicly."

Taking me by the arm, he leads me around the edge of the terrace and through a door that opens onto a private room that, by the looks of it, is being used as a cloakroom by the wedding guests.

My father takes my bag from me and places it on the floor beside a rail of coats.

"I've not been completely honest with you, *bambina*."

The way my father is refusing to look me in the eye has my stomach fluttering with nerves.

He's not a man of many words, and we don't have the closest of relationships, but we have always been honest with one another no matter what.

So, the fact that he's in distress over whatever it is he has failed to tell me has a lump forming in my throat.

"What is it, *Papino*?" I press, my voice barely above a whisper.

I watch as his shoulders sag, as his mouth opens and closes once, twice, before he lifts his eyes to mine.

"This isn't Rosanna's wedding."

"Okay..." A laugh threatens to escape my lips.

Is my father playing some sort of joke?

I've spent weeks going over guest lists and catering options with Rosanna. "Whose wedding is it?"

But the way my father's expression turns from one of guilt to sympathy has my knees almost buckling beneath me.

"It's yours."

2

ALEXEI

The first time I set eyes on my blushing bride was meant to be at the end of the aisle before we exchanged vows, not in the small confined space of an elevator.

Bride or Groom... I shake my head, chuckling, as I remember her asking me.

It's clear she had no idea who I am or who today is really for.

But I'm glad I got to have a moment alone with her before she has a chance to hate me when she learns the truth.

I didn't expect her to be as beautiful as she is, with the most luscious, rich brown hair and the brightest blue eyes. It didn't help that the gold slinky dress she was wearing brought out the warm hues in her skin and hugged every inch of her body.

Just the thought of her soft curves has me adjusting myself as I scan the terrace in search of her. Eventually, she appears from a side door behind her father, rage almost a wave emanating from her body.

"This should be good."

I catch her eye across the crowded terrace and watch with amusement as she shoots daggers in my direction.

She's clearly in the middle of an argument with her father. From the scowl that's plastered across her face, I'm guessing she's been caught up on today's agenda.

Getting married to a woman who's not only a stranger to me, but who's also the daughter of a rival mafia boss, should have my blood running cold. Legally binding myself to the Bellucci family puts not only myself at risk, but my brothers too.

But I owe Emilio Bellucci a debt.

He had valuable information about the Gilanto family. They destroyed my family.

And I'd finally found the last piece of information to destroy them once and for all.

So, I took the deal. The information Emilio had in exchange for protection for his family. His *daughter*.

I used what he gave me to enact my revenge. I tried to wipe them all out. I failed.

I need them gone. All of them.

Bianca storms toward me.

I let my eyes take her in—the way her dress hugs her shapely legs and how her full breasts bounce with each step as she closes the distance between us.

The fact that in less than an hour she's going to be legally bound to me has me adjusting myself *again*.

I guess I'm going to enjoy marriage more than I originally thought.

"Here we go." I chuckle under my breath as I lift my eyes back to Bianca's.

"You *knew*!" she spits, her blue eyes flashing as she slams her fists into my chest.

I reach for her small wrists, holding her in place as I

stare down at her. I don't fail to notice the way goosebumps break out over her arms at my touch, the way her mouth parts in surprise as she blinks up at me.

I can't help the smirk that tugs at my lips as I take her in.

"Trust me, *kisa*, this was not part of my plan," I murmur, stroking her wrists with my thumbs.

"What did you call me?" She bares her teeth at me.

Fuck, she's wild, and I'm loving every second. "*Kisa*. It means, pussycat."

"*Pussycat?*"

"You are hissing just like one, but your claws are not sharp enough to do any real damage."

She yanks her hands out of my grip and places them on her hips, dragging my attention once more to her body.

"You don't get to look at me like that either."

"Like what?" I fold my arms across my chest. I catch her eyes flicking to my biceps, and this time, I let a grin break out on my face.

"Like *that*."

"Can't a man admire his wife?"

Bianca's eyes flutter closed for a moment, as if she's trying to compose herself, which only adds to my amusement.

I'm not used to women fighting back, and I must say I'm very much enjoying getting a rise out of her.

"I. Am. Not. Your. Wife."

"Not yet, but whether you like it or not, in about half an hour you're going to be." I smirk. "I quite like the sound of Bianca *Koslov*."

"I'm not marrying you. And I sure as hell am not changing my name."

"You don't have a choice."

Bianca opens her mouth as if she's about to snap at me

once more, but then her eyes glisten and her lower lip trembles, and I know reality is starting to set in for her.

I fight the urge to reach for her, comfort her, when I know ultimately this marriage is nothing more than business.

Neither one of us really wants to get married here and now, but this is something that needs to happen.

And I can't afford to let feelings get in the way, so I keep my hands to myself and plaster a look of indifference on my face.

"If you want answers, *kisa*, speak to your father. He's the one who agreed to this deal."

"Oh, believe me, I'll be having words with my father. So, you can put this ridiculous notion that there will be a wedding today on hold until he explains what the hell is going on."

"Don't take too long, the wedding breakfast is being served in an hour."

Bianca offers me one last scowl before storming past me, her shoulder brushing against my own.

My breath catches as a sweet jasmine scent hits my nose, and I have to bite back a moan at the thought of burying my face in her hair, inhaling that scent as I sink myself deep inside her—

My brother Dimitri chuckles, slapping me on the shoulder and snapping me out of my fantasy. "She's a handful. Sure you know what you're doing?"

I clear my throat, shifting my weight between my feet as I watch Bianca storm back over to Emilio, her slender arms waving about as she rips into him.

"I know exactly what I'm doing."

My youngest brother, Danil, smirks. "I don't think I've ever known a woman *not* to throw herself at you, Alexei.

How does it feel to know your soon-to-be wife rejected you straight out the bat?"

"I like a challenge."

Mikhail laughs. "He's dying inside."

I roll my eyes and turn around to face all three of my brothers, shooting Mikhail a glare.

"Can't you all go and bother someone else?"

My brothers glance between each other and grin.

Sometimes, I hate being the oldest. It meant I had to be the one to grow up, to take over as head of the family while they got to cling to the last of their childhood innocence for a while longer.

I don't resent them for it. It wasn't their fault that our parents were taken from us. But I have a responsibility to them, to this family, and that's what I have to keep reminding myself of.

The only reason I'm about to sign my life away to the daughter of a rival crime boss is because it got me the information I need to finally get my revenge. For me and for my brothers.

I have a duty to my family, no matter how irritating they are.

Mikhail glances around the busy terrace.

"Whoever organized this little get-together did a good job. I'm thoroughly enjoying the open bar." He raises a half-empty glass of scotch that I hadn't noticed he was holding, his shirtsleeve rising slightly to show off his tattooed arm.

"It's not even midday." I reach for the drink.

Mikhail scoffs, rolling his eyes at me as he steps out of reach. "We're celebrating, brother."

I look to Dimitri for backup as the second eldest, but he only shrugs.

As I take my brothers in, it is clear that we all look similar in our dark suits.

Many of the guests here today are keeping their distance, not because they know who we truly are but because of the intimidating presence my brothers and I give off. If only they knew of the countless weapons we each have stashed on our persons on the off chance any unexpected guests decide to cause trouble...

In our line of work, you can never be too careful.

I shake my head at my brothers. "Try and stay out of trouble."

Mikhail and Danil simply grin at one another before stalking away in the direction of the bar, leaving me alone with Dimitri.

"Mom and Dad would've been proud," Dimitri says under his breath.

I glance sidelong at my brother, my throat thick as I think of our parents.

"Not only for honoring your promise to Emilio, but for how you've kept everything together since..."

I bow my head, hating the shadow that is cast at the mention of my parents.

They should be here, and even though it's been almost a decade since we lost them, it still feels like yesterday.

The nightmares haven't gone away yet. The grief still cripples me sometimes. Just like it's doing now.

"Thanks."

"Don't you wish it could be different?"

I turn to face my brother. "What do you mean?"

He gestures around to the decorated rooftop. "That your wedding would be with someone you..."

"Someone I love?"

He shrugs, folding his arms across his broad chest.

"Perhaps. But this deal with Emilio is more important. I have to honor it. Besides, you know as well as I do that anyone we bring into our lives needs to be aware of the risks. And do I really want to risk yet another person I love?"

"True. Especially since even with the information Emilio offered us, we still haven't taken down Mario."

I flex my fingers at the mention of the head of the Gilanto family. The last man standing. The one man I want dead more than anything. "The information was useful, even if Mario got away."

"It just seems to me that Emilio's getting a sweet deal here. Our protection, along with security for his daughter, when the one man responsible for destroying our family still runs free."

"A deal is a deal. He delivered, we failed to bank on it."

"Maybe we should've asked for Mario's head on a platter," Dimitri mutters, his jaw flexing.

"If anyone is going to kill Mario, it's me."

Dimitri holds his hands up.

I clap him on the shoulder, appreciating his concern.

Dimitri tilts his chin to somewhere behind me. "Apparently, we need to step it up. If we're not careful, Emilio might be the one getting killed today."

Frowning, my hand flies to my holster as I follow his line of sight. I let out a huff of a laugh as Emilio gets backed into a corner by his daughter.

"I think I may have to go and rescue my soon-to-be father-in-law from my bride-to-be before she murders him."

Dimitri laughs. "It wouldn't be a true Koslov wedding without a murder."

3

BIANCA

I'm living a nightmare.

This can't actually be happening. I can't be about to be wed to the Don of one of the most powerful crime families in New York.

Is he even a Don if he is Bratva, instead of Italian mafia?

Doesn't matter. Alexei Koslov cannot be my future husband. He can't be my future *anything*.

"*Papino*, how could you do this?" I swallow the lump in my throat.

I'm about to be married off to a complete and utter stranger.

"You should have warned me." I blink back tears.

"We needed an alliance with the Koslovs, *bambina*. For protection against the Gilantos."

A hysterical sob escapes me.

Of course it comes down to business. It always does with my father. Every time I think I might be his top priority, I'm always proved wrong...

When will I learn?

"And there was no other way?" My voice cracks. "Does

it have to be through marriage? I-I could go and work for them like I do with you. I could...I could do anything else! *Papino, please.*"

My eyes are stinging with tears as I look at my father.

Part of me is glad to see the guilt etched across his face, but knowing he didn't make such a bargain lightly does little to make me feel better.

If anything it only makes me feel worse.

What has my father gotten himself into that meant he had to sign my life away to the Koslovs?

I'm only twenty-three and nowhere near ready for marriage. Hell, my last relationship during my senior year of college turned out to be a complete dumpster fire, and I vowed to take a break from men for the foreseeable future.

"No, there was no other way, *tesorino*." My father sighs. "You are my only child. I had to offer them something of great value to me."

My chest tightens at his words—at the hidden meaning beneath them.

Only child.

My mother died giving birth to me, and my father has never remarried. He lost the love of his life the day I came into the world, and although he never blamed me for *Mamma's* death, I carry the mantle of guilt heavily on my shoulders.

Perhaps this is my way of finally making it up to him.

"You have to know this wasn't an easy decision for me, Bianca." He reaches for my hand. "I hope you know I'm not handing you over to the Koslovs lightheartedly. You are my world, and I'll do whatever I have to in order to keep you safe."

"This doesn't feel like keeping me safe, *Papino*." My

eyes fall to the floor. "It feels like I'm being fed to the wolves."

My father flinches, and my chest tightens.

But I should be hurt for a minute or two. I deserve it, don't I? I was forced to organize a wedding for months that I didn't know was my own until I got here.

I was betrayed by my whole family. And now I'm being given or sold for something that has nothing to do with me.

Does no one care?

"They will not harm you. I made it pretty clear to them that I wouldn't tolerate it."

"Is that meant to be reassuring?"

My father glances over his shoulder at the crowd of guests who will soon enough start to wonder where the hell the bride is. Little do they know she's in the corner about to commit a felony against her own father if he doesn't start talking.

Or maybe they all know and are avoiding looking at me because they pity me.

"Come with me, *stellina*." My father guides me back into the makeshift cloakroom, away from prying eyes.

"Do all the guests know whose wedding they're here for? Am I the only one not in on the truth?" I shake my head. "What about Rosanna? Was she in on it this whole time?"

"They know."

I'm about to throw up.

The hours I spent pouring over seating charts and food choices for my cousin's wedding, and Rosanna won't be the one walking down the aisle toward the love of her life.

I'll be the one walking toward a life sentence, because there's no other way to describe it.

My entire body is shaking so badly that I have to reach out and cling to one of the coat racks to steady myself.

The humiliation and betrayal are almost crushing me. And it doesn't help that Alexei Koslov's smirk when he realized I had found out the truth is playing on repeat in my head.

Asshole.

"You could have been straight with me from the start, *Papino*. Making me think I'm a guest when I'm really the one getting married is low, even for you."

"I couldn't risk you not showing up." He bows his head. "You overthink things, *bambina*."

"For good reason. Why couldn't you trust me enough to tell me? I'm not an unreasonable person. If you have a good reason for this marriage, then I deserved to know. I deserved to have the time to understand, to come to terms with it."

I look down at the floor, trying to stop the knot from forming in my throat. "After all this time, have I not proven myself? That I care about this family? I know what's expected of me, *Papino*. After all, I'm your only heir."

"You're right." My father sighs, rubbing at his jaw as he looks at me with pity in his eyes. "I should have gone about this another way, and I apologize for that."

"What exactly is being asked of me here, *Papino*? Do I just need to sign the marriage license and be done with it?"

He shakes his head.

I shake mine in return. "Of course not... It's not enough that I have to legally bind myself to a stranger, but I have to sign away my freedom too? You're making me give up my entire life, *Papino*. Everything I've worked so hard to build for myself..."

We both look at each other for a moment, and my shoulders sag with the weight of what's to come.

My life is being ripped out from beneath me, and there's nothing I can do about it.

"I don't even have Zara with me."

"*Bambina—*"

"No. It's my goddamn wedding day, and my best friend isn't even here! How fucked up is that?" My arms are flying around me now. "And how do you think she's going to feel when she finds out I got married without her even *knowing*?"

I laugh. "Of course, how could she if *I* didn't even know? How pathetic is that?"

"I couldn't risk you finding out. I had to pretend it was a family-only affair to stop you from learning the truth and bolting."

I stare into my father's blue eyes, so much like my own.

But he is nothing like me. He doesn't care. Did he ever?

There's no way I'm walking away from today without a ring on my finger. Emilio Bellucci always gets his way, no matter what.

"I hope you know what you are doing, *Papino*. And I hope this is worth losing your daughter over."

My father lets out a long sigh.

"I'm sorry, *bambina*." He reaches down to press a soft kiss to my cheek. "But this is the only way."

"Then let's get this over with." I fight the tears that are threatening to spill down my cheeks.

The last thing I want is for Alexei to see me crying. I can't show any weakness to this man and risk him using it against me.

My father leads me back over to the elevator and presses the button for the penthouse suite where my cousin Rosanna, the fake bride, is waiting to dress me. Her blue eyes are shining with tears as she rushes over to me and takes me by the hand.

"I'm so sorry, Bianca," Rosanna mumbles as she leads me into the luxurious bedroom.

My eyes fly to the white garment bag hanging on the back of the bathroom door and my knees almost give out beneath me.

"I wanted to tell you all this time, but your father made me promise... I'm so sorry."

I'm barely listening to Rosanna as I walk across the bedroom and run my fingertips over the garment bag. My stomach is in knots as reality starts to set in, and I fight the urge to run into the bathroom and hurl my guts up.

All I can think about is everything that I missed out on.

This is not *my* wedding. This is someone else's wedding that I planned and am now taking over.

None of this was done with me in mind. None of this is my choice. From my dress all the way to my fucking husband. This is not how it was supposed to be.

My wedding day was meant to be filled with happiness and *love*, but those things feel so far away.

My eyes flutter closed, and I picture Alexei's face as he towered over me in the elevator, his dark eyes devouring me as a smirk tugged at his full lips.

Something flutters in my stomach, and my eyes fly open as goosebumps break out over my skin.

Alexei Koslov is dangerous, and I would do well to remember that.

The moment I put on the wedding dress, I am just another pawn in his twisted game. And I'll play my part well.

"Your dad's an intimidating man. I didn't know how to tell him no." Rosanna continues to babble on, filling the silence with empty apologies as I stare and stare at the garment bag. "The dress will look just as lovely on you…"

I know she's only trying to ease her own guilt in the role she played in this, but I'm too tired to care. Too hurt.

In truth, I loved this dress, for Rosanna. It suited her curvy frame perfectly, and the strapless detail with her flaming red hair draping around her shoulders would have been breathtaking.

I never for a second pictured myself putting it on and walking down the aisle. Marriage was so far in the future for me, something I thought would happen when I felt ready to commit fully to someone I loved, someone who I wanted to build a life with.

Instead, it's moments away, and the man meeting me at the altar is one of the most powerful men in the city, and a complete and total stranger.

"I guess I better get dressed." I reach for the zipper with shaking hands.

I let Rosanna fix my hair, keeping with the slicked back updo, and touch up my makeup. I can barely look at myself in the mirror as she works, not wanting to see the haunted look in my eyes.

The moment I step into my wedding dress and Rosanna fixes the zipper, I feel as if the last bit of air has been ripped from my lungs, and I won't ever be able to take a full breath again.

I clutch at my stomach, my heart racing so fast I might pass out at any moment.

"You look beautiful, Bianca." Rosanna finishes fastening me into the dress.

I say nothing, my throat thick with tears as I wait for her to pull on the silky gold dress that I arrived in.

I lose count of how many times she apologizes for the

role she played. She shouldn't be the one walking with me to the elevator where *Papino* is waiting, or the one to stand beside me at the altar to take my flowers as I exchange my vows.

That was always meant to be Zara's role—my best friend since freshman year of college. She's my rock, my person, and she's not here.

How can I explain all of this to her without risking her safety?

I bite down on the inside of my cheek as I take my father's arm and step out of the elevator, my legs threatening to buckle with every step.

As we round the corner, I let out a whimper as every seat is now occupied, and I'm standing at the end of an aisle leading to my future husband.

I lift my eyes to find Alexei staring at me, a smirk tugging at his lips as his eyes flick over me.

My cheeks heat as he takes in my strapless dress that clings to my waist before fanning out into a long train.

I can't deny he's an extremely attractive man, with his broad stature and chiseled jawline. But there's also an underlying hint of danger that radiates from him. It's there, behind every smirk, every stolen glance.

Why do I feel like this man is going to be more trouble than he's worth?

4

ALEXEI

I try to ignore the feeling of hundreds of eyes on me as I stand at the altar with my three brothers beside me. I'm not usually one to be the center of attention, especially when I'm about to recite vows to a woman I've shared only a handful of words with.

But I made a promise.

And I *never* break my promises.

So, I stand patiently, waiting for Bianca to appear.

Dimitri leans into my ear. "You don't think she's made a run for it, do you?"

I shoot him a glare.

"Maybe she took one look at me and realized she's marrying the wrong brother?"

"Trust me, you wouldn't have a clue how to handle a woman like Bianca," I mutter under my breath.

"I'm not sure you do either, brother."

I roll my eyes, though part of me thinks he might be right.

Bianca is all soft curves and big eyes, but the moment

she opens her mouth... Fuck, it would send any normal man running for the hills.

But not me.

Most women I've encountered tend to have no clue about who or what I truly am, and I like to keep it that way for everyone's sake. But even without them knowing the truth behind my family name, many choose not to push me. They do exactly as I say in order to keep me happy.

I'm not ignorant of the fact that I radiate power and wealth, two things that many crave. But in my case, they bear consequences. And not ones they can deal with.

So, when Bianca did the opposite, challenged my intentions and spoke to me as if we were equals, it sent such a thrill through my body.

I'm still finding it hard to shake the arousal as I picture her plump lips pulled back in a snarl as she rips into me.

I can't seem to fight the smirk that tugs at my lips as I picture us later in the honeymoon suite.

She'll definitely give me a run for my money then.

Dimitri's arm lands on my shoulder. "Here she comes."

I turn and glance down the aisle at the same time a string quartet starts playing the entrance music.

My breath catches as my eyes land on Bianca, clutching her father's arm, as she stares at me.

I let my eyes trail over her bare shoulders, taking in the strapless silk dress that barely contains her full breasts, before hugging her waist and fanning out into a full skirt.

She's breathtaking.

And she's *mine*.

Her cheeks grow a beautiful shade of pink under the weight of my stare, which adds a certain innocence to her complexion.

I'm well aware of the fact that I'm ten years older than

her, and that I'm stealing a moment from her that most girls dream of since childhood. But in order to survive in my world, you have to make sacrifices.

Our eyes stay locked as Bianca makes her way down the aisle, which has been laid with a pale pink carpet to match the flowers. Her full lips are parted, and I know that the moment she stands beside me she's going to make another snide comment.

And I can't fucking wait.

"Here we go." Dimitri chuckles under his breath as Bianca and Emilio eventually reach the end of the aisle.

I glance at Emilio who nods his head once before taking his daughter's hand and offering it to me.

As I go to reach for Bianca's hand, she snatches it away, choosing to pick up the heavy skirt of her dress and move so that she's facing me.

"Forgive me, I didn't have a chance to write my own vows." She shoots me a glare.

Laughter titillates through the small crowd which only deepens her scowl.

"I took the liberty of writing some for you." I grin, reaching into the inside pocket of my jacket and pulling out a sheet of paper. "I think you'll find them satisfactory."

She frowns as she unfolds the paper and scans the vows that I jotted down for her while she was changing.

"Are you kidding?" She snorts. "What is this, the nineteen-fifties? There's no way in hell I'm saying any of this."

"You're welcome to make a few changes, but I suggest you stick to the gist of what I've written." I smile at her, but I know she can take a hint.

Bianca's blue eyes meet mine for a moment, and her cheeks instantly redden, and I know she's picturing what I mentioned in there.

As if she can sense my own thoughts, she clears her throat and looks back down at the vows.

"How about I agree to listen to you occasionally and that we have mutual respect for each other?"

"I guess that will do. For now." I raise my eyebrow. "But that second paragraph—"

"Is not going to happen."

Dimitri stifles his laughter next to me.

I bend down so that my lips are almost brushing her ear.

"The same would apply to you too, *solnyshka*. I'll be more than happy to take care of your every need and desire..."

The sound of her breath catching makes me grin.

I straighten and let my eyes flick down to her breasts which are rising and falling quickly as she tries to calm herself.

"Don't even think for a second that I'm wearing a ring."

"That's fine, *kisa*. Everyone will already know who you belong to."

She shoots me a glare that makes me bite the inside of my cheek to stop from smiling.

I like how easy it is to rile her up.

"Let's get this over with." She turns to face the very patient minister who seems rather concerned by the nature of this wedding.

Round one to me.

The moment Bianca Bellucci signs the marriage certificate in front of all two hundred guests and is officially declared my wife is a moment that is burned into my brain forever. Not because of how romantic or heartwarming it was, but because the moment she slams the pen down onto the table, she gets to her feet, storms off down the aisle, grabbing a rogue bottle of champagne from an ice bucket on the way and disappears inside the elevator without a backward glance.

I get to my feet, trying my best to hide my amusement at Bianca's attitude, and address the guests.

"Time to celebrate!" I exclaim, clapping my hands together. "If you all would like to make your way down to the ballroom."

I plaster a smile on my face as I watch the guests get to their feet and start to file out of the rows of chairs. Many of the faces are unfamiliar to me, though I know Emilio would have requested their attendance for a reason.

My marriage to Bianca sends a message. Two of the most powerful families in New York are legally bound together. You mess with one, you mess with both.

Dimitri hugs me. "I wonder how long it will take for Mario to learn of your wonderful news."

I shoot him a warning glare.

"Keep your mouth shut, Dimitri. You don't know who might be listening here."

I scan each of the faces of the guests that pass me as I make my way down the aisle, my brothers filling in behind me.

Looking to the corners of the rooftop, I catch the eyes of the only other people I invited to share my special day. Feliks, Micha, and my cousin Anton. They nod at me in turn, and I relax a little, knowing they got my back.

This may be a wedding, but that's never been enough to halt the workings of the mafia.

As we near the elevator, I turn to Dmitri. "Keep your eyes on Bianca."

She disappeared without a trace of security, and I don't like it.

I make a silent vow not to be so careless again.

She might not like being married to me, we may have nothing between us other than a piece of paper, but that won't stop me from ensuring she's protected at all costs. I have a promise to keep.

He frowns at me. "Isn't that your job, brother?"

"Just do as I ask." I step into the elevator.

Dimitri chuckles and steps in beside me, along with Mikhail and Danil, who presses the button for the ballroom.

"Congrats, brother." Mikhail slaps me on the shoulder.

Danil looks at me. "What's the plan now? When is she moving into the family digs?"

"Tomorrow."

Danil chokes, and Mikhail has to slap him on the back.

"I was joking."

"She's my wife, Danil." I tap my fingers against my thighs as the elevator goes down the ten floors.

"On paper," Mikhail reminds me.

"She has even more of a target on her head now that she's bound to me." I fold my arms across my chest. "I didn't think I would need to explain that to you, but so be it. She's part of this family now, and you protect her like she's one of our own, got it?"

I look each of my brothers in the eye. "Got it?"

"*Da, brat.*"

"And while she's living under our roof, you will treat her with the utmost respect. Regardless of everything else, she is still my wife. Am I clear?"

"*Da, brat.*"

"Good, now let's go and enjoy my wedding," I state as the elevator doors slide open.

Dimitri keeps to my side as we scan the ballroom.

It's like a florist blew up in here. It's perhaps a little much for my taste.

My eyes land on Bianca, and I can't help but smile.

She's holding a glass of champagne, not the bottle anymore, as she gently sways to the music with a vibrant redhead wearing the gold dress Bianca was wearing only a few hours ago.

"That must be the cousin," I mutter under my breath to Dimitri.

"Couldn't you have married her?" He smirks. "She seems more...mellow."

"Not a fan of redheads." I grin, deciding to finally approach my wife, hoping the champagne has calmed her down a little. Though by the way she glares at me as I approach her, I might be wrong.

"What do you want?"

I glance at the terrified redhead and offer her the warmest smile I can muster.

"May I have a moment alone with my wife?"

She nods, scurrying away, leaving me alone with Bianca in the middle of the dance floor.

"Care to dance?" I offer her my hand.

Bianca glances down at it and wrinkles her nose.

"You really do wonders for a man's ego." I chuckle, tucking my hands into my pockets.

"Surprise marriage or not, it takes more than a smile to win me over, *gattino*." She grins. "I need another drink."

"Little cat, huh? I'll take it, *kisa*." I wink at her. "Now allow me."

She rolls her eyes but falls into step beside me as we wade through the guests toward the bar at the far end of the ballroom.

I lift one finger to the bartender. "Champagne, please."

Bianca frowns at me. "You're not having one?"

"Not tonight. I think it's best if one of us remains sober."

"If you say so." She takes the glass from the bartender, draining half of it in one go.

I'm mesmerized as her throat bobs, and I can't help but picture running my tongue along the smooth column of her neck.

This woman is *intoxicating*.

"I'm not really a bad guy." I bow my head so I can whisper in her ear.

Bianca rolls her eyes as she glances at me.

"Some women would think me quite a catch, you know…"

"Perhaps if their standards were on the floor…" She takes another sip of her drink.

"I'm not the villain here, *ptichka*."

She frowns, and I grin as she briefly loses hold over her stone-like composure.

"Oh yeah?" Her eyes search my face. "How many weapons have you got stashed on you right now?" Her eyebrow quirks as she waits for my answer.

I give her my most seductive tone. "Only one, *solnyshka*…"

She slaps my arm as a soft pink tinge appears across her chest.

Fuck, she's thinking about my cock, and that makes it twitch.

She looks at anywhere but my face. "I'm being serious."

I reach for my jacket, pulling it open to expose the inside pocket where there is a very clear outline of a handgun.

"One." I pull open the other side. "Two."

Bianca's throat bobs as I reach to pull up my trouser leg where I have a knife strapped to my calf, the tip of the blade outlined beneath my sock.

"Three."

"Were you planning on using any of those if I said no?" Her eyes never stray from my jacket, as if she's trying to imagine me pulling a gun on her.

"You can't seriously be asking me that?"

Does she really see me as that much of a monster?

I try to ignore the way my chest tightens at the thought, keeping my expression neutral as she fumbles for an answer.

She shrugs her slim shoulders.

"You're a stranger to me, Alexei, I don't know what you're capable of."

I exhale, running my hands through my hair as I regard Bianca's cold expression.

"I made a vow to protect you, and I plan to honor it with my life."

"Hmm..." She presses her lips into a thin line.

I want to know what she's thinking. "Many would think such a declaration to be highly romantic."

"Perhaps if the man speaking wasn't a sadist."

I can't help but laugh as she scowls at me once more.

"In all seriousness, *ptichka*, whether you like it or not, we are married. And how that marriage goes is up to you. I've laid my cards out on the table, play them however you like."

"You called me that before. What does it mean?"

"*Ptichka?*"

She nods.

"It means little bird."

Bianca rolls her eyes.

"I meant it when I said I want to protect you. But as for how this whole marriage thing can go between us, give it some thought."

She tilts her head, almost as if she is assessing me, before she nods once and storms past me, clearly annoyed.

I want to follow her, to let her know... What?

It doesn't matter because Dimitri approaches with a grim look on his face.

I frown. "What is it?"

"Gilanto is pissed." My brother glances around in case any prying ears are listening.

"Word got back to Feliks. He had a guy trailing Mario's new second. He's well aware of who betrayed the information about his family's whereabouts. Emilio better get the hell out of town while he has a chance. Otherwise, he may just find himself with a bullet lodged in his skull."

"I'll take care of Emilio. Make sure Feliks and the others are on alert. I don't want this to get back to Bianca."

"Of course." Dimitri nods before disappearing into the crowd.

I take a deep breath and turn around, leaning against the bar as I scan the room for my new father-in-law. I thought perhaps we would have a few weeks before any threat would be made on Emilio's life, but it turns out the Gilantos wait for no one.

I find Emilio nursing a glass of scotch at one of the tables, his eyes trained on Bianca who has gone back to dancing with her cousin who seems to be moments away from breaking down into tears.

Sliding into the vacant seat beside my father-in-law, I clasp a hand on his shoulder. "It's time, Emilio."

He says nothing, lifting his glass to his lips as he watches Bianca.

It kills me, for both of them, but this needs to happen. And the sooner, the better. For all our sakes. "Mario knows."

After he drains his glass, we both get to our feet.

There's nothing but agony in Emilio's blue eyes as he glances once more at Bianca before looking at me.

"Take good care of my daughter." His eyes are pleading. "Promise me on your life that you won't let any harm come to her."

I get my right hand over my heart. "*Klyanus' svoyey chest'yu.*"

He frowns at me.

"I swear on my honor. Or should I say, *lo giuro sul mio onore.*"

I smile a bit as I reach out my hand, and Emilio grasps it and nods, his shoulders sagging.

"She's all I have," he chokes out.

"I will protect her with my life."

5

BIANCA

"*Bambina.*"

I whirl, almost spilling my fresh glass of champagne all over my father.

"*Papino?*"

"I have to go."

I frown as my father's eyes start to glisten. I'm frozen for a moment, wondering if the alcohol is making me hallucinate.

Is Emilio Bellucci about to cry?

"Don't be sad, *Papino.*" I sigh, reaching for his hand. "I know you didn't have a choice, and while it might take me a while to come to terms with this... situation, I still love you."

My father nods, taking my hand in both of his and squeezing tightly. "I'm sorry it had to be like this."

"I appreciate that."

His face remains riddled with devastation.

I'm taken aback by the level of emotion on my father's face.

He's not normally one to show such feelings, and the sight of him like this is making my stomach knot.

"It'll all be okay in the end, *Papino.*"

"I love you very much, *mia stellina.*" His smile doesn't reach his eyes.

I don't know what is going on. I want to laugh, but I want to cry too.

From the way he's acting, it's like he's never going to see me again. But it's not like I'll be moving to another country. We can still see each other all the time.

"I'll see you soon, *Papino.*" I stand on my tiptoes to press a kiss to his cheek.

He bows his head and turns, walking away without another word.

Before I have a chance to overthink my father's sudden expression of emotion, I head straight back to the bar, determined to drown my sorrows in unlimited champagne.

I MUST BE ALMOST TWO BOTTLES DEEP BY THE TIME A strong hand is on my waist and hot breath is tickling my cheek.

"I think it's time to call it a night, *wife,*" Alexei murmurs.

I let my eyes flutter closed for a moment, enjoying the heat radiating from his large body.

Perhaps it's the alcohol causing my body to arch back against him, to let out a contented sigh as both of his hands find my hips, his fingers digging into the soft flesh.

"Bianca..."

"Time for bed." I turn around to face Alexei.

My eyes trail up his broad chest until they lock onto his, the warm chocolate of his eyes devouring me whole.

He really is extremely attractive, and according to the state of New York, mine for the taking.

A grin pulls at my lips.

"What?" He frowns.

"It's our wedding night," I whisper.

A strangled sort of sound escapes his lips, and I laugh.

"That's your cue to go to bed." Alexei drops his hands from my waist and takes me by the arm, leading me out of the slowly emptying ballroom.

I hurry beside him, hiccups mixed with giggles escaping me as I imagine fucking *Alexei Koslov*.

My heart hammers in my chest as he drags me into the elevator, pressing the button for the penthouse suite.

I steal glances at Alexei as we ascend the nine floors to the top of the Waldorf.

His body is rigid, his shoulders set as he stands slightly in front of me. Let my eyes trail down his back, I linger on his ass which looks incredible in his suit trousers.

"Stop it," he warns without looking my way.

"Stop what?" A string of hiccups makes me giggle.

"Eye-fucking me from behind."

"You were eye-fucking me most of the day. I think it's only fair that I get my share, *husband*." I bite the inside of my cheek as Alexei's body tenses at my words.

If he turns around, will there be any evidence to suggest he liked what he saw?

But he remains still, reaching behind to take my arm as the elevator opens, and pulls me along as we step into the penthouse suite.

I can't stop the alcohol-induced giggles from spilling from my mouth as he leads me across the expansive living area to the bedroom at the far end.

One look at the giant bed and the giant of a man beside me has me squeezing my thighs together.

"Sleep." He drops his hold on me.

"I know I should be furious because of this situation I find myself in." I lick my lips as I run my fingertips across the soft sheets. "But as I think of what we could do in this bed, I'm struggling to stay mad." I sigh, glancing at Alexei.

His face looks pained as he regards the enormous bed before us.

"I think we should both get some sleep. We have a long day tomorrow." Alexei steps away from the bed, from *me*.

I pout. "I don't want to sleep."

I reach for the zipper at the side of my dress.

Alexei's eyes follow my movements, and his gaze turns heated as he watches me slowly pull the zip down.

"I was thinking maybe we could do another sort of bedroom activity."

"Bianca." Alexei's throat bobs.

I grin as I release the zip, and my dress pools to the floor, leaving me in nothing but a pair of pink lacy panties.

"Whoops." I chuckle, glancing down at my bare breasts. "Forgot I wasn't wearing a bra."

Reaching up, I cup my full breasts.

I look up under my lashes at Alexei and his expression is glazed as he watches me knead my breasts. Sighing, I roll my thumbs over my pebbling nipples.

I pull my lower lip between my teeth as Alexei takes in my body.

My eyes trail down his chest, pausing as I take in the impressive bulge in his pants.

A soft whimper escapes me at the sight, and I want nothing more than to sink to my knees and take him in my mouth.

"Alexei." I step out of the dress, taking a step toward him.

I need him. This feeling is all-consuming.

He keeps his arms plastered at his sides, clearly trying his best to restrain himself as I close the distance between us.

"Kiss me...*husband*," I murmur as I sink my fingers into Alexei's shirt and pull his mouth down to mine.

The moment his lips touch mine, my body melts.

I cling to his shirt, desperately trying to get closer to him, to feel the soft material of his shirt against my aching nipples.

My tongue darts out to trace his lower lip, urging him to part his mouth for me.

His hands grip my shoulders, and he pushes me away, leaving me confused.

"You're clearly drunk, *solnyshka*," Alexei murmurs. "I won't take advantage of you like this."

"We're married." My cheeks burn as I glance down at my almost naked body, wiggling my hips to try and entice my new husband into bed. "You vowed to satisfy my every sexual need."

Alexei huffs a laugh, the sound sending a shiver down my spine.

My nipples instantly harden as he takes a step toward me, his eyes burning into me as he takes in my curves.

"I did," he grunts, his hands moving to adjust his bulge.

I let my eyes follow his hand and gasp at the view.

"Well?" I press, my voice breathy as I rub my thighs together.

"While I'd want nothing more, *ptichka*, you have some issues to work out before we take things further. So, I suggest we both get some sleep."

The little nicknames he calls me do something to me, and I want more from him.

"You're not serious." I cross my arms over my chest to try and shield myself.

"I'm deadly serious."

"There's a naked woman practically throwing herself at you, and you're saying *no*?"

Alexei's eyes close for a moment, as if it's taking everything in him to keep himself composed.

I try to ignore the dull ache that is building between my thighs as I take in his huge stature.

The way he's rolled his white shirt to the elbows, exposing his muscular forearms. How he's undone one too many buttons to reveal a hint of dark chest hair that has my mouth watering.

He opens his eyes and takes another step toward me and bends down so that his breath is tickling my ear.

My back instantly arches, my nipples aching for any form of friction he can offer me.

"I am no stranger to that fact, *ptichka*, but you are now my *wife*," he murmurs. "And I refuse to use you when you are in a vulnerable state, especially to satisfy my own need for release."

A strangled sound escapes me at his words, filling my mind with all sorts of *filthy* thoughts.

I'm no virgin by any means, but my experience consists of a few sloppy one-night stands in various Manhattan club bathrooms, a summer fling during my sophomore year of college, and a yearlong relationship with a guy who ended up cheating on me with one of my friends.

The boys I've been with barely know how to put on a condom correctly, let alone get a woman off. I need a man.

I need Alexei.

He reeks of experience, and I know he'd need no guidance in getting me off.

"Now, don't make me tell you again, get some sleep."

My cheeks burn at his rejection.

I guess part of me was wanting to have some ounce of control over how this day ended, seeing as the rest of it was so far out of it. But as the alcohol is starting to wear off, and I realize I'm wearing nothing but a pair of panties in front of a man I met only a few hours ago who also happens to be my husband, I feel nothing but embarrassment.

"I'll take the couch," I mutter, walking past Alexei into the bedroom.

His eyes weigh on me as I grab my bag that has been put on the armchair and start rifling through it for something to put on before going to bed.

"There's no need for you to sleep on the couch."

I keep my back to Alexei as I pull an old college T-shirt on over my head and slide a pair of cotton shorts over my thighs, only because I don't want him to look at me like I'm some juvenile charity case.

"Well, it's more than obvious we're not sharing a bed." I adjust my T-shirt before turning to face him.

He's leaning against the doorframe with his arms crossed, a deep frown between his eyebrows as he looks over me.

"And stop looking at me like *that*."

"Like what?"

"Like I'm about to shatter into a million pieces."

"Bianca..."

I freeze at the sound of my name on his lips.

"You are far from fragile."

"Then why won't you touch me?"

"Because the first time I fuck my wife, I want her to be sober. I want to know it's her wanting me, not the alcohol."

My eyes flick up to meet Alexei's, and it's clear how he would take me.

There would be nothing gentle about it.

I fight a moan as I imagine him bending me over the edge of this bed and sinking so deep inside me I might break in two.

"I will not ask you a third time, *solnyshka*. Go to *bed*."

I scowl as his words break through my lust-filled fantasy.

To show my annoyance, I grab the comforter off the bed and tuck a pillow under my arm, intent on sleeping as far away from my husband as possible.

Though, I don't make it far.

Alexei grips hold of my arm as I pass through the door.

"Bed. Now."

I glance up at him, narrowing my eyes at his commanding tone.

"No."

He lets out a long breath, any amusement at my disobedience now replaced with irritation.

"If you are so adamant not to share a bed with me tonight, that's fine. But I will be the one taking the couch." He reaches for the pillow tucked under my arm.

I blink, too stunned to fight him as he reaches for the comforter.

"Good night, *wife*," he murmurs before stalking away toward the couch.

6

BIANCA

Despite the plush bed and silk sheets, my sleep brings little relief to my racing thoughts. I wake multiple times, confused about where I am. Then when I realize, the events of the previous day come flooding back, and I'm left feeling empty and alone despite Alexei being in the next room.

It's likely he didn't bother getting a separate room for fear I might make a run for it in the middle of the night. But realistically, where would I go? My studio? Zara's apartment?

I almost laugh at the thought of turning up at Zara's place in the middle of the night, informing her that I'm on the run from my new husband who also happens to be the head of one of the most powerful crime families in the city.

She'd think I had drunk a bottle of tequila, and from the pounding in my head, so would I.

Eventually, I must fall asleep as I wake to the sun starting to peek in through the curtains and a huge shadow cast over my bed.

"Morning, *solnyshka*." Alexei chuckles.

I groan, throwing the covers over my head. "You've got one hour to eat breakfast and shower before we leave for our new marital home."

"Can't wait," I mutter, wincing as my head pounds.

"I took the liberty of ordering you some food. It should be here by the time you're done showering."

"I don't need you to tell me what to do." I throw down the covers, glaring at a very fresh-faced Alexei.

He's wearing a fresh white shirt and dark chinos, and a waft of his musky cologne hits my nose as I sit up.

"What time is it?"

"Six thirty."

"Oh, hell no," I groan, falling back against the covers.

"Welcome to the life of a Koslov." Alexei chuckles. "Enjoy your shower."

"Asshole," I mutter.

Standing beneath the waterfall shower, my thoughts are plagued with memories of last night. How I practically begged Alexei Koslov to fuck me, and how he turned me down.

I run my hands over my face, mortified at how I acted.

And now I'm expected to live with the guy?

Whoever I pissed off in a former life must be having a hell of a good laugh at my expense.

The shower does little to clear the fog in my head, and when I eventually look in the mirror to brush my hair and teeth, I cringe at the slight grayish tone of my skin.

Drinking near enough two bottles of champagne on an empty stomach will do that to you. It's a wonder I didn't spend my wedding night with my head buried in the toilet bowl.

I do my best to make myself look somewhat presentable before emerging from the bedroom, wearing a pair of denim shorts and a tank top along with my red converse.

As I cross the living room to where Alexei is perched on the couch, my heart starts racing faster and my hands start sweating.

Yesterday felt like a game, a simulation, but now reality is starting to set in.

I'm married to Alexei Koslov.

My knees threaten to buckle beneath me, and I manage to grab hold of the back of the couch to steady myself.

Alexei glances over his shoulder, getting to his feet as he eyes the look on my face.

"Bianca?"

A knock sounds at the door, causing Alexei to curse under his breath.

"I'm fine." I close my eyes for a moment as I fight through the sudden feeling of nausea brought on by alcohol and fear.

Alexei hesitates for a moment before going to the door to collect our room service. The smell of pancakes and bacon wafts into the room as the hotel staff wheels the tray inside, and I groan.

"Perhaps we should skip breakfast and hit the road." He turns the staff away and closes the door.

"Unless you want the inside of your car to look like a toilet bowl, I think that's wise."

He chuckles softly under his breath. "You can sleep on the ride over to the house, I promise."

He lifts one of the tray covers to steal a piece of bacon.

"And where exactly is my new house?" I maneuver to perch on the edge of the couch arm.

"Forest Hills."

"Where?"

"In Queens."

I choke on a laugh.

"Of course, it is."

My heartbeat is ringing in my ears, and my chest is so tight it hurts to take a full breath.

I swallow, my throat scratchy and raw, but I ignore it. Ignore all the feelings that are coursing through my body, all the needs that I'm neglecting. *Especially* the one that I so badly wanted Alexei to fulfill last night.

That cannot happen again. I can't afford to let my guard down for one second around this man, no matter how many times he says he's going to protect me at all costs.

I fall asleep in the backseat of Alexei's Range Rover if only to stop myself from saying anything else I might regret.

He informs me that the drive will only take half an hour if we don't hit any traffic.

Why the hell did he wake me so early, then?

But the short power nap does rejuvenate me a little so that by the time we're pulling up outside his ridiculously huge mansion, which backs onto the Forest Hills park, I'm in a better mood to appreciate my new home.

"It's just you that lives here?" I climb out of the car, choosing to ignore the fact that Alexei opened my door. I crane my neck as I take in the house.

The property is stunning, with windows that span over all three stories, thick pillars on either side of the double front door that must be almost twice Alexei's height, as well as expansive grounds that surround the house.

"It's my family's main residence in New York, but my

three brothers often choose to stay at our penthouse apartment on the Upper East Side. I've told them to stay away from here for a few days at least so as not to...*overwhelm* you."

"Ah, yes, because meeting new brothers-in-law really can tip a girl over the edge."

Alexei ignores my comment, and I frown as he guides me up the front steps to the house. He seems less playful than he did yesterday, or was that side of him merely a ruse to help ease me into the idea of marrying him?

I cross my arms over my chest, fighting the lump in my throat as I watch the man I was forced to marry open up the front door to our new home.

He stands to the side, holding the door for me as I cross the threshold, and his rich musky scent hits me as I brush past him.

My breath catches, but I quickly distract myself by taking in the expansive foyer of my new house.

"It's... It's..." I have no words as I glance around, taking in the rich mahogany detailing, the dark jewel tone colors of the walls.

I'm no stranger to wealth, my father isn't exactly short of money, but the Koslovs are on a whole new level of wealth.

My mouth hangs ajar.

This is my new home.

"I have a more old-fashioned eye when it comes to interior design." Alexei moves to my side.

I try to ignore the fact he's standing so close, the rich sandalwood scent that hits my nose as I take a breath.

"The kitchen and bathrooms are fairly modern, but I prefer a more cozy feeling to the main living spaces."

"Ah, yes. A three-story mansion screams cozy."

Alexei chuckles, the sound sending a shiver racing down my spine and a warmth spreading through my core.

I cough, snapping myself out of my scent-induced trance.

"I have some rules that I want to lay out before we go any further." I fold my arms across my chest, turning to face my husband.

Alexei's eyes gleam, but he signals for me to continue.

"I want my own room."

"Done."

"And I want free roam of the house."

Alexei narrows his eyes for a moment but eventually nods.

"You are not a prisoner here, *ptichka*. This is your home now, but I will add to this rule."

"Go on."

"You are not to leave the premises without me knowing, and without security."

I scoff. "You're not serious..."

"In case you haven't realized yet, I don't take the matter of your safety lightly. So if that makes me the bad guy here, then so be it. I'll do whatever it takes to keep you safe."

"Fine." I know there's no point in fighting him.

In truth, Alexei is starting to remind me a lot of my father. Overprotective alpha male types seem to be a running theme with the men in my life.

"Anything else?" Alexei asks.

"Yes." I take a deep breath. "I want a place to work on my art."

Alexei's brows lift.

"You paint?"

"Among other things." I shrug.

"You'll have to show me some of your work."

I shake my head, fighting a smile. "Only my *closest* family and friends get to see my work. 'Strange man who I was forced to marry' does not fall into either of those two categories."

"Perhaps I'll fall into the category of muse." He flashes me a wink, and I fight the urge to picture him posing nude for me. Nothing but rippling muscle and hard lines.

I swallow, averting my eyes.

"You're too cocky for my taste." I fight a smile.

"Really?" He lifts his eyebrows, his dark eyes twinkling. "I didn't get that impression last night."

My cheeks heat from the memory. Of Alexei's lips on mine, of the hardness of his body up close as his fingers dug into my hips.

"W-why don't you give me a tour?"

The smirk Alexei offers me tells me he knows exactly the sort of thoughts plaguing my mind, but he humors me nonetheless.

I try not to look dumbfounded or starstruck as he takes me around the expansive kitchen, dining room, multiple studies and lounges and many of the bedrooms that his brothers tend to occupy when they visit.

It's a massive property. It even has a pool, tennis court, a basement, which has its own gym, private garage, and acres of land.

"What's on the third floor?" I look up the stairs.

"My office, the library—"

"You have a library?"

Alexei nods, that infuriating smirk gracing his lips.

"Impressed yet, *solnyshka*?"

"It's not bad." I shrug, not wanting him to know the truth.

Alexei chuckles as we step onto the elevator by the stairs.

"Maybe this will change your mind."

As we get to the top floor and open the first door on the right, I can't stop the gasp from escaping my lips as I take in the towering bookcases and plush leather armchairs.

There's even a fireplace, and suddenly I can see it—evenings spent curled up in one of those chairs, drinking hot chocolate and losing myself in a book.

"What about now. Impressed?"

I lift one shoulder.

"Can I see my room?" I glance over my shoulder at Alexei.

"It's just down the hall."

I turn and walk past him, but I pause when I notice the three other doors on this floor. "What else is on this floor?"

"This door—" Alexei moves to the one opposite the library. "—is my study."

"Another one?"

Alexei ignores my comment, strolling down the hall, his footsteps almost silenced by the dark blue rug that runs the length of it.

"This one—" He pauses at the door on the far left. "—is my room."

I frown, glancing once at the door and then letting my eyes fall to the one opposite.

"Let me guess... The last one's my room?"

Alexei grins, and I fight the urge to slam my fist into his chest.

"So many bedrooms, and you had to give me the room opposite yours?"

"Like I keep saying, *ptichka*, I take your safety very seriously." He crosses the hall and opens the door to my room.

"And like I keep saying, you're an *asshole*." I don't hide my groan of frustration as I storm past Alexei and into my room.

I pause, surprised by the pale cream walls and rose-colored detailing. I blink, glancing at the enormous bed which looks like it's made of marshmallows from the color scheme of the bedding and plush pillows. There's a large vanity littered with products, a chaise longue, and a large bookcase filled to bursting with books. A cream fluffy rug covers most of the floor, and I itch to slip off my shoes and sink my toes into the soft fabric.

"The door on the right leads to your own private bathroom, which has a jacuzzi tub and waterfall shower, and the door on the left leads to your walk-in closet which I took the liberty of stocking for you."

"Did you pick out the color scheme too?" I walk over to the bed and run my fingers along the comforter.

"Yes, but you're welcome to decorate however you want if it's not to your taste."

It's exactly my taste.

"It'll do, thank you," I mutter. "Now, if you don't mind, I'd like some time alone."

"Of course."

I glance over my shoulder to find his eyes searching mine.

He seems hesitant to leave, but something on my face makes the decision for him because he offers me a curt nod before closing the door, leaving me alone in my new room.

I perch on the edge of the bed, glancing around my room with nothing but a growing sense of dread in the pit of my stomach for company.

"How the fuck did I end up here?"

7

ALEXEI

Five mornings in a row I've come down to the kitchen to find Bianca brewing coffee, wearing everything from a long T-shirt that barely covers her ass to micro shorts and a tank top. Her long brown hair is normally piled messily on top of her head, and I itch to pull it free and run my fingers through the silky strands.

She's trying to kill me.

I know it's in part because of my rejection on the night of our wedding. In truth, I wanted nothing more than to fuck her senseless, but she was drunk and vulnerable. And despite what she might think, I'm *not* an asshole.

So instead, I get to admire the Bianca show every morning, leaving me sporting a constant semi at the thought of those ridiculously small shorts and the tank tops that leave very little to the imagination.

It doesn't help that I know exactly what's beneath said tank tops, and it's enough to have me jumping in a cold shower every day to try and calm the fuck down.

"Morning." I slip onto a stool at the breakfast bar.

It's barely seven, but it seems this is our new routine for

now. It's clear that sleep is not coming easy to Bianca from the dark circles that have started to appear beneath those beautiful blue eyes, but I'm giving her a week. A week to adjust to the house, the marriage, *me*.

Then if there's no improvement in her mood, I'm going to take matters into my own hands.

I set my hands on the counter. "How did you sleep?"

Bianca ignores me as she loads the filter into the machine and turns it on.

I smirk as I watch her, my eyes flicking down to take in her delicious curves.

How I had the strength to turn her down is beyond me.

"I tossed and turned all night." I slide off my stool to give her a hand.

I reach into one of the overhead cupboards and take out two glass mugs, all the while glancing sidelong at Bianca to gauge her reactions. But she stays quiet as she moves to the fridge to get the creamer. "Maybe it's because I know you're just across the hall wearing those skimpy little shorts..."

She freezes, her hands gripping the handle of the fridge so hard her knuckles turn white.

There it is.

"Do you want me to picture you in those shorts, Bianca? Is that why you parade around here with your ass practically on show?"

"I wear them—" She yanks open the fridge and pulls out the creamer. "—because my pig of a husband stocked my wardrobe with clothes that barely cover my ass."

I bark a laugh, enjoying the sight of that scowl on her face once more. It's better than the blank look I sometimes catch in her eyes when she thinks I'm not looking.

I'm well aware of the fact that she's in my home against her will. That if she had a choice, she would leave in an instant, no matter if there is a hint of a spark between us that I am so desperate to explore.

I took away her choice, but it's for her own good. A target was placed on her head the moment her father spoke out against Mario Gilanto. And when I failed to take him down, I only made his thirst for blood even worse.

I won't risk her life. So, I'll deal with her bad moods and snide remarks for as long as it takes for me to put a bullet in Mario Gilanto's skull.

"What are your plans for today?" I reach for the fresh pot of coffee and pour us both a cup.

Bianca remains a few feet away, leaning against the marble counter with daggers in her eyes as she watches me.

"Let me see..." She sets the creamer down on the counter and lifts her right hand. "See my friends. Check. Go on a date with a guy I met in a bar. Check."

I grind my teeth together at the mention of her going on a date when she's legally bound to *me*.

I shouldn't be jealous. I have no right to be. This marriage is nothing more than business. But that doesn't stop my instincts from screaming at me to mark my territory.

"I get your point."

"Do you, Alexei? Because my life has been completely turned upside down, and I don't see it ever returning to normal."

I lean back against the counter, digging my fingers into the cold marble and letting out a long breath to try and keep myself calm.

She's hurting. Be patient.

"I get you're frustrated—"

"I'm done having the same patronizing conversations

with you." She grabs her coffee cup and the bottle of creamer off of the counter and storms out of the kitchen.

I don't see Bianca for the rest of the day. I busy myself in the study on the ground floor, not wanting to seem too overbearing if I take residence in my actual study up on the top floor.

I check in with Dimitri and Anton, but neither of them have any updates of note other than the fact that Emilio is in hiding and is safe. For now. I keep that information tucked away to offer to Bianca when the time comes. She's under the impression she'll be visiting with him soon, and I don't have the heart to take that away from her too.

When dinner is served later that evening, Bianca takes a seat at the table opposite me but barely eats or speaks. It's like I'm rooming with a zombie.

Something has to change because I can't stand to be the reason behind the haunted look in her eyes every time she actually glances my way.

"I'd rather eat in my room," Bianca states after ten minutes of awkward silence. "Eating dinner at the table every night with you makes me feel like a charity case."

"We eat at the dinner table in this house." I pour myself some water from the pitcher between us.

The table is large, big enough to seat ten people, but I had the maid lay up two seats opposite one another to try and make the dinner appear more intimate. Not that it seems to be making the blindest bit of difference.

"And you most certainly aren't a charity case, *solnyshka*."

"So, there's no other girl you'd rather be wining and dining with?"

"Only you." I dip my chin.

I wait for her cheeks to heat, her breath to catch, but she simply drops her gaze to her plate.

After another ten minutes of silence, Bianca excuses herself after barely eating her food. I watch her leave with a painful ache in my chest.

I need to do something to cheer her up.

Two days later, I gently knock on Bianca's door. It's just after midday, and I haven't seen her since our morning coffee in the kitchen. I try to hide the smile on my face at the surprise I have planned for her, hoping it'll make her feel more at home in this house.

"Bianca?"

"Go away."

I take a deep breath before knocking again. "I have something to show you."

Footsteps shuffle across carpet on the other side of the door before it flies open to reveal Bianca wearing a pale blue sundress with thin straps to show off her delicate shoulders, her hair piled up on the top of her head. A few loose strands frame her face and I almost reach out to tuck them behind her ear.

"What?"

"Come with me." I flash her a wink.

For a moment, I think she might slam the door in my face, but she steps out of her room and follows me down the stairs to the landing below.

I pause outside what used to be Danil's old bedroom, my hand hovering over the door handle. "Ready?"

Bianca looks up at me with a confused expression. "I guess?"

I bite the inside of my cheek to hide my smile as I open the door and usher her inside. She stands frozen for a moment, taking in what I've done to the room.

"You... you did this for me?" she whispers as she walks into the center of the room.

I nod.

"This is your home now, *solnyshka*. I wanted it to feel like it."

She gazes around at the makeshift art studio I have created. This room has the best view overlooking the pool, with its own balcony where I set up a table and chairs so she could work outside if she wishes. I put in a huge set of drawers filled with every type of art supply I could think of —chalk, paint, charcoal, pencils as well as shelves filled to bursting with canvases and paper. I set up a large easel and work stool in front of the large glass doors as well as a loveseat against the right wall for a more comfortable option.

For a moment, I see a flash of happiness in her eyes as she takes in the room.

I should have known better than to think a bedroom would be enough. She needs a way to fill her time, to have a creative outlet for all the emotions she's been experiencing.

But then it's as if she catches herself starting to feel happy and steals her expression back to one of icy indifference.

I frown as she rounds on me, her hands on her hips as she shoots me a glare.

"I don't need state-of-the-art everything," she states.

I blink. Is she being serious?

"You're actually mad right now?"

"You can't buy my affection, Alexei."

"Why should I when you were so ready to give it away

for free on our wedding night?" I know it's a low blow, but I need her to meet me halfway here.

Does she honestly think I enjoy this arrangement? I'm not exactly thrilled about being married to a stranger either, but at least I was trying to do something thoughtful.

"Are you seriously going to bring that up every fucking time we have a conversation?" She throws her hands up in the air.

"I can't help it, *kisa*. You make it so easy for me." I cross my arms over my chest.

Anger flashes in her eyes, and I find myself taking a few steps back until I'm in the doorway, watching as she storms toward me.

A sharp thrill courses through my body at the sight of her in that dress with such fire in her eyes and a wicked smile on her lips.

There you are, solnyshka.

But then she's reaching for the door and slamming it in my face.

I thought organizing a private art space for Bianca would have her warming up to me, but it seems to have done the opposite.

Raking my fingers through my hair, I let out a steadying breath as I walk away from the door, glancing out one of the windows as I descend the stairs. I pause when I catch sight of my youngest brother in the backyard.

"What is he doing here?"

My brothers were under strict instructions to stay away from the house until told otherwise, but I shouldn't be surprised. Danil never likes being told what to do. He's the typical youngest sibling, and it doesn't help that he had me as a parental figure during adolescence.

"I didn't realize you were here." I cross the freshly mown grass.

He's sitting cross-legged beneath a cherry blossom tree at the edge of the lawn, his eyes gazing up at the house, his expression telling me he's lost in thought.

"I told you not to come until I said so," I remind him, but then I halt in my tracks, gazing up at the blossoming flowers.

"It's today, isn't it?" I glance at Danil.

He lifts his eyes to mine and nods once.

My eyes flutter closed for a moment as a wave of grief hits me so hard my legs threaten to give out.

"I miss them." His voice brings me back, reminding me that I have to be the strong one here.

I take a seat beside my brother, bringing my knees up and resting my forearms on them as we look to the house.

My eyes wander to the window of Bianca's studio, wondering if she's looking down at us right now.

Part of me hopes she is.

"Do you miss them?" Danil asks.

"Every day." I swallow the lump in my throat.

"Me too."

I ball my hands into fists, sinking the nails into the palms of my hands.

Sometimes, I hate the fact that my brothers were old enough to remember my parents, to remember the night that they were ripped away from us.

Would it have been kinder if they were children with hardly any memories to cling to?

Danil was fifteen when our parents were murdered, and I know he remembers it like it was yesterday.

I sure as hell do.

"Mom loved this house." Danil sighs. "I remember her

saying that she couldn't wait for all of us to marry and fill the place with grandkids for her to spoil."

I huff a laugh, though there's nothing light about the sound.

What would she think if she were here now? To learn that I have a wife purely out of business obligations, not love?

I know it's not what she would have wanted for her son, but it became my responsibility the moment I took over as head of the family.

"I know you told us all to stay away," Danil mutters. "But this is the only place I feel close to them."

"It's okay." I ignore the guilt of not realizing what day it was. "Let's go and have a drink to honor their memory."

"The way dad would've wanted us to."

"Exactly." I sigh, my eyes wandering to Bianca's window as I think of my family.

8

BIANCA

The clock on my bedside table informs me that it's 1 a.m., and I'm wide awake. I've been tossing and turning for hours, my mind racing as I stare at the ceiling.

I've been cooped up in this house for over two weeks, and I'm losing my mind, despite my very fancy new art studio, courtesy of my husband.

I cringe at the thought.

I know I shouldn't have blown up at Alexei like I did when he showed me the space he had set up for me, but the rage that's constantly bubbling just beneath the surface is starting to frighten me.

Everything is out of my control—from what I wear down to what I eat.

I went from living in a studio apartment in the center of New York, seeing my friends multiple times a week, going to museums and coffee shops, to being stuck in a house with one of the most dangerous men in New York.

Who also happens to be one of the most attractive men I've ever seen.

I thought I'd escaped a lifetime of control. My father

was exactly the same—always wanting to know where I was at all times and who I hung out with. It's a miracle I even had any friends before I turned eighteen and went away to college.

But it seems all I've done is swap one controlling man for another.

A shiver runs down my spine as Alexei fills my thoughts.

My fingers automatically move to my lips, the phantom feeling of him still lingering there even two weeks later. That's how incredible of a kiss it was.

The way he kissed me was possessive, and I hate that I've thought about it every night since.

His rejection of my advances still stings, and it doesn't help that he likes to bring it up at every given opportunity. I think the asshole actually enjoys the fact that he turned me down and took a knock to my ego. Though I know it's probably for the best.

This marriage is purely for business, and I can't afford to give my heart away to a man who will likely tear it into shreds.

Alexei Koslov doesn't scream relationship material.

Ignoring the heat pooling low in my belly, I screw my eyes shut and try to think of anything other than Alexei. I won't give him the satisfaction of fantasizing about him.

He doesn't deserve my orgasm when he stole away my freedom.

So, I try to sleep.

When the clock turns two, I decide enough is enough. It's clear I need to give my brain something else to think about.

Throwing back the covers, I slip on the pink silk robe that hangs on the back of my door and sneak out of my room. I hesitate in the hall, my eyes wandering to Alexei's door.

There's no light coming from the crack beneath, so I assume he's asleep, though I know he likes to work late into the night.

There have been a few times where I've heard him creep past at all hours of the morning, the sound of his footsteps making me hold my breath.

On a few occasions, I swear he paused outside of my room, and I silently wished he would open the door and slip into the bed beside me.

I dreamed he would climb on top of me, enveloping me in his strong arms as he sank his cock deep inside my throbbing heat.

My thighs automatically rub together, snapping me back to reality.

"Get a grip, Bianca," I mutter under my breath as I turn my back on Alexei's room and head down the stairs to my studio.

I quietly open the door and flick on the light, illuminating the space in a warm glow.

A few finished canvases already line the wall on the far left, though I'm still waiting for the oil paint to dry on a picture of the view from the window. I know Alexei picked this room specifically for my studio because of the view, and I've spent many afternoons this past week sitting on the balcony with a sketchbook on my lap taking in the vast expanse of greenery surrounding my new home—in particular, the cherry blossom tree.

It's breathtaking, and I know it must mean something to Alexei.

There's only one, and I caught him and one of his brothers sitting below it the other day.

Even if I stood all the way up here, the sadness on their faces was still so clear as they talked. Eventually, they disappeared inside the house, and I didn't see Alexei again until breakfast the next morning, with him choosing to skip our evening meal.

I cross the room to take a seat at my easel where my current work in progress is waiting for me.

It's a portrait that I started a few days ago, and it's really starting to take shape.

Grabbing the tubes of paint I'll need, I load up my palette before taking a seat on the wooden stool and getting to work.

I must not have been working for more than half an hour before the skin on the back of my neck prickles. I sigh and put down my paintbrush.

"What are you doing here?" I glance over my shoulder to where Alexei leans in the doorway.

He's wearing his usual white shirt and black pants, despite the hour.

Perhaps I was wrong, and he wasn't in his room at all.

"I saw the light was on." He pushes off the doorframe.

I quickly turn back around to avoid his gaze, picking up my paintbrush and dipping it into the white acrylic.

"Did I wake you?"

"No. I've been in my study."

"Do you ever sleep?"

"Do you?"

"I used to..." I mutter.

Alexei is quiet for a moment, so I continue to work quietly, adding some white detailing to my portrait.

"That's really amazing. She's beautiful."

"Thank you."

"She looks like you." My chest tightens as I add some white to the eyes.

"That's my mother." A lump forms in my throat. "Everyone always says that my father gave me his eyes, but the rest is all her. I had this picture of her beside my bed, and I wanted to recreate it. I never want to forget even if pictures are the only memories I have." I don't know why I say it, but the knot in my chest loosens just a touch as I talk.

"You never met her." It's not a question.

I shake my head, swallowing down the lump in my throat.

"She died giving birth to me." My voice noticeably cracks as I speak the words out loud, but I don't want to stop. "So no, I never met her."

"And your dad didn't remarry?" Alexei moves to stand beside me, and the heat radiating from his body surrounds me as he towers over me.

I almost lean into him, craving some connection as I think about the greatest loss in my life.

"She was the love of his life." I close my eyes for a second. "And I took her away from him."

The words spill from my mouth before I have a chance to stop them.

"Bianca..."

"It's okay." I shake my head. "I know my father loves me. But I know I also make him feel sad because every time he looks at me, he sees her."

"You are not responsible."

"It's hard not to feel like it."

"You are *not* responsible. What you are is extremely talented."

A warm hand is on my shoulder, squeezing it softly, and

my eyes flutter closed at the touch, at the warmth of his fingers seeping through the thin material of my robe.

I try not to squirm in my seat, suddenly all too aware of the fact that I'm wearing nothing beneath my robe.

"Thank you." My cheeks heat up at the compliment.

So much for trying to empty my mind of thoughts of Alexei when all he's doing is filling it back up.

"You should not waste a talent like this."

"Good thing I have an extremely rich husband who can finance my hobby." It's a weak attempt to lighten the mood.

I'm glad Alexei knows about my mother. I know it's important to talk about her to try and keep her memory alive, and I hope eventually I'll be able to think of her without any trace of guilt.

But I'm not there yet.

"It's a good investment," Alexei chuckles. "So, do you prefer to paint portraits?"

I bite the inside of my cheek as I glance over at the wall to where my other paintings are drying, lingering particularly on the painting of the cherry blossom tree.

"I like a mixture. Though I do enjoy portraits. I like bringing someone to life, to focus on all the details that make them unique." I cringe at my own babbling.

Why am I so nervous?

Because Alexei has yet to remove his hand from my shoulder, and my skin is starting to burn from the heat of his touch.

I shift on my stool, aware of the heat building between my thighs. I'm glad he can't see my face, at the heat that is creeping up my neck.

"I've never had someone paint my portrait." He removes his hand from my shoulder and strolls over to the cream loveseat. He turns, eyeing me with amusement as he tucks his hands into his pockets.

My breath catches as I imagine him posing while I paint him, lounging on the loveseat, his powerful thighs spread as he runs his hands through his dark hair...

"I could always paint you... nude." I bite the inside of my cheeks. Alexei's eyes widen just a fraction at my words, and I think I might actually have taken him by surprise. "Unless, of course, you're too embarrassed..."

Alexei lets out a low, breathy chuckle.

The sound makes me shiver as I let myself imagine painting him in the nude.

But then he's reaching for the buttons on his shirt, his eyes locked on my lips as he slowly undresses himself.

"I told you before, *ptichka*." A smirk tugs at his full lips. "I'd be more than happy to be your muse."

He shrugs out of his white shirt, revealing the most deliciously broad, tanned chest and chiseled abdomen that I've ever seen. He even has those V lines that disappear down into the waistband of his pants that make me involuntarily lick my lips.

As if he followed my gaze, he reaches for his belt and begins unbuckling his pants.

I swear I don't breathe the entire time he undresses, and the asshole seems to know it from the smirk on his face.

"Do you like what you see?" He steps out of his pants.

My eyes fall to his cock, and a strangled sound escapes my lips as I take in his enormous length.

He chuckles. "I'll take that as a yes."

Heat instantly pools in my belly as I think of what it would be like to climb on top of him and sink down on his cock, taking him deeper than I ever thought possible.

"I need some more paint," I choke, getting to my feet.

I can feel his eyes on me as I grab a fresh palette and canvas and load it up with nude tones, my mouth filling with saliva as I think of the colors of his skin, his hair.

Goosebumps break out over my skin, and my nipples pebble against the soft silk of my robe, desperate for some friction.

Why the hell did I suggest painting Alexei nude? Am I trying to torture myself?

At least it gives me something else to think about at night other than our one drunken kiss…

"Are you comfortable?" I ask as I choose a few brushes.

"Oh, I'm very comfortable." I glance at him and see his signature smirk tugging at his full lips.

Alexei is draped across the loveseat, his body nothing but rippling muscle, and it takes everything in me not to stare.

I can't give him the satisfaction.

So instead, I take a seat at my easel and swap out the portrait of my mother for a fresh canvas.

"This might take a while," I warn him, turning my focus back to the blank canvas.

"I have incredible stamina, *solnyshka*, don't you worry."

Oh, my god.

9

ALEXEI

I don't fail to notice the blush creeping up Bianca's chest and neck as I lie on the couch. I also get immense satisfaction when her blush intensifies every time her eyes flick to my cock. I shift my position, doing my best not to get aroused as she sets up a fresh canvas.

"Can you lie back a bit more?" she asks from behind her easel.

I grin as I catch her peeking at my abs, which I make sure to flex even more.

"Of course." I spread out even more, resting my arms along the back of the couch as I spread my thighs, giving her ample view of my cock. "Is that better?"

"Y-yes." She hides behind the canvas.

Chuckling, I enjoy the turn my night is taking.

I had been holed up in my study for hours, not wanting to give in and go to bed because I knew sleep would never come. The dreams and flashbacks never fail to plague me, but they're particularly bad in the days surrounding the anniversary of my parents' murder.

I've found if I work myself to exhaustion, whether in my

study or in the gym, then I can grab a few peaceful hours before the nightmares eventually rouse me.

Tonight, I'm hoping my dreams will be plagued with something else.

We're both silent as she works.

She's shifted her position slightly to gain a better view, meaning she's no longer completely hidden behind her canvas, giving me the most delicious view. She perches on her stool with one leg crossed over the other, her silk robe hitching up to show most of her upper thigh.

I swallow at the sight of her smooth skin, desperate to lift that robe higher.

Is she wearing anything underneath?

My eyes roam upwards, and I have to bite back a groan as I notice the outline of her pebbled nipples.

I think that's my answer.

My mind goes blank as I look back down at her thighs, my fingers itching to trace her skin.

My tongue darts out to moisten my lower lip as I realize there's only a thin piece of material keeping her pussy shielded from me.

I swallow, my body feeling like it's on fire with the need to take her.

It was torture enough having to turn Bianca down on our wedding night, and the memory of her full breasts, the feeling of her mouth on mine as she pressed herself against me, has had me taking myself in my hand every night since.

But it's not enough.

I'm not sure I could show the same restraint if she were to stand and slip off that robe to reveal her luscious body to me.

A soft chuckle snaps me out of my haze.

"Is something funny?"

"Sorry. It just seems as if we're blurring the lines between art and erotica."

I glance down to see that my cock is at full attention.

I bite back a groan as it throbs painfully, desperate to spill.

My mind fills with images of Bianca's breasts, and I can't help but take my cock in my hand and squeeze it hard.

"Maybe you need to come over here so I can make things clearer for you." A smirk tugs at my lips.

Bianca stares at me wide-eyed as she watches me pump my length, her mouth falling open as I roll my hand over the head and let out a deep, guttural groan.

I watch her intently as her gaze turns hazy, and I know she wants this as badly as I do. That she's imagining what it would be like to have me thrust my cock into her mouth and spill down her throat.

I think perhaps she might walk away from the way she's hesitating. But as I roll my hand once more over the tip and suck in a breath, she sets her paintbrush down and walks over to me.

Continuing to work my cock, I admire those shapely legs.

"Come here." I release my cock to sink my fingers into the soft silk of her robe, pulling her closer to stand between my thighs.

Her hands find my shoulders to steady herself, and I shudder at the warmth of her touch, my cock twitching at the thought of what I might find beneath this robe.

I tug at the ties, letting the robe fall open to reveal smooth skin and soft curves that are begging to be explored with my tongue.

"Take off the robe." My voice is gravelly as I try to steady myself.

My cock is practically screaming at me to pull Bianca down onto my lap and let her ride me until we're both gasping with release, but I need to take my time.

Bianca's eyes remain locked on mine as she shrugs out of her robe, the pale silk falling around her feet.

I swallow a groan as I take in her naked body—my eyes roaming over the soft swell of her breasts, those perfect hard peaks that I'm desperate to suck on. Trailing lower, I admire the curve of her waist before glancing down at the apex of her thighs.

"So fucking beautiful."

Leaning forward, I press a soft kiss to her belly.

She gasps, her fingers sinking into my shoulders as my tongue darts out to lick her skin.

I chuckle as she starts rubbing her thighs together. I can only imagine how wet she must be for me.

My mouth waters.

I move my fingers to her hips, squeezing them softly. "I think it's my turn now to show you *my* talent."

I press another kiss to her stomach as I trail my hands up to her breasts, tracing the soft underside with my fingertips before brushing my thumb over the sensitive peaks.

She gasps, arching into my touch as I continue pressing kisses to her stomach as I start working her breasts.

"I wanted to do this on our wedding night," I murmur against her skin.

She sighs as I knead her soft flesh.

"I also wanted to do this." I bring my right hand down to her hip, squeezing it once before dipping between her thighs.

We both gasp as I run two fingers along her drenched core.

"Ptichka moya," I groan, my cock throbbing with the need to sink deep inside her wetness.

I bring my fingers up to her swollen clit and start rubbing lazy circles around it, reveling in the way it makes Bianca squirm. I know she's desperate to be filled from the way she's rubbing her thighs together but not yet. I'm enjoying teasing her too much.

"Please."

I look up and almost come at the look in her eyes.

"What do you want, Bianca?" I reach forward to trace my tongue up her abdomen as I continue kneading her right breast, taking her nipple between my thumb and forefinger and tweaking it hard.

"More," she groans.

"So greedy." I chuckle against her skin as I let my index finger circle her entrance before dipping inside.

She moans, clinging to me as I sink my finger inside, all the way to the knuckle.

Her pussy clenches around me, and my eyes flutter closed as I try my best to stay calm.

I want to take my time exploring her body, to get her off before my cock comes anywhere near her.

"Can you take another?" I rub her clit a little harder.

"Yes," she gasps.

"Good girl." I sink another finger inside her pussy as I continue to work her clit.

She lets out a whimper as I curl my fingers, letting them graze those sensitive inner walls.

"Oh fuck!" Her hips grind against my hand as her orgasm starts to build.

She's so wet, and the sound of my fingers slipping in and out of her pussy is making my cock start to leak.

I want nothing more than to take my shaft in my hand, but this isn't about me.

She comes first. Always.

"That's it, *ptichka*."

I drop my hand from her breast to wrap around her waist to try and keep her steady.

Her movements are becoming hurried as I quicken my pace, pumping in a third finger as I rub her clit, and I know I'll only have to curl my fingers once more, and she'll reach her pleasure.

"Are you ready to come for me, *solnyshka*?"

"*Yes*," she groans, her nails painfully clawing at my shoulders.

I chuckle, loving how responsive her body is to my touch.

If she's like this with just my fingers...

"Come for me, Bianca." I curl my fingers, pressing my thumb hard against her clit.

She cries out, clinging to my shoulders as her hips buck, riding out her orgasm as I continue to finger her.

My hand is drenched with her arousal, making my cock throb so painfully that I have to shift my hips so that I'm brushing the tip against her thigh to try and relieve the ache.

She's gasping for breath as she comes down from her pleasure, her legs shaking as I slowly pull my fingers free.

I look up, locking eyes with her as I bring my fingers to my mouth and suck.

"Mmm..." I groan, my eyes almost rolling at the sweet taste of her arousal. "Fuck, *ptichka*, you taste *incredible*."

A soft whimper escapes her as I lick my fingers clean.

"Can I taste?" she whispers, her eyes flashing with need.

"Come here." I take her by the hips, pulling her toward me.

Bianca wraps her arms around my neck as she straddles my lap, hovering just above my cock.

She bends down to press her lips to mine, her tongue darting out to trace my lower lip.

I instantly part them so that our tongues tangle together, both of us moaning at the taste of her arousal.

"Do you like tasting yourself on my tongue?" I whisper against her lips.

"It's...sweet." Her cheeks flush.

"I can't wait to try it straight from the source."

I trace my tongue along her jaw and down her neck.

She arches against me, giving me more access, so I press my lips to the curve between her neck and shoulder and suck.

Her skin has a slight sheen from her orgasm, mixing her sweet vanilla scent with a salty taste. It's intoxicating.

"Are you going to ride me, *ptichka*?"

"Yes." She rests her forehead against mine.

I grin, squeezing her hips as I lower her just enough for my tip to tease her entrance.

"Mmm..." She wiggles her hips.

"Before we go any further, *solnyshka*, I need to hear you say that you want this." I look deep into her pools of blue. "Tell me you want me to fuck you, Bianca."

Her eyes glaze with pleasure as she nods.

"Say it."

"Fuck me, Alexei."

"Thank fuck," I groan as I tighten my hold on her hips and pull her down onto my cock with one hard thrust.

She cries out, her head falling back as I fill her to the hilt.

So fucking tight.

I grit my teeth to try and keep myself from coming right then, especially as her hips start moving.

But I still her, rubbing soothing circles on her hips with my thumbs. "Let yourself adjust, *ptichka*,"

"I'm so *full*," she moans, her eyes fluttering closed.

"I know. You're taking me so well."

"I-I need more." She opens her eyes to gaze down at me, her blue eyes so glazed with pleasure.

"Ride me, *solnyshka*."

Her body shivers, but her hips start moving as she slowly begins to grind on my cock.

I glance down to where we're both joined as she lifts herself off me until my head is barely inside her before she slams herself back down.

We both let out a moan as I fill her once more, and then she's rocking her hips, finding her own rhythm.

"S-so good."

"You feel like silk," I groan, thrusting my hips so that I can take her deeper.

Her eyes roll at the sensation, so I do it again, watching in awe as her breasts bounce with each movement.

I move my right hand so that I can circle my thumb over her clit, my other arm wrapping around her waist as I thrust up into her.

Bianca matches my thrusts, slamming down onto my cock so perfectly, the inner walls of her pussy clenching me so hard I know I won't last long.

And from the sweet moans that spill from her lips, I know she's close.

"Alexei," she groans, clawing at my shoulders.

I bury my face in her breasts, sucking and licking at them as she bounces up and down my length.

Hearing my name fall from her lips as she chases her release is my undoing.

"Fuck," I groan. "I'm close."

"*Yes!*"

I work her clit harder, faster, feeling her tighten even more around me.

Our movements become sloppy, and I have to tighten my arm around Bianca's waist to keep her steady as I pound my cock into her.

"That's it, *ptichka*, come around my cock," I growl, taking her nipple into my mouth and sucking hard.

"*Alexei!*"

Her crying my name as her pussy pulses around my cock is heaven, and it only takes me one more hard thrust before I'm spilling inside her.

"Fuck, yes," I groan, pulling Bianca tight against me as her pussy takes every last drop from me.

"Oh, my god," she moans, burying her face in my neck.

I trace my fingers up and down her back as we catch our breath, loving how flushed her skin is from her orgasm.

"Incredible." I kiss her shoulder.

She chuckles. "I thought sex was meant to suck once you got married."

"Maybe we need to keep testing the theory, just to be sure." I move my hips slightly, my cock still buried inside her heat.

"Mmm..."

I love the way she's clinging to me, as if she never wants to let me go. I know at this moment, I don't either.

"We should get some sleep, *solnyshka*."

She lifts her head and presses one last kiss to my lips, the gesture so soft it takes me by surprise.

The moment she lifts herself off me, I'm already craving

more. But I keep still, watching as Bianca bends to pick up her robe, her skin so flushed and glowing that I can't seem to take my eyes off her.

"What?" She ties her robe. "I know my hair probably looks a mess."

She smoothes her tousled brown locks with her hands.

Fuck, she's gorgeous. I want to wake up to her on my bed every day.

What? Where did that come from?

I shake my head, trying to clear the post-sex haze that is clouding my mind.

"I have some more work to do." I get to my feet, quickly pulling on my clothes.

"At this hour?"

I don't miss the hurt in her voice as I hurry to dress, but I can't tell her the truth.

"Yes."

I have to get away from her before I fully lose myself to her. So, I keep my eyes down, focusing on re-buttoning my shirt and zipping up my pants to avoid her gaze before walking over to the door.

"Get some sleep, *solnyshka*. I'll see you for breakfast."

I glance over my shoulder to meet her eyes.

All evidence of the bliss she felt moments before is gone, replaced by icy indifference as she regards me.

Good. This is just an arrangement, I need to remember that.

10

BIANCA

"I have a request."

Alexei's at his usual seat at the counter, watching me over the top of his coffee mug as I potter about the kitchen.

He watched me in silence as I made the coffee which unnerved me. I was expecting a few teasing comments about what we did last night, but so far there's been nothing.

His gaze has been almost indifferent.

Does he regret what we did? Was that why he left so abruptly afterwards?

I stayed in my studio and worked on the painting of him to try and sort through my emotions.

We shouldn't have slept together, it crossed so many boundaries. But the way he was looking at me like he wanted to devour me had me losing control of all my morals.

It's been so long since someone looked at me like *that*.

"A request?" Alexei raises an eyebrow.

"Yes." I lean against the countertop, clutching my own coffee to keep my hands busy. To stop myself from crossing the distance between us and sinking my fingers into the soft fabric of his shirt.

His hands will go to my hips, lifting me onto the counter where he'll pull down my shorts and bury his face between my thighs, sinking his tongue deep inside my pussy...

"Bianca?"

"Huh?"

"You had a request for me?" Alexei chuckles, as if he can read every thought racing through my mind on my face, and from the way his gaze darkens, I know he's thinking the same thing.

"Uh, yes. I do." I clear my throat. "I want to see Zara."

"Zara?"

"My best friend."

Alexei frowns, setting his mug down and folding his arms across his chest.

"I haven't seen her for weeks, and she doesn't even know I'm married."

"Bianca—"

"I know what you are going to say, but Zara can be trusted. I've known her most of my life and to have gone through such a huge life change without her has been hard. I just... I want my old life back, or at least part of it. I haven't even been able to call her. You took away my phone, my car, everything! If I can only go and visit her, I promise I won't tell her the truth behind our marriage, and I'll even take security with me if you really want."

Alexei contemplates me for a moment, his eyes searching my face.

It takes everything in me not to look away.

"This is important to you."

"Very."

His shoulders heave as he lets out a long breath.

"I have terms."

My stomach flutters as I realize seeing Zara might actually be a possibility.

"She will come to the house, and I will have someone collect her in a car to bring her here."

I open my mouth to object, to demand that he not be so controlling, but I also want to acknowledge the fact that he's meeting me halfway.

"I appreciate that."

"And I hope this goes without saying but you cannot, under any circumstances, tell her the real reason behind our marriage, *ptichka*."

"I'm not sure I even know the real reason."

My stomach is a bundle of nerves as I put on some makeup at my vanity to try and hide the dark circles under my eyes.

Zara's going to be here any minute, and I have no idea how I'm going to explain to her that I got married and moved out of the city without telling her a damn thing.

She's going to be pissed as hell.

I quickly run a brush through my hair and throw it up into a ponytail before hurrying down the two flights of stairs at the sound of car tires crunching across gravel.

"She's here." I'm almost vibrating.

Zara's more than a best friend to me. She's my rock. My ride or die.

Growing up an only child and with a father as overbearing as mine meant I was lonely a lot of the time.

But when I went away to college and met Zara when we were rooming together freshman year, it was like I had found the sister I had always wanted.

So, to have gotten married without her even knowing…

I swallow the lump in my throat as I open up the front door and plaster a smile on my face as Zara climbs out of the ridiculously obnoxious blacked-out Hummer and stalks toward me.

Her green eyes are narrowed on me as she climbs the few steps up to the front door, her arms folded across her chest as she looks over me.

"I think somebody has some explaining to do." She raises her eyebrows.

Where I am petite and dark-haired and tan-skinned, Zara's the opposite. With pale skin, blonde hair, and legs to die for, she's like a walking Victoria's Secret model.

I huff a nervous laugh and open the door wider.

"Coffee?"

Zara follows behind me, deathly quiet, as I take us through to the kitchen and get to work making a fresh pot of coffee.

She perches at the counter, in the very seat Alexei was in only a few hours ago, and I briefly fill her in on my news, keeping the details as minimal as possible.

"Married?"

I cringe at the tone in her voice, but nod.

"Yes."

"You got married."

"It was a last-minute thing—"

"You got *married*?"

"Zara, you need to understand—"

"I didn't even know you were dating anyone."

My chest feels like it's being cracked open at the hurt in her eyes.

"Well, I wasn't, really…"

"But you got married."

"You keep repeating it."

"Because it doesn't make any sense!" Zara huffs. "You weren't dating, but you married a guy? A guy who, by the looks of it, is fucking *loaded* and requires me to travel with a bodyguard just to see you for coffee! You haven't answered any of my texts or calls for weeks. Honestly, if it wasn't for the fact that your dad told me you lost your phone, I would've called the police. Seriously, B, what the hell is going on? Because this is starting to freak me out."

I open my mouth to reply, but I don't have the words to explain. Not in a way that would make Zara not feel so betrayed.

"Why didn't you at least invite me?" Her voice wobbles. "Did you not want me there?"

"Zara." I sigh, crossing over to the island and sliding into the stool beside her.

Reaching for her hand, I clutch it tightly, hoping that she can hear the sincerity in my voice. "I wish you were there. But in truth, it wasn't even really a wedding. We signed the documentation and that was it. It was all so rushed, I barely had a moment to get my head around it."

"Did he force you into this?" She glances over her shoulder as if worried we might be overheard.

Knowing Alexei, there are cameras in every room in this house, so it would make no difference. I wouldn't be surprised if he was up in his office watching over this entire interaction right now.

"N-no, nothing like that." I force my mouth into a smile that I hope reflects more 'marital bliss' rather than 'arranged marriage with mafia lord.' "Trust me, you're the only person I would've wanted there."

"This is a lot to take in." She sinks her teeth into her lower lip. "I don't even know the guy."

Neither do I.

"I know, Zara. I'm so sorry. I hope you can forgive me." My voice cracks at the thought of Zara not being able to let this go.

What if we can't get past this?

"We're best friends. Of course, I forgive you."

"You do?"

She wraps her arms around my shoulders and hugs me tightly.

I screw my eyes shut to try and keep the tears from falling.

"Of course. I mean, it might take me some time to get used to all of this—" She gestures to the enormous kitchen. "—but it's not worth losing you over. I'm sure you had a good reason to keep this quiet."

"I don't deserve you," I mumble into her shoulder, clinging to her so tightly.

"Marriage has turned you into a weeping mess, B." She chuckles softly, and the sound is like music to my ears. "Now, how about a tour of the new digs?"

We tour the ground floor of the house, and with each room Zara's eyes get bigger and bigger to the point I'm worried they might pop out of her head.

"What is it your husband does again?"

"He, uh... He's an entrepreneur." I try not to visibly cringe.

Before Zara has the opportunity to ask any more questions that I don't have the answer to, we reach my new studio.

I open the door and step inside, my blood heating as my eyes land on the cream loveseat against the wall.

"Holy shit."

"I know." I smile, looking around the room.

"What is *that*?" Zara points at the canvas resting on my easel.

My cheeks burn as images of last night flood my mind.

"Uh... That..."

"That is a very naked man!" Zara laughs, hurrying over to the easel to admire the portrait.

After Alexei left last night to go back to his office, I stayed working on his portrait until my eyes were so heavy with fatigue that I eventually crawled into bed at almost 6 a.m. Though my body clock had me up less than an hour later.

"Yes, it is." My cheeks are blazing.

"I didn't realize you painted such...*erotica*."

"It's not erotica." Though what followed certainly was.

"Wait a minute..." Zara's eyes narrow as she studies the painting. "Is that your husband?"

She glances over her shoulder at me.

I sheepishly nod, and her eyes light up.

"He's... Wow, is it to scale?"

"Zara!"

"What?" Zara laughs. "I need to know that the man my best friend married is satisfying her."

"Oh my god," I groan, burying my face in my hands. "I'm starting to regret inviting you over here."

"I have no regrets." Zara places her hands on her hips, tilting her head to the side as she admires my work. "I can see why you married the man on the spot, with a dick like that."

"*Zara!*"

"Maybe I should get into painting." She laughs.

"There is no way you'd be able to stare at a naked man for hours on end without fucking him."

"True... But I bet it would make for incredible foreplay." She looks at me with a knowing look in her eye.

"I wouldn't know..." I choke out.

"I need details, *now*."

My cheeks are burning hot by the time Zara and I head back to the kitchen following our very detailed conversation about Alexei's cock. It only intensifies when we walk into the kitchen to find Alexei leaning against the counter sipping a double espresso.

I had hoped that one night with Alexei would be enough to get it out of my system. That it was the mystery of him that I was so intoxicated by.

How wrong I was...

Knowing what it's like to feel his warm skin beneath my fingertips, to have the sounds of his rough grunts as he fucks me ring in my ears has me so wet and hot between my thighs that I have to stifle a moan.

Alexei's eyes darken as he looks at me, and I know that he's thinking the exact same thing.

"Hi, I'm Zara."

Alexei blinks and turns to face my friend, the picture of ease as he sets his cup down and strolls over to us.

"Pleasure to meet you, Zara, I'm Alexei." He holds out a hand for her to shake. "I trust you arrived here okay?"

I glance at Zara and notice a pink tinge to her cheeks as she looks up at Alexei.

"I felt like a celebrity." She laughs.

Amusement dances in Alexei's eyes as he observes Zara.

"And this house is *incredible*."

"Thank you." Alexei dips his chin. "You're welcome any time."

His eyes snap to mine, and my breath hitches in my throat at the warmth in his expression.

"Thank you," I mouth, and he flashes me a wink.

But then his eyes flick to something behind us, and his jaw instantly clenches.

"Aren't you going to introduce me?" a deep male voice sounds from behind us.

I whirl, my hand going to my chest as I take in the towering presence of who I can only assume is one of Alexei's brothers, given the dark hair and impressive build.

"And who is this?" Zara raises her eyebrows.

"I'm Dimitri." He crosses the room in a handful of strides and offers a hand for Zara to shake. "Alexei's brother."

I try to hide my surprise as Zara takes Dimitri's hand.

I catch Alexei's eye, and he's frowning as he sinks his hands into the pockets of his pants.

"Good to see you again, Bianca." Dimitri flashes me a grin.

I force a smile, trying to hide the fact that this is the first conversation I've shared with my now brother-in-law.

How I would get around explaining *that* to Zara I have no idea.

Alexei folds his arms over his chest. "Dimitri was just leaving."

"Was I?" Dimitri's eyes lock back on Zara.

I don't miss the way they rake over her body, and I'm instantly reaching for her arm to pull her away. The last thing I want is for Zara to get caught up in the twisted web that is the Koslov family.

"Yes, you were," Alexei warns.

"Shame." Dimitri's tongue darts out to lick his lips. "You look like you know how to have some fun."

Zara looks him up and down. "And you look like you have too much fun."

I freeze, but then Dimitri is throwing his head back and howling with laughter.

"Oh, I like her." He grins. "She can visit more often."

"Maybe when you're not here," Alexei mutters.

"Well, I can always give you my number, *pcholka*, and I can show you how much fun I am."

"Dimitri..." Alexei groans, but his brother only grins.

"Thanks for such an incredible offer, but I think I'll pass." Zara shrugs. "I can spot a player a mile away. Besides, I prefer my men when they're not riddled with sexually transmitted diseases."

I glance at Alexei who's trying to fight a smile as Dimitri is shocked into silence.

I bet he doesn't get turned down very often, looking the way he does. Perhaps he'll do well to have Zara knock his ego down a peg or two.

"I'll walk you out." Alexei places a hand on his brother's shoulder and guides him out of the kitchen.

"Well, I think you've officially won over Alexei." I laugh as Zara watches Dimitri be escorted out of the kitchen.

She frowns. "And the brother by the looks of it."

Zara stays for most of the afternoon, and she fills me in with life back in the city.

I try to seem happy as I listen to her ramble on about our favorite spots for coffee by Central Park and the new workout classes she's tried, but it only makes me feel resentful.

How could my father have ripped my life out from underneath me like this?

What hurts even more is that he hasn't bothered to reach out since the wedding, which hurts more than I care to admit. We might not be the closest, but I would have at least thought he'd want to make sure I was okay.

So, I decide to take matters into my own hands.

I no longer have a cell after Alexei confiscated it the night of our wedding, but that doesn't mean there aren't other options.

Zara is about to leave, but before she does, I take my chance.

"Zara, since I lost my phone, is it okay that I use yours to call my dad? I haven't talked to him in forever."

She smiles. "Sure." Rummaging through her bag, she retrieves it and hands it to me. "Here."

I dial the number to my dad's cell and step away from my friend to try and get some privacy.

My stomach starts to knot as the phone begins to ring, anxious about what I might say.

I know we left things amicably on the night of my wedding, but I still can't shake the betrayal I feel that he would give me away to a stranger as easily as he did. The fact that I've also now slept with Alexei Koslov complicates things a little, but my father does not need to be made aware of that information.

After a minute, my father still hasn't picked up, and I realize that perhaps he might be avoiding me.

When it hits voicemail, I hang up the phone. "You can't hide forever, *Papino*."

11

ALEXEI

"I think my brother might have a thing for your friend." I lean against the doorway to the kitchen that evening.

Bianca rolls her eyes as she continues tucking into a bowl of chocolate ice cream. She's wearing a floral sundress that is hitched up around her thighs, exposing her tanned skin to me.

I can't stop the feeling of blood rushing to my cock as I watch her slowly lick the spoon, aching to lick the chocolate smeared around her full lips.

"He's not allowed anywhere near her." She lifts her eyes to mine. "I mean it, Alexei."

"I couldn't agree more. Zara had my brother figured out in seconds." I chuckle. "Dimitri is not one to commit and settle down."

"And you are?"

"I am now."

Bianca rolls her eyes and looks away.

"I thought you wanted your brothers to stay away while

I'm here." She dips her spoon back into the ice cream and pops it back in her mouth.

I dig my nails into my palms as I watch her.

"I did, but my brothers don't like to follow rules. I'm sorry if his being here made you uncomfortable. I will kindly remind my brother of such a request. He stopped by to drop off some paperwork, and I thought he had let himself out, but clearly he had other ideas."

She shrugs, keeping her eyes down.

"It's his house."

"It's *your* house."

She's quiet for a moment, tapping the spoon against her lips. Her delicate shoulders are hunched over and that lightness I saw in her eyes only a few hours ago has been dimmed once more.

"Are you glad Zara came to visit?"

"Yes and no." She sets her bowl down beside her. "It was hard lying to her."

"I'm sorry you had to lie."

"She's my family, Alexei. Her and my father. They're all I have." Her voice cracks and she sets down the spoon on the counter before burying her face in her hands, her dark hair falling in front of her face. "You don't know how lucky you are to have siblings."

I push off the doorframe and close the distance between us. I know it's selfish of me to want to be close to her when she's feeling so vulnerable, but I hate the fact that I'm the reason for it. That marrying me has taken away the people that she loves the most in this world.

"Now that you've married me, you have three brothers by default."

I reach to brush her hair behind her ear, and she leans

slightly into my touch, dropping her hands to her lap and glancing up at me beneath dark lashes.

I smile. "Be careful what you wish for."

"I suppose you're right."

"Did you find it hard growing up as an only child?"

Bianca nods. "I was very lonely. My father isn't the most affectionate man in the world, and losing my mother the way I did... I always felt responsible, like I had killed her."

"What happened to your mother was in no way your fault." I take her hand, knowing firsthand how difficult it can be to lose someone you love. "Grief can make us feel and do crazy things."

"Like marrying a complete stranger?" Bianca jokes.

I chuckle and move closer to her. "Admit it, you're warming to me."

She frowns, looking up at me with those beautiful blue eyes.

"Why did you leave so quickly last night?"

My chest aches at the hurt in Bianca's voice, but I know she deserves an answer.

"I felt guilty..."

"Why?"

"Because I took advantage." I curse myself for being so selfish. "You were vulnerable and—"

"Stop." She places a hand on my chest. "You didn't take advantage. I wanted it too."

"Do you regret it?"

Her eyes search my face for a moment, lingering a little longer on my lips. "No. Do you?"

"My only regret is that I didn't get a chance to taste you more." My voice rasps as I imagine running my tongue along her slick pussy.

Bianca's eyes glaze over, and a feral grin tugs at my lips.

"Do you want that, Bianca? Do you want me to bury my face between your thighs?"

Bianca lets out a soft gasp, and a soft blush creeps across her skin.

"Alexei... This complicates things."

"Perhaps, but I'm willing to risk the consequences if you are."

She hesitates for a moment.

Last night was different. It was clear we both wanted to get it out of our system, have it be a one-time thing.

But I knew the moment I left her studio last night that I wouldn't be able to resist her now that I know what it's like to have her come around my cock.

"I want this, Alexei."

"Lie back on the counter, *solnyshka*."

My cock is already hard and aching, desperate to be buried inside her tight pussy, but I need to taste her first. From the source this time.

Bianca lets out a soft, breathy whimper but she does as I ask. She unravels her legs and lies back on the cold marble, and I wrap my hands around the backs of her knees, spreading them wide.

"I've been able to think of nothing but your pussy all day." I dip my head to press a kiss to the inside of her thigh.

She gasps, her back arching under my touch.

"Have you thought about my cock, Bianca?"

"Yes."

I graze my teeth against her skin as I run my hands up her thighs, hitching her dress higher to reveal a tiny pair of purple lace panties.

"I can tell." I trace a finger along the damp seam.

I groan as my cock strains against the zipper on my

pants, aching to be set free, but I know the moment I do, I won't be able to stop myself from taking her right here on this counter.

"I-I've been aching all day."

I move to graze my finger over her clit through the thin material.

"You were so *big*."

"Mmm, you took me so well, *solnyshka*." I kiss her inner thigh. "Once you've come on my tongue, I'm going to take you upstairs to my bed and fuck you. Do you want that, Bianca?"

She moans, her hips grinding as I lick along her inner thigh.

As I get to her covered pussy, I dip my head and wrap my lips around her clit through the material and suck hard.

She cries out, her hands going to my hair as I flick my tongue over the swollen bud.

"Alexei, please."

I have to grit my teeth as my cock throbs painfully. I'm desperate to take it in my hand as I devour Bianca's pussy, but I want all of my attention on her pleasure.

I softly kiss along her core, the sweet taste of her arousal on her panties making me groan.

"You're so wet, *solnyshka*. Is it time to take off these panties?"

"God, yes."

I keep my eyes locked on her pussy as I dip my fingers into the waistband and pull her panties down her thighs.

"Fuck, *ptichka*, look at you," I groan at the sight of her glistening core.

I pocket her panties and lean forward, throwing her legs over my shoulders as I run my tongue along her center.

We both groan simultaneously, the sweet taste of her making my cock start to leak in my pants.

I reach down to grasp my throbbing length through my pants to try and ease the ache as I continue to devour Bianca with long, slow licks.

"Oh god." Her fingers knot in my hair as she starts to slowly grind against my face.

I move my hands to grip her ass, bringing her closer against me as I sink my tongue inside her pussy, my eyes rolling as her arousal starts to run down my chin.

Fuck going upstairs, once I'm done making her come on my tongue, I'm going to bend her over this counter and fuck her from behind.

Just the thought of getting to sink myself inside her gets me working her clit faster.

I dip my tongue inside before running it along the center and flicking it over her swollen bundle of nerves.

Bianca's breathing is coming in short pants, and I look up to find her pulling her dress down to expose those perfect breasts.

"*Solnyshka*," I groan, almost coming at the sight.

She whimpers as she kneads her swollen breasts, her thumbs rubbing back and forth over her pebbled nipples.

"I'm close," she gasps as her back arches.

"Maybe this will help." I take my right hand and sink two fingers inside her as I take her clit between my teeth.

"Yes!" she cries, her pussy clenching around my fingers as I start to pump them inside her.

Her thighs are starting to shake, so I increase my pace, sucking and licking her clit as I continue to sink my fingers deep inside her.

"Come for me, *ptichka*." I curl my fingers inside her,

brushing those delicate inner walls that I know tip her over the edge.

Bianca arches off the counter, her hands moving to grip my hair so tightly as her orgasm hits.

I can't get enough.

The way she grinds against my face and moans my name as I work her through her climax has me almost feral with the need to be inside her.

Once she's collapsed back against the counter, her breathing coming in heavy pants, I slide my fingers out of her pussy and press a kiss to the inside of each thigh.

"Come here, *solnyshka*." I lock her shaking thighs around my waist, wrapping my arms around her to lift her off the counter.

She wraps her arms around my neck and kisses me deeply, moaning as she tastes her arousal on my tongue.

Her hips instantly move against me as my cock grazes her bare pussy and when she feels how ready I am for her, she moans even louder.

"Do you like tasting yourself on my tongue?" I sink my fingers into her hair and angle her head so I can deepen the kiss.

"Mmm..." she sighs as our tongues entwine. "I want to taste you."

My hips buck at the thought of Bianca getting on her knees and taking my cock into her delicate mouth and working me with her tongue.

I can feel her wetness through my pants, and I let out a deep guttural sound as I try to calm myself down long enough to get her upstairs and onto a bed.

"Not yet," I choke.

She chuckles against my lips as she grinds her pussy against me again.

"If you keep doing that, I'm going to come before I'm even inside you," I growl.

Bianca's eyes darken, and she takes her lower lip between her teeth.

"Is that what you want, *ptichka*? For me to come inside you?" I grunt.

"I want you…" She leans forward to kiss me softly. "To come on my breasts."

"Fuck," I hiss, my eyes fluttering closed as I try to ignore my aching cock.

"And then…" She kisses me again. "I want you to come in my mouth."

"*Bianca.*"

She kisses me once more, laughter falling from her lips as she arches against me so that her nipples can brush against the fabric of my shirt.

"And then… I want you to come inside me."

12

ALEXEI

I BARELY REGISTER THE FACT THAT MY FEET ARE moving.

Bianca trails soft kisses along my jaw and neck as I carry her up the stairs, the soft sighs falling from her lips like music to my ears.

She's addictive, and that should scare the fuck out of me, but right now as she's wrapping her legs around my waist, all I care about is pulling my cock free and sinking so deep inside her that I see stars.

I kick open the door to her bedroom and toss her down on the bed, her legs splaying open to reveal her slick pussy to me once more.

"Take off your clothes." My voice is hoarse with need as I make quick work of removing my shirt.

Bianca moves to a kneeling position and takes the hem of her dress and lifts it up over her head.

I grind my teeth at the sight of those perfect breasts, the soft skin of her belly, so desperate to have her beneath me.

"Lie back and spread your legs for me, *solnyshka*."

Bianca's throat bobs, her eyes flicking downwards to watch me as I start undoing my pants.

"Now."

She does as I say, and as I'm pulling my pants and boxers down over my thighs, she parts those delicious thighs to reveal herself to me.

My cock springs free, the tip already glistening with my arousal, and I'm instantly taking it in my hand, pumping myself hard and fast as I revel in the sight before me.

"So fucking beautiful," I growl.

Bianca lifts herself onto her elbows and gasps as her eyes fall to my cock. She starts to close her thighs, no doubt desperate to rub them together to relieve the ache, but I won't allow it.

"Keep them open, *solnyshka*." I step out of my pants, moving to the edge of the bed, all the while still working my cock.

She bites her lower lip but widens her thighs, her eyes pleading with me to relieve her ache.

"Good girl."

I watch her for a moment, loving how worked up she's getting as she watches me fist my aching length.

"Are you ready for me, *ptichka*?" My voice is gravel as I try to steady myself.

"Yes," she gasps, her eyebrows pinching together as I climb onto the bed and settle myself between her thighs.

I wrap my left hand around the back of her neck and rest all of my weight on that side as I reach for my cock and line it up with her entrance, rubbing the tip teasingly across her clit.

"Oh!" She arches into me so that her nipples brush my pecs.

Letting a smile tug at my lips, I watch her eyes flutter closed with the small amount of pleasure I'm allowing her.

I repeat the motion once more before running my head down her core and slowly pushing inside her tight heat.

"Fuck," I hiss as I shift my weight onto both elbows and slowly thrust my hips, groaning as Bianca grips me so tightly I almost come.

"This is how I should've taken you last night," I murmur, bending down to press a kiss to her mouth as I slowly slide my cock in all the way to the hilt. "Slow and deep."

"*Alexei.*" Bianca's pussy clenches around my cock.

I bury my face in her neck, the sound of my name spilling from her lips almost too much to bear.

But I keep the pace slow, trailing kisses along her jaw and neck, my hands moving to knead her full breasts as we move together.

When my balls start to tighten, I reach around the back of her knee and lift her leg over my shoulder so I can thrust even deeper. From the way Bianca is clawing at my back with each stroke, I know her climax is building, but I don't want her to come just yet.

"What do you want, *solnyshka*?" I nip at the delicate skin beneath.

"Harder," she gasps, her nails sinking into my shoulders.

"Where are your manners, *ptichka*?" I pull my cock out until the tip is barely grazing her entrance.

Bianca squirms beneath me, desperately trying to push her hips upwards, but I keep her still with my hands.

"*Please,*" she moans.

I run my nose along her jaw, inhaling her sweet vanilla scent. "Please...?"

"Please fuck me *hard*," she groans.

"My pleasure, *solnyshka*." I chuckle as I move to cover her mouth with mine as I slam into her so hard the headboard crashes against the wall.

There's nothing sweet or tender about my movements and from the breathy sounds that spill from Bianca, I know she's about to fall over the edge.

She's so wet my cock is begging for me to spill inside her.

My jaw aches from clenching it so hard as I fight the urge to come.

Not yet. She has to come with me.

I want her to clench around my cock and milk every last drop of cum from me.

"Oh, yes. Fuck, I'm close!" she cries.

The base of my spine starts to tingle, and I know it's about to be game over, especially when Bianca reaches between us and starts rubbing her clit.

"Oh, *ptichka*," I groan.

I watch as Bianca's eyes roll into the back of her head, her beautiful breasts bouncing with each thrust of my cock. And when her mouth parts, and her orgasm hits, she cries out my name, and I'm instantly spilling inside her as her pussy pulses around me.

"Shit." My hips buck as I give her every last drop.

When Bianca's thighs slacken around me, I slowly pull out as I softly kiss her.

"Let me get a towel," I murmur.

She sighs happily, her eyes closed and her cheeks flushed as I climb off the bed and dart into the adjoining bathroom.

I can't help but chuckle at how spent Bianca is as I clean her between her thighs, taking extra care of her sensitive flesh. I finish with a kiss to each thigh and one to her swollen bundle of nerves before climbing onto the bed beside her and pulling her against me.

"Any regrets, wife?" I run my hands through her tousled locks.

"Definitely not." She sighs, wrapping her arms around my waist and closing her eyes.

It doesn't take long for Bianca to fall asleep in my arms, and I hold her there for a while, enjoying the feeling of her warm body against mine.

But I know I should get back to work.

The point of this marriage was not to spend every night in her bed.

I might grow to regret crossing a line with Bianca, but not right now. Right now I want nothing more than to stay tangled up with her, slowly wake her up with kisses to her neck before climbing on top of her and fucking her until she's screaming my name again.

But this marriage was to provide protection for our new ally while we continued our work on taking down Mario Gilanto, which won't happen if I don't get out of my bed and get to work.

Once I'm dressed, I pull a blanket off the couch and drape it over her naked body.

"Sweet dreams, *solnyshka*." I press a kiss to her hair before slipping out of her room.

I decide to go and make myself a cup of coffee before heading to my office.

It's late, almost midnight, and I will likely have a few more hours of work to do before I can crawl into bed myself.

Not that I'll get much sleep.

What I don't expect to find when I walk into the kitchen is my three brothers standing around the island, all looking particularly sheepish.

"What the fuck are you doing here?"

Dimitri shoves his hands into his pockets. "We need to talk."

He's wearing a black shirt and pants, his signature look, though his dark hair is a little messier than usual... I pray he didn't follow Zara out of here and get himself tangled in something he can't walk away from.

Plus I think Bianca might actually castrate him if she ever caught wind that he had defiled her best friend.

"I thought you went back to the penthouse." I shake my head as I run my hands through my hair.

Danil catches my eye and gives me a knowing smirk.

Is it obvious what I just spent the last hour doing? Were they downstairs the whole time? I fucking hope not.

"I did, though I'd have much rather gone back to Zara's place." Dimitri chuckles.

I shoot him a warning glare, and the amusement instantly fades from his eyes.

"I need to change the fucking locks," I mutter under my breath.

"It's our house too." Mikhail looks like he's come straight from the gym, wearing black shorts and a T-shirt that are still damp with sweat that show off his full sleeves of tattoos.

"Not when Bianca Bellucci is sleeping upstairs it's not. I don't trust a single one of you assholes."

"I'm offended," Danil mock gasps.

"Can we get back to why we're here?" Mikhail butts in. "*Brat*, I think we should talk in your office."

I shake my head, not liking how close they'd all be to Bianca's very naked body. "We can talk in the lounge."

We walk out of the kitchen and across the large foyer until we reach the lounge at the far end of the house.

I take pride in knowing it's as far as we could get from Bianca, so I relax a little as my brothers take a seat on the two leather sofas, and I get to work pouring us all a drink from the bar cart in the corner.

"What's the issue that has you breaking into my house at gone midnight?" I take a drink over to Mikhail and Danil.

"We got an email through about an hour ago." Dimitri frowns. "Which you would know if you bothered to check your phone."

"I was busy."

I hand Dimitri a vodka and take a seat opposite him, beside Mikhail.

I glance between each of my brothers.

Danil and Mikhail both fail to meet my eyes. Even Dimitri's usually playful air has turned somber.

"Spit it out."

"The person we thought was responsible for *Mamochka* and *Papochka*... It turns out they were innocent."

Everyone is quiet for a moment as I take in what Dimitri is saying.

How is this possible?

"Says who?" I take a long sip of my drink.

"We received an anonymous tip with information about the real killer."

Danil flinches at Dimitri's words, and I hate that he's now old enough to sit in on these business talks.

It's a brutal game we have to play, and I tried to protect his innocence as long as I could.

But ultimately, he is a Koslov, and that comes with a price.

"How credible is this tip?" I look at Mikhail.

"I'm having one of my guys look into it. I forwarded him the info the moment it arrived in my inbox."

"Good." I down the rest of my drink, hissing as the alcohol burns my throat.

"What if it's Mario just messing with us?" Danil asks.

Dimitri shifts to face Danil, his broad body taking up most of the two-person couch.

Danil looks so young, with his clean-shaven face and leaner limbs, compared to the rugged build of Dimitri.

"Maybe this is his way of trying to mess with us."

I frown. "It's a pretty fucked up way of going about it."

"It's Gilanto's style," Dimitri growls. "He plays even dirtier than we do."

Danil glances nervously at me. "Do we take the bait?"

I shake my head. "Not until we can confirm if this information is legit."

Dimitri scoffs. "It's not like you not to take a swing at Gilanto. Since when do we need a reason?"

"We don't." I get to my feet to refill my glass. "But I don't want to take any unnecessary risks."

Mikhail shifts in his seat. "Because of Bianca."

"Yes, because of Bianca. I made a promise to her father to keep her safe and while she's living under my roof, I'm damn well not going to run straight into the lion's den without any legitimate reason. So, until your guy can confirm anything, none of us is to make a move against Mario Gilanto. Do I make myself clear?"

They each nod, though I don't miss the look they share between them.

I'm letting my feelings for Bianca get in the way of business, which is the exact opposite of what I wanted to happen.

I only hope Mario Gilanto doesn't decide to use that against me.

13

BIANCA

Alexei perches on a stool beside me as I paint. "Did you go to college?"

I think he secretly likes watching me paint, especially when the subject is his naked body.

"Yes, it's where I met Zara."

"Did you study art?"

I can't help but laugh at his question as I dip my brush into my jar of water.

"What's so funny?"

"My father would never let me study art." I shake my head. "He thought it was a nice hobby to keep me out of trouble, but when it came to picking my major, I had to study marketing and advertising so I could go into the *'family business'*."

I give Alexei a knowing smile, and he nods.

"It's a shame you weren't encouraged to pursue your art when it's clear you have a talent for it."

I shrug. "I gave up on my dream of ever pursuing a career in art a very long time ago. I was always destined to work for my father, being his only child and all."

Alexei is quiet for a moment, watching me as I start to add some shading to his abdominals.

My cheeks warm as he leans in close, his thigh brushing against me as he regards my work.

"It's so detailed." He glances at me.

I ignore his gaze, focusing instead on mixing the perfect shade of pink to add some dimension to his skin tone.

"You paid very close attention."

"Stop being crude."

Alexei laughs, and I can't fight that smile that pulls at my lips.

It's nice how easy we've become in each other's company over the last few weeks. Though I suppose when you're stuck in a house with no one else to talk to, you're likely to form some sort of relationship.

And the mind-blowing sex is also an added bonus that I wasn't expecting from this arrangement.

Alexei looks at the painting again. "Have you considered taking an art class at a local college in the evening?"

"Not really. My dad worked me very hard so I never had a lot of free time." I frown at my use of past tense.

It feels as if I'm talking about someone else's life rather than my own. A life that no longer exists to me.

"Hmm..."

I frown as Alexei gets to his feet and pulls his cell out of his back pocket and starts tapping away.

"What are you doing?"

He ignores my question as he continues to scroll on his phone, his eyes narrowed as they dart back and forth across the screen.

"Alexei?"

"They have an art class at Queen's College twice a week in the evening."

"So?"

Alexei looks up at me and nods his chin in the direction of his painting.

"So, I think you should nurture this talent, Bianca."

"You want me to go to an art class?"

"Yes, I think it would be good for you."

"Uh..." I'm so taken aback by Alexei's suggestion that I don't know how to respond.

I'm not used to people encouraging me like this. Sure, both my father and Zara think I'm talented, but my father has already laid the path of my life out for me, and Zara is realistic, and life as a creative is not sustainable in her eyes.

"I-I'll think about it."

"It's running tonight and it starts in an hour."

It's like he hasn't even heard me.

"Alexei." I sigh, setting down my paintbrush. "I appreciate you wanting to help but—"

"This will be good for you, Bianca." He tucks his phone back into his pocket. "And it's close by, so I can drive you there myself."

"Are you serious?"

"Yes. We leave in thirty minutes. That should give us enough time to sort out the enrollment fees and documents before the class."

I KNOW I SHOULD BE EXCITED TO BE LEAVING THE house for the first time in almost four weeks, but the truth is I'm not. Because once again the terms of such freedom have not been dictated by me.

I'm still a prisoner. Just a prisoner on a leash being driven to what I assume will be an overpriced still-life-painting seminar with a bodyguard who also happens to be my husband.

"I wish you'd let me look through the syllabus before making a decision," I mutter as Alexei pulls into the parking lot of the arts building.

He was quiet the entire drive over to the campus, and I was too busy sulking to care.

I glance around and notice a few students leaving the building carrying portfolios of their work and cases of supplies. I don't miss the fact that they glance at Alexei's car.

He was set on taking some ridiculous supercar, but I refused to get in.

I already feel out of place, and rocking up to class in a car that costs more than the tuition fees made me want the ground to open up and swallow me whole.

We compromised on a blacked-out Range Rover which isn't much better, but the look Alexei was giving me implied that he would throw me over his shoulder and carry me to campus if he had to.

"Sometimes, it's better to just be pushed," Alexei says. "So many people become paralyzed by indecision, they never take a step forward."

"And you assumed I would be like that? I'm not being funny, Alexei, but you don't know me at all."

"I know you enough."

I ball my hands into fists and stare straight ahead, my stomach knotting at the sight of the sign on the front of the building before us.

Queen's University Art Department.

This has been all I've ever wanted, to study art and spend my days painting. So why can't I be more excited?

Perhaps it's due to the fact that Alexei Koslov is the one to see me for who I am, and that scares the hell out of me.

The man has barely known me for four weeks, and yet he's actively going out of his way to nurture my talent.

My eyes start to prick with tears.

This is something my father should have done, but instead, he took this choice away from me too.

"If you're only doing this out of guilt, then don't bother." I swallow the lump in my throat.

"What do you mean?" Alexei unbuckles his seatbelt and turns in his seat to face me, but I keep my eyes forward, not wanting him to see me so upset.

"You feel guilty for marrying me, for taking me away from my life. So, you're trying to ease your conscience by giving me the chance to paint."

"I'm giving you the opportunity to nurture your talent. Something you weren't allowed to pursue because your father decided otherwise. I thought you'd be more pleased?"

I bow my head, hating the fact that *I* feel guilty for even questioning his motives.

I wish I could be more detached, but I ruined any chances of that the moment I sat down at the easel he bought me.

"You're right. I'm sorry. I'll see you after the class." I unbuckle my seatbelt and open the car door.

Alexei's eyes stay on me as I walk over to the red-bricked building, but I don't give him a second glance before I open the double doors and head inside.

It's fairly quiet as it's almost seven in the evening and most classes are finished for the day. But there's a door at the far end of the hall which is ajar, and there are quite a few people milling about inside.

My stomach is a bundle of nerves as I walk down the

hall, taking in the artwork that's hanging on the walls on either side of me. There's a mixture of abstract work, still life, and portraits, and the level of skill is enviable.

I wish Alexei had given me more time to think about this.

Art has always been something just for me, a creative outlet that helps me work through my emotions when I can feel myself falling into a dark place.

Though I thought about studying it before, it's not necessarily something I want to be graded on.

It seems Alexei called ahead and spoke to the head of admissions, as the moment I knock on the door and peer around into the classroom, a woman in her late thirties rushes over to me, a huge grin plastered on her face.

She has a mass of dark curls piled on her head, and she's wearing paint-covered overalls and a white T-shirt.

"You must be Bianca." She holds out her hand.

There's at least one ring on every one of her fingers, and heavy bangles hang from each of her wrists. "I'm Ella, I'll be running this class."

"Hi." I force a smile as I glance behind her at the rows of easels laid out.

Most of the other students are already sitting at one and pulling out their supplies, their projects already started.

My stomach sinks.

Was I meant to bring my own paints?

Ella seems to follow my train of thought as she drops my hand and wraps it around my shoulders, ushering me inside.

"All supplies will be provided for you, don't worry. But you're always welcome to bring your own if you prefer your own paint brushes or paint." She brings me over to a vacant stool at the back of the classroom. "You've only missed the first week, so you're not behind."

I glance to the person beside me, a girl around my age with blonde curly hair. She's working on a painting which seems to be very harrowing, with lots of dark colors and blood dripping down the edges.

"The theme of the first few weeks is grief," Ella explains.

I almost roll my eyes.

How on brand for me.

"You're welcome to use whatever medium you wish, I only ask that the piece reflects your own experience with grief. Not what you *think* grief is, but what you *know* it to be."

"Sounds great."

"Have fun!"

I take a seat at my stool and glance at my empty canvas.

A cart of supplies is beside me, with everything from chalks to watercolors.

I run my fingers over the tubes of paint, my mind already racing with ideas for my piece.

I settle for filling my palette with various shades of yellow, wanting to create a sort of contrast between the life I was meant to have and the one I ended up living.

The one where I ended up marrying Alexei Koslov...

I clear my throat and dip my brush into the paint, letting myself fall into a rhythm, enjoying the hustle and bustle around me as the other students work.

It's such a contrast to the quiet studio at home. Suddenly being surrounded by people after only seeing mainly Alexei for the past four weeks has me feeling nervous to talk to anyone.

The girl beside me leans in a bit. "You're new, right?"

I look over at her and nod, feeling my cheeks flush.

"Is it that obvious?"

She laughs, shaking her head of blonde curls.

"Sorry, I didn't mean it like that." She chuckles, her brown eyes crinkling as she regards me. "I'm Marnie."

"Bianca."

"It's nice to meet you." She smiles.

"You too. Are you studying at this college or…"

"I'm studying Art History, but I'm taking some extra art classes in the evening to build up my course credits. I'm hoping to graduate a few semesters early."

"Good for you." I look over at her canvas.

"What about you?"

"I graduated from NYU last spring. I majored in marketing and minored in advertising."

"Whoa, that's very different from art."

I sigh, picking up a fresh paintbrush. "It is. But this is my true passion."

"Good for you for making time for it. Many people don't. They just get sucked into the corporate world and leave everything that makes them happy behind them in exchange for a paycheck at the end of the month."

"I suppose…"

"What's your piece going to be on?"

I hesitate, putting down my brush and looking at my piece. I've done a rough outline of the shapes, though it still doesn't make much sense even to me.

"My mother died giving birth to me." Grief coats me. "So, I want to paint a contrast between two lives. One with her and one without."

"I get that."

I look to her and find her eyes filled with sympathy.

"My mom died when I was eight. We were in a car crash, and I survived."

"Oh god, I'm so sorry."

She waves me off. "It was a long time ago, but I've felt guilty for living ever since."

It's as if Marnie reached into my own mind and shared what she found out loud.

No one has ever understood what it meant when I spoke such feelings, and to know someone else feels the same is comforting.

"I know exactly what you mean."

We fall into an easy conversation as we work for the rest of the hour, choosing to share a little of our pasts but mostly our love for art.

As the class starts to wrap up, Ella gives us instructions on where to put our canvases to dry, and we get to work, tidying away our supplies.

"It was great having someone to chat with." Marnie smiles as we tidy our supply carts. "Maybe we could swap numbers or something?"

"Uh…" I no longer have a cell phone. Alexei took it after the wedding, and I've not been given a new one.

I try to ignore the anxious feeling in the pit of my stomach as I think of how little autonomy and freedom I actually have.

"It's cool if you don't want to—"

"No! It's not that. Sorry, I lost my phone and haven't got a new one yet. So, why don't you write yours down, and I'll text when I sort out my new number?"

"Sounds good." Marnie smiles. She scribbles down her number on a scrap piece of paper, and I tuck it into the pocket of my dress. "See you next week?"

"I'll be here." I offer her a genuine smile in return.

Maybe this wasn't such a bad idea after all…

14

BIANCA

As soon as I walk outside, Alexei is getting out of the car and walking around to open my door.

He has a smug look on his face as I slide into my seat, and I watch him as he walks back around to his side, trying not to admire how hot he looks in those black pants that he always wears.

Asshole.

I sink into my seat and fold my arms across my chest as Alexei pulls out of the parking lot.

He's rolled his sleeves up to his elbows, exposing his muscular forearms as he grips the steering wheel with one hand.

I grind my teeth and keep my eyes forward, annoyed that such a small thing could get me so worked up.

His eyes fly to me and back on the road after a few minutes of awkward silence. "Are you going to tell me how it went?"

"No."

He chuckles, glancing sidelong at me, but I keep my eyes forward.

"Are you punishing me?"

"Yes."

"*Solnyshka...*"

"Don't call me that."

"Would you rather I call you wife?"

Oh, he is definitely walking on thin ice.

"I'd rather you stay the hell out of my life."

Alexei, for once, remains quiet, and the moment he pulls up outside the house, I'm throwing open my door and climbing out of the car.

I don't bother waiting for him as I stomp across the gravel and climb the steps up to the front door.

His feet crunch the gravel behind me. "Are you seriously ignoring me?"

I throw open the front door and head inside.

My footsteps echo around the expansive foyer and soon, Alexei's join mine as I head to the kitchen.

"I think someone enjoyed themselves, and they just don't want to admit it."

At the door, I whirl around, folding my arms across my chest as I stare at Alexei.

His mouth is pulled up into a grin and amusement dances in his dark eyes.

I hate how handsome he looks when he smiles like that because it makes me want to forget that we're fighting and drag him upstairs to my bed.

"You don't need to act like a know-it-all asshole all the time."

Alexei grins wider.

I turn to walk away. "Screw you."

"I can't help it if I'm always right."

I scoff, glancing over my shoulder and shooting him a glare as I walk into the kitchen to make a cup of tea.

"Your modesty is admirable."

Alexei chuckles, the sound making me shiver as I open one of the cupboards and pull out the box of peppermint tea and a mug.

"I knew it would make you happy."

My stomach flutters at his words.

How is it that this man seems to know me better than I do?

"I know what else would make you happy."

"Oh, yeah?" I unwrap the tea bag and plop it into my mug. "What's that?"

Warm hands wrap around my waist, pulling me back against that deliciously hard body, and I can't fight the sigh that escapes my lips as Alexei presses a soft kiss to my neck.

"This." His breath tickles my skin.

His hands trail up my stomach to cup my breasts, and I'm instantly arching into his touch, my ass pressing back against his hips.

I moan as his hardness digs into me.

I want to push him away so badly. I want him to realize that he can't win me over with art classes and sex, but fuck, when he grinds against me like that, I lose all control.

"I'm sorry if I pushed you," he whispers in my ear as his hands continue to knead my breasts through my dress, his thumbs brushing over my sensitive nipples. "But you are so talented, *solnyshka*. And I don't care if it makes me a selfish prick, but I want you to be happy."

His words make me melt.

He has no reason to care for me. Our marriage isn't one of love or affection, and yet the lines are becoming more and more blurred. It's making it harder for me to stay mad at him.

"Alexei." I sigh.

He removes his right hand from my breast and reaches beneath my dress to cup me between my thighs.

I gasp, arching against him as he bites down on my neck, sucking hard as he moves my panties aside and dips two fingers inside me.

"What if someone walks in?" I gasp as his fingers curl inside me. "Your brothers—"

"Will have the good sense to leave if they hear the sounds that are about to fall from your lips, *ptichka*."

He grunts, and I know it's because he realizes how ready I am for him.

"I want you to be happy, *solnyshka*."

My eyes flutter closed as he starts pumping his fingers inside me. His thumb starts brushing lazy circles on my already swollen clit, and I know I can't fight it.

He knows exactly what to do to get me off.

So, I give in.

I reach behind me to cup his neck and angle my head so that I can kiss him. I run my fingers though the soft hair at the base of his neck, groaning as his tongue forces its way into my mouth.

"I know what you need, *ptichka*," he murmurs against my lips as he presses his hardness into my backside.

I whimper, my orgasm already starting to build from only a few strokes of his fingers.

"Fuck, you're always so wet for me."

"Alexei," I gasp, leaning back against his solid chest as he increases his pace.

He removes his hand from my breast and wraps it around my waist, pulling me harder against him.

"I know, *solnyshka*." He trails kisses along my jaw and neck, leaving goosebumps in his wake.

His touch is like nothing I've ever experienced, and it terrifies me how much I crave it.

But I can't walk away, not when it feels this good.

"I'm so close already," I moan, my hips rocking against his hand as he works my clit.

"The sooner you come, the sooner I can bury my cock inside you."

"Oh *god*."

My pussy starts to clench around his fingers.

Alexei grunts as he grinds his cock against me, and knowing how badly he wants me too sends me crashing over the edge.

I cry out, arching against him as his fingers work me through my orgasm so well. A rush of wetness floods my thighs, and the sound that spills from Alexei's mouth makes my knees buckle.

"*Fuck.*" He slides his fingers out of me. "I need you, Bianca."

I turn around so I can face him, my hands trailing up his broad chest to cup his beautiful face.

His dark eyebrows are pulled together as his chocolate eyes search my face.

Despite all the hard lines and rippling muscle, I'm beginning to learn that there's a very different side to Alexei Koslov one I'm certain hasn't been shared with many, if at all.

I reach up on my tiptoes and kiss him, wrapping my arms around his shoulders as his lips part for me.

The moment his tongue brushes against mine, I lose control once again, my body melting against his as I explore his mouth.

The taste of him is intoxicating, and I need more, no matter how badly I wish I didn't.

"Fuck me, Alexei," I murmur against his lips. "Please."

A deep, guttural sound spills from his lips as he reaches down to wrap his hands around the backs of my thighs and lift me up.

His mouth crashes against mine, claiming me as he spins us and the next thing I know, my back is against the wall, and he's grinding his erection against the slickness between my thighs.

"I'm very glad I stocked so many of these dresses." His hand cups me through my panties.

"Me too," I gasp as I rock my hips.

"The only problem is that you insist on wearing panties."

"Would you rather I didn't?"

"*Solnyshka*," Alexei groans, his thumb brushing over my clit.

My panties are soaked, and the warmth of his fingers mixed with the damp fabric against my clit has me groaning so loudly that Alexei has to cover my mouth with his own.

"Would you be able to concentrate if you knew I was walking around with nothing covering my pussy?"

Alexei tightens his arm around my waist and grinds his hips against me to show me exactly how he feels about it.

"I would be able to think of nothing else. I would always be ready for you," he growls. "Would you like that sweetheart?"

"Oh, yes."

"Are you going to let me bend you over the counter and fuck you from behind?"

My pussy clenches at his words, and I whimper at the ache between my thighs.

I'm so desperate for him to fill me that I unwrap my legs from around his waist.

His brow furrows, but he gently lowers me to the floor, and I step out of his hold to walk over to the island.

"*Solnyshka—*" Alexei freezes the moment I reach beneath my dress to pull down my panties, pulling them over each foot and tossing them onto the counter.

His breath hitches as I lift the hem of my dress up over my ass and bend myself over the counter, spreading my thighs wide to give him ample view of my drenched pussy.

"*Fuck.*"

I rest my cheek against the cold marble top, fighting a smile as I slowly sway my hips from side to side.

Alexei's groan echoes around the kitchen followed by the sounds of his belt buckle.

I glance over my shoulder to see him stalking toward me, his hand working to pull his cock free as he devours me with his eyes.

I'm desperate to rub my thighs together as his thick length springs free, so hard and ready that my mouth waters.

When his hands find my hips and the tip of his cock nudges my entrance, my eyes flutter closed, and I push back against Alexei, not wanting him to take his time.

I slide myself onto his thick length until he's buried all the way to the hilt and both of us groan.

"Bianca."

"Fuck me."

My breath is already coming in heavy pants, and I'm so wet that my arousal starts to drip further down my thighs.

Alexei pulls his cock all the way out before slamming back inside me, grunting as he stretches me so perfectly.

His thrusts are brutal, but I can't get enough.

He sinks his fingers into my hips to keep me steady as

he fucks me, his cock brushing my G spot every time he slams himself inside me.

I didn't know he could get so deep inside me, and every time he pulls himself free, I cry out with the need to be filled.

"Fuck, *ptichka*, I'm not going to last much longer," Alexei grits out.

I moan, pushing back against him to meet him thrust for thrust.

"I want to feel you dripping down my thighs, Alexei."

"You want a Koslov to claim you, don't you, *solnyshka*?" His thrusts become sloppy and desperate as he chases his own release.

"Yes." I can barely think straight, my whole body feels like it's about to explode from pleasure.

"Who do you belong to, *solnyshka*?"

"Y-you."

"Say my name. Tell me who owns you."

"You do, Alexei."

"Fuck right. You're *mine*," Alexei growls as he thrusts himself once more inside me, sending us both over the edge.

My legs buckle as my orgasm hits, and Alexei moans as I clench around his cock, milking every last drop from him as he spills inside me.

Wave after wave of such intense pleasure courses through my body that I can barely take in a breath, a thin sheen of sweat breaking out over my skin as I ride out my orgasm.

"You took me so well, *solnyshka*," Alexei murmurs, leaning forward to press a kiss to my shoulder as he slowly pulls his cock free.

I push myself off the counter and turn around, my legs

still trembling from my orgasm. Alexei's cheeks are flushed, and his eyes are heavy with lust as he looks at me.

"An orgasm doesn't automatically make me forgive you, you know?"

"What about two?" He chuckles as he tucks himself back into his pants.

I keep my eyes on his face as I know the moment I glimpse his glorious length, I'll want him to take me again.

"It gets you halfway there." I bite my lower lip.

"You're hard work, you know that?" He shakes his head, a hint of a smile playing on his lips.

"I take that as a compliment." I reach for my panties and stalk from the kitchen without a backward glance.

15

ALEXEI

"You know you don't have to drive me to the class. It's barely a fifteen minute walk."

"I like spending time with you." I slow the car down as we approach a stop sign.

"You're insufferable."

I fight back a laugh as I look over to find Bianca scowling at me, her arms folded across her chest.

"And you're incredibly sexy when you're mad."

My eyes glance down to her chest where I can see the soft swell of her breasts beneath her tank top.

My tongue darts out to wet my lips, wanting nothing more than to pull the car over and take her in the back seat.

"Eyes on the road, Koslov."

I grin as I turn my attention back to the road, shifting slightly in my seat so that my hardening cock doesn't scrape against the zipper of my pants.

"So, tell me about your class. It's been a week and you still haven't told me."

Bianca fills me in on the current piece she's working on and about a new friend she's made, a girl called Marnie.

My skin bristles at the mention of her. Having grown up in the world that I have, I'm not nearly as trusting as Bianca is, and I make a mental note to have Feliks run a background check on this girl.

I can't take any chances when it comes to Bianca.

"That reminds me, I want my phone back."

"You can't."

"Why?"

"Because I had Mikhail throw it in the Hudson."

"You *what*?"

"Bianca," I sigh. "You were coming to live in my family home. I couldn't risk someone tracking you or hacking into your phone in order to get information. I would expect you to understand that."

"You sound more and more like my father every day." She pouts.

"Why do you need a phone?"

"To speak to my friends, my dad, to check Instagram? I would expect you to understand *that*."

I run my hand through my hair before signaling for the turnoff to the house.

I appreciate how well Bianca has adapted to her new life, to *me*.

"Fine, I'll get you a new phone. But I'm putting a tracker on it, and I'm pre-approving any people who you give your number to."

"Like I said before, insufferable."

I reach across to squeeze her thigh, and she squirms beneath my touch. I'm tempted to roam my fingers higher to get a feel of her delicious pussy, but as I pull down the driveway to my home, I spot two black SUVs parked out front.

"I need you to go straight up to your room, do you

understand?" I race down the drive, gravel spraying up around the car as the wheels spin.

"I do, but I'm not going to listen."

I take a deep breath, trying to stay calm as I pull up behind the SUVs.

"Bianca, please—"

She throws open her car door and climbs out.

I hit the wheel. "Fuck!"

By the time I'm out of the car, she's already up the steps and throwing open the front door.

My heart is hammering in my chest as I race after her, my right hand reaching inside my jacket to check for my gun as I climb the steps.

Bianca's fast. She's springs across the foyer, her red trainers squeaking against the wooden floor as she runs toward the kitchen.

"Bianca!"

But it's already too late.

The sounds of my brothers' voices echo out into the hall, and I curse under my breath as I round the corner and see Danil pulling her into a hug.

I see nothing but red as his fingers brush her bare shoulders. "Walk away, Danil."

Dimitri throws his head back and laughs as Danil winks at me.

I'm across the room in an instant, wrapping my arms around Bianca's waist and hauling her back against me.

"Hey!" She slams her elbow back, but I grip her arms, holding them against her sides.

"All of you, my study, *now*."

Bianca scoffs. "Why won't you let me talk to your brothers?"

Mikhail smirks. "Because he's threatened by our ridiculously good looks."

I shoot him a warning glare, but he doesn't even flinch.

"You better have a good reason for showing up here unannounced, *again*."

Dimitri dips his chin, his expression turning serious as he looks at me.

"Maybe we better talk in your office, *brat*."

His eyes flick to Bianca, who I'm still holding in my arms.

I lean forward, my lips almost brushing her ear.

"If you go to your room, I promise to make it up to you."

"I'm not a fucking child." She yanks her arms free of my grip and whirls to face me. "I want to stay."

I grind my teeth, but I know from the way she's standing with her hands on her hips and her face set in a scowl, the only way I'm getting her away from this meeting is by throwing her over my shoulder and carrying her to her room.

Danil shrugs. "Let her stay."

I glare at him. "That's not your decision to make."

"Alexei, I'm part of this family now. I have a right to know if I'm in danger or if my family is in danger."

Hearing her refer to my family as her own makes my chest swell.

I glance at my three brothers, and they all nod.

"Fine, what is it you need to say?"

Dimitri sinks his hands into his pockets. "Mario is planning some kind of attack on us. We caught wind of the threat from Micha. He was following a few guys known to be on Mario's books, and they let slip that he has something planned regarding, as he put it, '*those Koslov bastards*'."

"What kind of attack?"

My mind's racing with every possible way he could harm my family.

I ball my hands into fists, trying to keep them steady as I try to push down the rising sense of panic that's threatening to take over my rational thought.

Danil shakes his head. "It could be anything, from a drug interception to a potential hit-and-run. We don't know."

Mikhail's eyes flick to Bianca. "But we shouldn't take any chances."

"I agree." I frown.

I have to protect my family at all costs.

Bianca looks between us. "Can these guys be persuaded to 'work both sides' as my father used to put it? For the right price, most of these guys can be persuaded to change their loyalty. At the end of the day, all they care about is their paycheck, not who it comes from."

My brothers look at Bianca with stunned expressions.

I huff a laugh, impressed by her confidence.

"It's true, and something we'll likely consider. In the meantime, I suggest we tighten our security."

This time, Bianca doesn't miss the way my brothers glance at her.

"Oh, hell no, if you think you're taking anything else from me, you can think again."

"Can you give us a minute?" I look at my brothers.

Bianca glares at me, her blue eyes filled with loathing.

I keep my eyes locked on her as my brothers surprisingly leave the room without any complaint.

"I'm going to have to cancel your art class for the time being, and Zara should stay away too—"

"No."

"This isn't up for debate, Bianca. My decision is final."

Her eyes widen, and she laughs. "Your decision? You're the one who pushed me to go to the fucking class in the first place, and now you want to take it away?"

"For the time being."

"No." She shakes her head.

A few strands of her dark hair fall from the knot on top of her head, and I itch to tuck them behind her ear.

"Alexei, there's always going to be some sort of threat on either one of us. It's the nature of our family, so we need to find a way to exist with it, otherwise I'm going to go crazy."

"Can you please cooperate on this? For me?"

"No."

"Fine. You can go, but I have Feliks or Micha accompany you to the class, including sitting in on it while you're there."

She shakes her head, her jaw clenching as she stares me down.

"I don't need a babysitter."

It takes every ounce of strength I have to keep my cool.

Does she think I enjoy taking away her freedom?

"Your father trusted me to keep you safe."

I blink as Bianca laughs.

"You mean the father I haven't heard from since my wedding? Fuck what he says."

I try to keep my face neutral. I want nothing more than to assure her that he cares, but I can't risk her knowing the truth behind his silence.

I sigh, searching for a way to diffuse the situation.

"If I let you continue your class, will that make you happy?"

"It's the only thing I have that is mine right now."

"Fine," I give in. "But I drive you there, and I pick you up, and I wait outside the class. No arguments."

"And my phone?"

"I will arrange a phone for you." I shake my head as a smile starts to creep across her face.

"You're going soft, Koslov."

"But that's it."

"Can I go and visit Zara if she can't come here?"

"I'm sorry, but that is a hard no."

"Alexei, I'm getting tired of being stuck in this damn house!"

"In case you don't get it, there is a threat hanging above our heads right now, and you might not care about what happens to you, but I do."

"But—"

"Look, you have an incredible new art studio to keep you occupied. Plus, I can think of many other things to keep you occupied, you won't even notice you haven't left the house."

"Like what?" Bianca asks, raising her eyebrows.

"How about you come over here, and I'll show you?"

Bianca rolls her eyes but drops her hands from her hips and stalks toward me.

My body instantly relaxes as I wrap my arms around her waist and bring my lips to hers, sighing at the sweet taste.

I let my hands roam down to cup her ass through her shorts, and she moans, sinking her hands into my hair.

A voice comes from the door. "Shit, sorry!"

Bianca pulls away, her cheeks flushing red as we turn to find Dimitri standing in the doorway covering his face with his hands.

"Oops." She chuckles, biting her lower lip as she steals a glance at me.

I flash her a wink, though I know my brother is about to give me absolute hell for what he just witnessed.

"I suggest you two keep your affections to the bedroom, unless you want everyone to know your business."

"Don't worry, Bianca loves an audience." I grin.

"Hey!" Bianca slaps me on the arm.

"You can give me a show any time, *golubushka*." Dimitri chuckles.

"Okay, I take it back." She glances at me. "He is the insufferable one."

"What did I do?"

"Did you need something, Dimitri?"

"I needed a word." He gives me a knowing look. The one that says this information is for us eldest brothers only.

While Mikhail and Danil play a crucial role in our family business, they're still young and some things are better kept from their knowledge.

"Bianca, why don't you go and get Mikhail to sort you out with a new phone. I'm sure he has a few new ones on hand in his room."

She rolls her eyes at me but for once, doesn't fight my order. She stalks out of the room, and I can't help but admire her ass in those denim shorts as her hips sway with each step.

Dimitri clears his throat, snapping me out of my lust-induced trance.

He lifts an eyebrow, chuckling. "Somebody has clearly crossed a line."

"This is the business you needed to talk about?"

Dimitri smirks, folding his arms across his broad chest. "No, this is me giving my big brother shit."

"There's no reason to give me shit. I'm not crossing any lines."

"The way you're looking at her ass tells me otherwise."

"I can't admire her?"

"You can... But I'm guessing you've also fucked her?" Dimitri's eyes dance with amusement, and I scowl at my brother.

"Marrying Bianca was something I had to do to gain information on Gilanto. Our situation is purely business, nothing more." My chest tightens at the lie.

Dimitri simply shrugs.

"That's not how it looks to me, but if you want to live in denial, then it's your problem. We have bigger things to worry about."

"I take it you've got more on that email?"

Dimitri nods, his face grave.

"Spit it out, then."

"It was sent by some guy named Matteo Ricci."

"Ricci?" I run my hands through my hair, trying to place where I've heard that name.

My brother leans against the wall. "Does the name Igor Ivanov ring a bell?"

Fuck.

"That Pahkan back in Russia?"

"Yeah. The one who was recently exiled and went underground. No one has seen or heard from him since. Turns out, this Ricci guy used to work for him."

"Shit."

"I've got Feliks trying to track him down, but I thought I should give you a heads up. For whatever reason, it's likely this guy has some intel on what went down with our parents."

"Get Micha on it too. I don't want to waste any time."

My ears are starting to ring at the mention of my parents.

I tuck my hands into my pockets to hide the fact they're shaking. "I'll look into Igor myself."

"You sure?"

"Yeah. This is just something I have to do alone."

16

BIANCA

MARRYING BIANCA WAS SOMETHING I HAD TO DO TO GAIN information on Gilanto. It was the price I had to pay, Dimitri. Our situation is purely business, nothing more.

I'm not stupid. It's not like Alexei and I are in love, but to hear him talk so callously has my stomach twisting with nausea.

I thought perhaps there was mutual affection starting to blossom between us. The way he's nurtured my passion for art, how he's sat and listened to me talk about my mother, I thought he was actually starting to care for me.

Have I really been that blind? Did I trick myself into thinking there was something more between us because the alternative was too painful to consider?

I shouldn't have listened in on Alexei and Dimitri's conversation.

Then again, I shouldn't have done a lot of things, like sleep with Alexei Koslov, but it seems I'm all about the bad decisions these days.

Having Alexei's brothers here and hearing the news

about Mario Gilanto seems to have pierced the sex-hazed bubble I've been in for the past few weeks.

It was meant to be a one-time thing. To scratch an itch and nothing more. But one taste of what it was like to have Alexei Koslov buried so deep inside me, to have his tongue devouring me, had me losing all sense of control.

Perhaps I wanted to forget how dangerous Alexei was, and what it was to be associated with his family, to be a *part* of his family, to ease some of my guilt for crossing the line.

But that doesn't mean I can let my guard down. I would do well not to forget that Alexei's first loyalty is to his family, no matter the promise he made to my father.

I fight the tears in my eyes as I head back toward the living room where Mikhail and Danil are lounging on one of the leather sofas.

"Mikhail?" I force a smile. "Alexei said you might be able to sort me out with a phone?"

It doesn't take Mikhail long to set me up with a new phone. Alexei was right, he had a stack of brand new iPhones in his desk drawer.

I know there was no point in asking him not to put in a tracker. His loyalty is to his brother, not to me. So, I watch him work in silence, trying to swallow past the lump in my throat as Alexei's words play on repeat in my head.

"He's a good guy, my brother." Mikhail turns the new phone on. "Whatever he said or did, he would've had a reason."

Am I that easy to read?

I say nothing, trying my hardest to not let the tears fall in front of Mikhail. I don't want it getting back to Alexei.

So, I bite down on the inside of my cheek and dig my nails into my palms to give me something else to focus on other rather than the endless ache in my chest.

Mikhail doesn't press me any further, so once he hands me my brand new iPhone, I mutter a thanks and dart upstairs to my bedroom, locking the door behind me.

I cross the room to my bathroom, locking that door behind me also. I know it won't be enough to actually keep Alexei out, but I want to put some distance between us, to try and sort through the mess that is my head.

There's only one person who's able to bring me back to reality when I start to spiral like this, and that's Zara. She's my voice of reason, and she's detached enough from this world that she'll be able to talk to me rationally. To help me make sense of what's going on between Alexei and me.

I quickly turn on the shower, hoping the running water will drown out the sound of my voice as I unlock my phone and type in Zara's number.

She picks up after two rings.

"Hello?"

The sound of my best friend's voice has the last of my walls crumbling.

"Zara?" My voice cracks, and the floodgates open.

I sink to the floor of my bathroom, leaning back against the tub as my emotions take full control, the sound of the water running doing little to calm me down. I can barely catch a breath as tears stream down my face.

"B? Is that you?"

"Y-yeah." I wipe my cheeks on the back of my hand.

"Honey? What is it? What's wrong?"

She shuffles about on the other end of the phone, the TV goes silent.

"Everything." A sob tears from me and I clasp my hand over my mouth to try and muffle it.

"Is it Alexei? Did he hurt you?"

My throat feels tight and every time I open my mouth, another strangled sob escapes.

"That's it! I'm coming over."

"N-no, you can't." My chest heaves as I try to catch a breath. "I-it's... I'm fine."

"Bianca, what the hell happened? Because you do not sound fine."

I close my eyes for a moment and focus on the sound of the shower running.

There's no way I can explain what's wrong without telling Zara the truth about my marriage. And if I do that, she'll be in danger.

The fewer people who know the truth, the better.

But the weight of my reality is starting to crush me, and I need my friend more than I need to keep my promise to Alexei.

"Bianca, you're scaring me."

"If I tell you something..." I press a calming hand to my chest. "I need you to promise to keep this to yourself. You can't tell *anyone*. I mean it, Zara."

"I promise, now tell me what the hell is going on."

Once I open my mouth, I can't seem to stop. Everything comes rushing out, and I can barely keep up with my own racing thoughts.

Zara lets me explain the truth behind mine and Alexei's marriage.

I bypass most of the details surrounding our two families and why our union was needed in the first place, but I tell her the truth of what happened on my wedding day. How my own father blindsided me into marrying a man I had never met, and how over the past few weeks I had grown to care for him.

"I thought he was starting to feel the same. And I know I shouldn't have slept with him, but I was so lonely, and he was always there. He genuinely acted like he cared about me. I'm so *stupid*."

Zara is quiet for a moment after I finish.

My bathroom has steamed up from the shower, and a thin sheen of sweat starts to coat my top lip from the heat. But I don't want to turn it off just yet.

Zara clears her throat. "This is... a lot."

"I know. I'm sorry I didn't tell you the truth. I thought I had it handled, but—" My voice cracks.

"How could Emilio do that to you?" Zara snaps. "He really gave you no warning?"

"Nope."

"And you'd never met Alexei before?"

"Never."

"Fuck. Oh, B, I'm so sorry. I knew I should've forced you to come back with me after I saw you. Something just didn't feel right, but I didn't say anything. I'm so sorry I let you down."

"I promised my father I would play my part, but then things got complicated..."

"When you slept together."

"Yeah... Fuck. I should have known better."

"He really told Dimitri that your relationship is purely business?"

"That's what I overheard," I mutter as a fresh wave of tears falls down my cheeks. "Was I that delusional? I mean, was all the art stuff just a way to keep me occupied and quiet so I didn't do anything stupid?"

"Perhaps..." Zara sighs. "But the fact is he's been by

your side pretty much every day since you moved in when he doesn't need to be... Doesn't he have security to keep tabs on you?"

"Yeah..."

"Have you ever seen them?"

I frown.

"They've not been needed because Alexei is always with me..."

"There you go! It sounds like he really does have feelings for you," Zara says. "I think he's likely covering his own ass by playing it down for Dimitri, especially if your relationship is meant to be purely business. I mean, he went to all that trouble to build you an incredible studio, and now he's even enrolled you in classes, which is something you've dreamed of doing since you were a kid. That does not sound like someone who isn't invested, B."

"I don't know... I-I've been so wrong before."

"Bianca." Zara sighs. "He's not Jack."

I flinch at the mention of my ex.

I thought he was the love of my life, until the day I found him fucking another woman in our bed. I always thought people who said you could die from a broken heart were ridiculous and dramatic. Until I witnessed the worst kind of betrayal and felt that pain for myself.

Not only was Jack cheating on me for months with one of our mutual friends, he got her knocked up too.

My father eventually found out and took care of Jack himself, but it didn't help. My trust had been broken, and I've never been able to stitch it back together.

"I know you have a tendency to think the worst."

"That way you're prepared, Zara. I never want to be blindsided like that again."

"Look, I can't tell you what to feel. Ultimately, this is a

very unique situation, and now it's become even more complicated because feelings are involved."

"I know..."

"What is your heart telling you?"

It wants Alexei.

The thought scares me more than it should because it shows how bad of a job I've done at protecting my heart.

I knew from the start that getting involved with Alexei would be dangerous territory, but I did it anyway, and now I'm going to have to suffer the consequences.

"It doesn't matter what it's telling me." I try my best to build the wall back around my heart. "I can't have him, at least not in any way that truly matters. I need to keep reminding myself of that rather than jumping into bed with him at every opportunity. It's only making me more confused."

"I get it, but listen to me, B. The way Alexei looked at you... That wasn't someone who's only in this relationship for business. Trust me, I think Alexei Koslov is falling for you."

"You have no idea how much I wish I could believe that."

17

ALEXEI

My solnyshka is avoiding me.

She's barely spoken two words to me since the other night when my brothers decided to show up unannounced.

I thought we had established some sort of truce by including her in the conversation about Gilanto, but it seems to have done the opposite.

Every time I enter a room, she leaves, no matter if she's sitting at the table, eating a meal, or painting in her studio. It's as if she suddenly can't stand to be in my presence.

I should be glad. Growing close to Bianca was never the plan because it would be too much of a risk to both of us. I've let myself lose focus and forget about the promise I made to Emilio, the promise I made to myself.

Protect Bianca at all costs.

I find her sitting at her easel, her back to me as she works on a new piece.

She's still sketching it out, so I can't work out what it is yet.

I gently rap my knuckles on the door, and her back stiffens. I try to ignore the sinking feeling in my stomach as she doesn't even bother to look around.

"I have to go into the city tonight. Micha is downstairs." *To keep an eye on you.* I don't say the second part out loud—it'll only make her sulk more.

I hover for a moment to see if she might try to fight me, to demand to come along and remind me that she's now a part of this family.

But she doesn't.

She simply picks up her paintbrush, dips it in the red paint, and smears it across the blank canvas like blood.

I head down to where Micha is waiting.

He's a big guy, almost six foot seven, with a shaved head, and full sleeve tattoos on both arms.

"She's in her studio."

He nods, crossing his arms over his chest.

"She'll likely stay there until I get back."

Another nod as Micha leans against the banister as I double-check my weapons tucked inside my jacket. "Any word on Ricci?"

My teeth grind together at the mention of Ricci.

Even if it turns out that the man I thought was originally responsible for my parents death was not the one, he is far from innocent. The fucker is a vengeful and sadistic monster, and he deserves to die either way.

But what I want most of all is justice. For my parents. For my brothers who had to grow up with only me to guide them.

And for myself, who had to go through all of this and grow up from one minute to the next.

"I'm counting on my brothers to have some new information for me this evening."

Other than my brothers and our cousin Anton, Micha

and Feliks are the only two people I trust to keep my family secrets. Having a constant target on your back means it's hard to find people you can trust, who won't betray you in exchange for money or protection.

"I'm meeting Asim tonight."

"Alone?" Micha's dark brows pull together.

"I can handle him." I chuckle, tucking my handgun back into my right breast holster.

"He's a snake."

"Even snakes have their uses," I remind Micha. "We're meeting at the Russian Tea Rooms."

"Aleksandr is working?"

"Yes, I made sure of it."

Micha nods.

"I expect updates." I glance up the stairs.

He nods. "*Da, Pahkan.* I hope you make Asim sweat."

I ARRIVE AT THE RUSSIAN TEA ROOMS TO FIND ASIM already waiting for me.

It's one of the few places in the city where I feel comfortable enough to have meetings. Many of the staff are on my books, and I can trust they'll be discreet.

"Have you been waiting long?" I slide into the red leather booth opposite Asim and unbutton my jacket.

The lighting is low, with a single candle on the table between us, casting Asim's face in an orange glow.

He takes a sip of his neat vodka as he regards me.

I know exactly how long he's been waiting. Aleksandr sent me a message the moment Asim arrived.

"Not long." He's almost double my age, with graying hair and faded tattoos creeping up his neck beneath the collar of his white shirt. His dark eyes have a certain haunted quality to them, one I know only too well.

I've been working with Asim since my parents died ten years ago. He was one of their most trusted allies, and when I took over as head of the family, he decided to stay.

Many didn't, but I don't blame them. I was barely in my twenties and tasked with raising three younger siblings as well as running all of my father's businesses.

Many wanted to see me fail. Which only fueled my desire to succeed.

"How is your new... situation?" Asim has a smirk tugging at his lips as he takes another sip of his drink. "The Bellucci girl settling in okay at casa del Koslov?"

I lean forward in my seat, resting my forearms on the table as I glance around.

The place is packed so there's no chance of us being overheard, but that doesn't ease my discomfort.

"I'd rather we keep the topic of conversation to the matter at hand."

"Of course." Asim nods.

A waitress appears and sets a rocks glass in front of me. "Double vodka for you, Mr. Koslov."

Her lips are painted blood red, and her platinum blonde hair is pulled back into a tight ponytail. Her eyes stay on me as I lift the glass to my lips.

Before Bianca, I'd have gladly given her my attention. I'd have taken her back to my penthouse and shown her a good time. But not anymore.

Though it might scare me, my disgust at the thought of sleeping with someone else doesn't surprise me. The moment I had a taste of Bianca Bellucci, I knew there was no going back.

"*Spasiba*." I dismiss the waitress.

Asim smirks as he watches her walk away.

"Now, I suggest you start talking before my brother arrives."

Asim lifts his drink to his lips and downs the rest, flinching as the vodka burns his throat.

I brace myself for whatever it is he's about to share with me.

"Thirty years ago, your father surrendered two of his properties back in Russia over to Ivanov." He sets his glass back down on the table.

"Surrendered?"

"We couldn't find any trace of any money being exchanged."

"He just handed them over?" This doesn't make any sense.

"It looks like it."

"Those properties would have been worth a fortune. Why the fuck would he just hand them over? Was he being blackmailed?"

My father was the most powerful Pakhan in New York. It would have taken a very powerful man to blackmail him.

"I'm still looking into that. I knew your father well, and this doesn't add up."

"I need to know everything you can find out about this Igor Ivanov."

Asim nods before getting to his feet.

"Good to see you again, Alexei." He reaches out a hand for me to shake before slipping out of the booth.

I down the rest of my drink and order a full round ready for my brothers' arrival.

Dimitri takes Asim's vacant space ten minutes later. "Uh oh, you look pissed."

Danil slides in beside me, and Mikhail takes the spot beside Dimitri.

We're all wearing identical black suits, our hair styled into neat parts. Though Mikhail and Danil are clean-shaven, Dimitri and myself are sporting more stubble than usual.

There's no denying the Koslov genes are strong.

"Asim just left."

Mikhail nods. "Did he have anything useful to say?"

I quickly fill them in on the information Asim shared with me.

Dimitri looks pissed as hell, leaning back in the booth and bracing his hands against the table, his large biceps flexing beneath his shirt.

Danil glances between me and Dimitri. "What does this mean?"

"Igor clearly had something on *Papochka*, something big."

Dimitri frowns. "It makes no sense, he never mentioned this guy."

I shrug as I swirl my vodka around my glass to keep my hands busy.

"He kept a lot from us," I remind him. "We were kids."

"A heads-up would've been nice."

"Yeah, well, murder can be a bitch. People can't plan for it."

Dimitri takes that as his cue to drop the subject.

"Any word on Ricci?"

My brother shakes his head.

"*Fuck.*"

"I do have another lead I'm following, though, so I'll have some new information for you soon, *brat*."

I wave him off, suddenly too tired to talk business.

It seems I'm just being handed more and more threads that are seemingly leading nowhere. Yet, I can't afford to ignore any of them, not when the lives of those I care about most might be attached to the other end.

I stay for one more drink with my brothers before heading back home.

I could have stayed at the penthouse in the city, but I feel uneasy at the thought of leaving Bianca. I trust Micha completely, but I want to be close to her. Even when she's not speaking to me, I feel calmer just knowing she's around.

So, I race back to Queens in my Maserati, to my *solnyshka*. My little sun. The only light in my life right now, other than my brothers.

I relieve Micha the moment I walk in, tossing him the keys to my car as a thank you for taking good care of Bianca.

He catches them and nods. "She's asleep."

I clap him on the shoulder as I pass him to make my way up to the top floor.

Her bedroom door is closed, so I tread carefully along the wooden floor.

My fingers itch to open the door, to catch a glimpse of her as she sleeps.

"Just one look..."

I slowly turn the handle and push open the door.

The low light from the hall illuminates the bed, and I bite back a groan at what I find.

She's naked, the silk sheets wrapped around her torso and between her thighs, giving me the perfect view of her soft curves.

Her heavy breasts rise and fall with each breath, her soft, pink nipples so inviting my mouth starts to water, and my cock starts to harden.

The only thing that's hidden from view is her pussy, and I'm desperate for a fix.

I stay in the doorway for a moment, watching her sleep.

As if she senses me there, her back arches slightly, and her thighs rub together, the silk sheet stuck between them.

"*Solnyshka...*" I moan under my breath as I squeeze my throbbing cock.

A soft whimper escapes her lips, and I have to rub my erection through my pants, running my palm up and down my length to try and ease the ache.

I know if I were to toss aside the sheet and expose her bare pussy, I would find it glistening with her arousal, so ready for me to sink inside her...

I'm crossing the room before I have a chance to stop myself.

Kneeling at the edge of the bed, I peel back the sheet that's draped over her torso and gently untangle it from between her legs, careful not to wake her.

The moment I remove the sheet from between her thighs, she stretches out, spreading her soft thighs wide and exposing her glistening pink sex.

"Oh, *ptichka*," I groan under my breath.

She's so ready for me, but I don't want to wake her. So, I'll give her what she needs and take care of myself later.

I slowly move to rest my forearms on either side of her thighs and gently lower my mouth to her pussy, running my tongue softly along her core.

She moans, her hips instantly bucking against me, so I do it again, biting back a moan as she squirms beneath my touch.

I lick her in long, slow strokes so as not to wake her fully.

She's already soaking, as if her own dreams were plagued with thoughts of us.

I bite back a moan as I sink my tongue deep inside her pussy, tasting her sweet juices as she softly grinds against me, sighing.

She's so fucking perfect.

My cock is straining against my zipper, desperate for me to pull it free, but I can't.

My pleasure will come later. Right now, I want to make sure my *solnyshka* has the sweetest of dreams.

I slowly pump my tongue in and out of her core before dragging it up her center.

She moans so loudly as I wrap my lips around her clit and gently suck.

When her fingers drag through my hair, I shudder as she starts to slowly move her hips against my mouth.

I fucking love that Bianca gets off both when it's hard and fast, but also when I take my time and build her release so slowly it gets her absolutely dripping wet. I glance up and find her breasts heaving, her breath coming in fast pants, and I know she's close.

Come for me, solnyshka.

A rush of wetness pools between her thighs as she climaxes, her legs shaking on either side of my face as she rides out her orgasm.

"Mmm..." She continues to grind her hips against me.

I continue to lick her pussy so slowly, lapping up her arousal as she slowly relaxes back against the bed as she falls back into a peaceful sleep.

With one last kiss to her clit, I get to my feet and drape the sheet back over her body. There's such a beautiful pink flush to her skin, and she has a faint hint of a smile on her face as sleep pulls her under once more.

"Goodnight, *solnyshka*," I whisper as I creep out of the room.

I'm desperate to take care of my own release, so I head across the hall to my room and immediately go into the ensuite. After turning the shower on, I strip out of my clothes, my erection springing free and growing even harder with the extra room.

I glance down, and the tip is already glistening with precum.

Fuck, I want nothing more than to go back across the hall and bury myself between Bianca's soft thighs.

But I need her to come to me.

Whatever it is that's plaguing her mind has made her want to keep her distance from me.

If I wasn't such a selfish bastard, I would let her go. But now that I've had a taste, I don't think I can ever give her up.

I groan as I take my throbbing length in my fist and pump it hard as I climb into the shower.

Pressing my left hand against the cold tiles to steady myself, I start working my cock hard and fast with my right hand as the water cascades over my tense muscles.

With the taste of her pussy still on my tongue, it doesn't take long for my balls to tighten and the base of my spine to start to tingle.

My hips buck as I fuck my hand, my grip painful as I roll my thumb over my slit.

"Bianca." My eyes flutter closed as I imagine her in the shower with me, bent over as I fuck her from behind.

She would take me so well, crying out with pleasure as my cock hit her inner walls over and over.

The feeling of her pussy clenching around me as she comes...

"Fuck." I increase my pace, picturing her across the hall,

still slick between her thighs. Did she wake up after I left? Is she still aching for more and having to dip her fingers between her legs to take care of herself?

Such a thought has my eyes rolling in my head as my release hits me.

Her name falls from my lips as I spill, my body shuddering as I pump my cock over and over to get out every last drop.

I can't even convince myself this relationship was only ever about business. I think from the moment I set eyes on Bianca Bellucci in that elevator at the Waldorf, my hand had already been dealt.

Now I just need to work out how I'm going to play it.

18

BIANCA

The sun's streaming through the window, warming my face, as I slowly wake.

I let out a contented sigh as I stretch my limbs, my thighs rubbing together as I remember the most amazing dream I had last night.

A soft moan escapes my lips as I find them slick with my arousal.

I'm not surprised when the dream I had involved a certain Koslov...

I remember it vividly.

Alexei came in while I was sleeping and knelt between my thighs, running his tongue over my aching core. He got me off so slowly, taking his time as he licked my pussy, and it was one of the most intense orgasms I'd experienced.

I only wish it was real...

Ignoring the ache that's building between my thighs, not wanting to give Alexei the satisfaction of reaching down to rub my throbbing clit, I throw back the thin silk sheet that was barely covering my naked body and climb out of bed, only to notice that my door is ajar.

"That's weird..." I hurry across the plush carpet to slam it closed.

I remember closing it last night because Micha was down the hall in Alexei's office, and I wanted some privacy from my 'babysitter'.

Did Alexei come in after all?

My cheeks burn at the thought of it being real.

I might be pissed as hell at him, but I can't deny that the thought of him getting me off while I slept makes my body come alive with desire.

"I need a cold shower..."

Marnie and I pack up our supplies after class. "There's a small art exhibition being held nearby if you fancy going? It's on Friday. It's showing some up-and-coming artists who recently graduated from the program. It'll be a good networking opportunity too. I think most of the class is going."

"That sounds like fun." Supporting newer artists and getting the chance to meet new people in the area is a great opportunity.

Fuck. I can't simply make this decision on my own, I have to ask Alexei first.

Marnie seems to notice my mood souring.

"It's ok if you're busy."

"No, I-I need to check..." I leave off the 'with my husband' part, not wanting Marnie to think I'm weird.

"Just text me." She throws her bag over her shoulder.

"I will." I force a smile.

She offers me a wave before leaving me alone to tidy up my things.

As I walk out of the art building, the sight of Alexei leaning against the bumper of the Range Rover with his arms folded across his chest should have had me crumbling with desire.

He looks gorgeous in his black pants and white shirt, which he's rolled up to his elbows to expose those muscular forearms.

I don't miss the way a few of the girls in my class pass by us, their eyes lingering on Alexei.

I shoot them a glare, which makes Alexei chuckle.

"I'm surprised you weren't waiting outside the classroom." I smooth my hands over my sundress.

"I thought about it."

"There's an art show being held nearby on Friday that I want to go to."

"No." He pushes off the hood of the car to stalk toward me.

"It's literally being held at a small venue ten minutes away. Most of the class is going—"

"My answer is no."

"Why?" I fold my arms across my chest.

"It's too dangerous." He mirrors my body language.

I shake my head, trying to shake off my desire to run my fingertips over those powerful forearms.

"What if you came with me? Or Micha? Or the whole fucking Koslov family, I don't care. Just *please*, let me go."

"No."

"You didn't even think about it."

"There's nothing to think about. It's too dangerous, and I won't compromise on your safety."

"It's a fucking art show!" I throw my hands up in the air.

Alexei glares at me as his eyes dart around.

I don't give a flying fuck if I'm making a scene.

"It's not like I'm asking to come into the city with you. It's in Queens, for fuck's sake!"

"We can discuss this when we get home." He reaches to take my arm, but I step back. "Bianca, get in the car."

"No."

His eyes flash.

"If I have to throw you over my shoulder and put you in the car, I will."

I shrug, refusing to budge. "Let me go to the art show."

I take another step back.

Alexei's restraint seems to snap, and I'm not fast enough to escape his grip.

He wraps his hand around my wrist and pulls me to him, bowing his head to whisper in my ear, "Stop acting like a fucking child and get in the damn car."

His breath tickles my neck, and I have to fight the urge to lean into him, reveling in the power in his voice.

How is it that this man can have me seeing red one moment, then wanting to melt in a puddle at his feet the next?

"Fine." I shrug out of his grip, storming over to the passenger side.

He follows behind me, waiting until I'm in the seat before reaching for the belt.

"I can do my own fucking belt."

Alexei ignores me and leans over to buckle me in.

My breath hitches in my throat as his hand brushes my bare thigh, and I catch the scent of his musky cologne.

He closes the door, and I watch as he stalks around the front of the car and climbs into the driver's seat.

"Stop sulking. You should consider yourself lucky that I'm letting you go out at all." He slams his door shut.

I can't stop the hysterical laugh that escapes my lips. "*Lucky?*"

"I don't think you're taking this threat against our family seriously enough." Alexei buckles his seatbelt. "Otherwise, you wouldn't be questioning me on this."

"Is this how life is going to be from now on? Me having to ask your permission for everything?"

Alexei says nothing, keeping his eyes forward.

"Oh, fuck you."

He unbuckles his belt and turns in his seat to face me.

I've never seen him look so pissed off. His strong jaw is set as he grinds his teeth, his eyes roaming over me as if he can't quite decide how he wants to handle me.

Every inch of this man screams power and control.

For a moment, I ignore the anger and let my eyes take in those deliciously broad shoulders. The fabric of his shirt strains against his biceps, and I want nothing more than to rip it clean off his body.

"If you think looking at me like that is going to make me let you go, then you're wrong." Alexei shifts in his seat.

My eyes flick downwards, to his strong thighs that he's spread wide to accommodate the very noticeable bulge in his pants.

Heat pools in my lower belly, turning my anger into lust as I imagine leaning over and taking him in my mouth right here in the parking lot.

"Talk to me, Bianca."

"No, I don't want to talk anymore." I undo my seatbelt. "It never seems to get us anywhere."

Alexei's eyes widen as I start to climb over the center console.

Fuck, this is the last thing I should be doing, but I don't care.

I've been aching all day after my dream last night, and it's clear he wants it too as his hands find my waist to help me maneuver onto his lap, my thighs resting on either side of his.

"What are you doing?" he growls.

"Taking control." I reach for the ties on my sundress.

"Bianca," he groans as I pull the ties free, letting my dress pool around my waist.

My breasts are heavy and aching, but he keeps his hands on my thighs.

That won't do.

I lean forward to press a kiss to his neck, the slight stubble rubbing against my cheek.

"The windows are blacked out, right?"

"Yes." He digs his fingers into the soft flesh of my thighs.

"Good, because I'm not wearing any panties," I whisper in his ear.

Alexei groans as his strong hands stroke up my thighs and disappear beneath my dress.

"And I'm so ready for you, Alexei."

I pull back to watch Alexei's face as he dips his fingers between my folds to find out exactly how ready I am.

His eyes glaze over as he sinks two fingers inside my pussy, all the way to the knuckle.

I rock my hips as he slowly pumps them inside me, working me just how I like it.

"Come here." He leans forward to take my nipple in his mouth.

I cry out as he scrapes his teeth against the sensitive bud, my back arching to give him even more.

"Is this what we do now?" I gasp as he takes my other breast in his hand and gently kneads the swollen flesh.

"Fight and then have sex when we can't find a compromise?"

Alexei chuckles, his breath tickling my nipple.

"Works for me." He pulls his fingers free.

I cry out at the emptiness, but watch in awe as he takes those fingers into his mouth and sucks.

"Do you want to fuck me, Bianca?" His eyes are filled with such desire that warmth pools between my thighs.

"Yes." I fumble with his belt, so desperate to get to his cock that I'm struggling to undo the buckle.

"Let me, *solnyshka*," Alexei murmurs.

I whimper as I rest my hands on his biceps, watching eagerly as he undoes his belt with one hand and makes quick work of his zipper.

When he reaches inside and pulls his cock free, a strangled sound escapes my lips.

He's so thick, a bead of precum already glistening along his slit.

My pussy clenches, desperate to sink myself down on top of him.

I reach out and grip his shaft.

"Fuck, Bianca," he groans as I pump him hard, running my thumb over the tip.

I grin, loving the way his eyes glaze over as he watches my hand work his cock.

"Mmm..." I release his shaft to bring my thumb to my lips.

I lick it clean, moaning at the salty taste of him. "You taste so good."

"There's plenty more where that came from, *ptichka*." He chuckles. "You can suck my cock any time you like."

"You're so big." I reach for him once more.

My fingers barely wrap around his shaft, and the

thought of taking him into my mouth and sucking him has me throbbing between my thighs. "I don't think you'd fit in my mouth."

"We'd take it slow, *solnyshka*."

My eyes flutter closed as I work his cock, my mind filling with images of me on my knees as he slowly pumps himself into my mouth.

I want that more than anything, but I need to satisfy the growing ache between my thighs. I need him to fill me, to claim me.

"I-I need you." I lean forward to crash my lips against Alexei's.

I part my lips, and his mouth claims mine, sucking and licking as I take hold of his cock and line it up with my entrance.

"You set the pace, *ptichka*," Alexei murmurs against my lips, his fingers digging into my hips as I slowly lower myself down on his cock.

I try to relax, but my thighs are spread so wide, and Alexei's stretching me so much as I take another inch that I wince.

"Relax, *solnyshka*."

Alexei softly runs his hands up and down my back as I take my time, holding onto his shoulders for support.

"That's it," he praises as I sink all the way down onto him.

I moan, leaning forward to rest my forehead against his shoulder, my breathing coming in heavy pants as my body adjusts to the size of him.

He wraps his strong arms around me, holding me against his body, waiting for me to move.

I hate how good he feels, how much I crave his touch.

Maybe because it makes me feel so protected. I know

there isn't anything this man wouldn't do to keep me safe, as much as that pisses me off.

I don't care if he said this was only business, because I'm starting to think Zara was right.

He's lying to himself because I've never experienced sex this good before, and he's just as hungry for it as I am.

I cling to his body, wrapping my arms around his shoulders as I slowly lift myself off his cock before slamming back down.

"Oh, *fuck*!" I cry out as he fills me once more.

Alexei's lips find my nipples, and he starts sucking and licking at the sensitive buds as I find my rhythm, bouncing myself up and down on his thick shaft.

He feels incredible at this angle, hitting me so deep it's almost too much to bear.

"That's it, *ptichka*, ride my cock." He moves his hands to my waist to help lift me off his cock.

He bucks his hips, thrusting back into me so hard I can't hold back the scream that escapes my lips.

I'm so wet, and the sound of him sliding in and out of me has my clit throbbing so badly I have to reach between my thighs to soothe the ache.

"Let me." He moves my hand back to his shoulder before dipping his hand between us to start working my clit.

I groan as I grind my hips against his hand. I'm so fucking close to falling over the edge, my thighs shake as I increase my pace.

"You're doing so well, *solnyshka*."

"*Alexei*," I moan, my head falling back as my pussy starts to clench.

Alexei groans, thrusting his hips harder and faster as he rubs my clit.

"Oh, fuck, I'm coming," he growls, reaching down to take my breast in his mouth.

"Yes!" I cry out as my orgasm hits me.

I collapse against Alexei's chest as wave after wave of pleasure rolls through my body.

My pussy pulses around his cock as he comes, spilling into me so hard I feel it drip down my thighs.

"Shit." His body shudders. "That was fucking incredible."

I lift my head to find the windows of the car have steamed up.

"I think I won that round."

19

ALEXEI

Fucking Bianca in the front seat of my Range Rover was hot as fuck. I don't think I've ever come so hard.

I'm well aware of the fact it's not healthy to avoid fighting by fucking, but if Bianca wants to climb onto my lap in the front seat of my car to take a ride on my cock, there's no way in hell I'm saying no.

I'm already growing hard inside her again, desperate for round two.

But I know it isn't safe to let my guard down so much in public.

Anyone could have ambushed the car, and I would've been hard-pressed to stop them.

So, as reluctant as I am to pull her off me, I do, only to drive us home and take her up to my bed.

Where I bend her over the edge and fuck her so hard she's screaming out my name as we both come.

What makes it even more perfect is the fact that afterward she crawls into my arms and falls asleep snuggled beside me in my bed.

I've never had a woman stay the night. Normally, once I've finished with a girl, I send her on her way, or I'm the one to leave.

But waking up to find Bianca's arms wrapped around my waist, her thigh draped over both of mine has a warmth spreading through my body.

I pull her closer against me, inhaling the sweet scent of her hair which is fanned out over my chest.

"Mmm..." She snuggles closer against me.

"Morning, *solnyshka*," I press a kiss to her hair. "Did you sleep well?"

She lets out a contented sigh, and I chuckle, stroking my fingers up and down the soft skin of her back.

I'm already hard, my cock twitching as Bianca rubs her nipples against my chest. I'm so desperate to pull her on top of me, but I know we have some things that we really need to talk through first that we can't keep avoiding with sex.

"I'm surprised you wanted to stay," I murmur.

She stirs a little more, moving to rest her head on my chest so she can look up at me.

"What do you mean?" Her voice rasps from sleep.

Fuck if it isn't sexy as hell.

"You've been avoiding me the last few days, and then yesterday, about the art show..."

She frowns.

"Oh right..." She shifts out of my hold and slides out of the bed.

I instantly miss the warmth of her body, though I watch her silently as she grabs my discarded white shirt from the dresser and pulls it over her head.

I bite back a groan as she wiggles, her breasts bouncing as she struggles to pull it over her body. It falls to mid-thigh, and the hard peaks of her nipples poke through the material.

"Do you want to tell me what's going on?" I push myself into a seated position.

The sheet barely covers my naked body and does little to hide my very prominent erection, but Bianca keeps her eyes on the floor.

I hate when she doesn't look at me, when she tries to shield her emotions as if she's worried about what I might say.

If only she realized that all I care about is making her happy.

"I overheard you speaking with Dimitri the other night." She plays with the buttons on my shirt.

I frown at her, trying to think what conversation she's talking about. But then it dawns on me. "You were listening to our conversation?"

Her eyes flick to mine, flashing. "I was on my way to the lounge to talk to Mikhail about my phone, and I heard my name. If you want privacy, maybe close the door next time."

"I would've thought it was a given not to listen in on other people's private conversations."

"And I thought it was a given to be straight with your wife. But then again, this isn't exactly a marriage of norms."

"You're right, it isn't."

She's silent for a moment, her cheeks flushed as she regards me.

I sigh. "I'm sorry you heard what you heard."

"I don't want some fake ass apology, Alexei. I shouldn't have been surprised by what you said."

"I keep thinking that if I can convince myself this is only business, then you can't be used against me."

"Is that all it is?"

"You don't know what these men are willing to do to get what they want, Bianca. If they hurt you—"

"I grew up in this world, Alexei, which is why your words mean jack shit to me." She takes a breath, running her hands through her hair.

I can tell she's trying hard not to cry, and my chest tightens at the thought of her being upset.

She shakes her head. "I hate that I let myself get caught up in this."

"Trust me, I never thought for a moment that I would cross the line with you, but I can't seem to fight it. Whatever *this* is." I gesture between us.

"Me neither."

"I lied to Dimitri." Fuck it all. I never want to be the reason Bianca cries again. "I wanted to get him off my back. You and I both know this marriage is no longer purely about business. At least, it isn't for me. Hasn't been for a long time."

She looks up at me under dark lashes as she takes her lower lip between her teeth.

"It isn't for me, either."

I shift over to the edge of the bed, not caring to cover myself with the sheet. I just want her close, to feel her skin beneath my fingertips.

I reach for her, and she stalks toward me, moving to stand in between my thighs, her arms resting around my neck.

"I care about you, Bianca." I run my hands up and down the backs of her thighs. "This is just all new to me. I mean, you're the first woman who I've actually spent the night with."

She blinks. "Really?"

"Really. I'm terrified of getting close to someone and

then having them ripped away from me. I've felt that pain before and I don't know if I could survive it again."

"I understand. My last relationship... He cheated on me and got the girl pregnant. I've never felt pain like it, and I never want to feel it again." She shivers. "When I heard what you said, I panicked that I had gotten in deep, and you were going to toss me aside like he did—"

Her voice cracks, and I'm instantly pulling her into my lap, cradling her against my body as I stroke my hands up and down her back.

"I will never hurt you like that, Bianca. I promise."

"Okay..." Her eyes are downcast.

"And I'm sorry that I upset you so much. That was never my intention. I hope you'll let me show you how sorry I am." I press a soft kiss to her collarbone.

"I think I can feel how sorry you are." She chuckles, snuggling into the crook of my neck.

"Trust me, *zhizn' moya*, this is going to be all about you."

I move to lean back against the pillows.

Bianca squeals as she moves to straddle my lap.

"Now, come here." I grab her by the backs of the thighs, shuffling her up my body until she's perching on my chest.

"What are you doing?" She laughs, the sound going straight to my cock.

"Hold on to the headboard."

Bianca does as I say as I slide down between her thighs until she's hovering above my face.

"Alexei," she gasps as she realizes what I want.

"Let me show you how sorry I am." I press a kiss to each inner thigh.

Trailing my hands around to her backside, I knead the

soft flesh as she slowly lowers herself down until my lips wrap around her clit.

She whimpers as I pull her against me, sucking and nibbling the swollen bud.

"Are you going to ride my face, *zhizn' moya*?"

"Oh god, yes."

"Good girl." I chuckle as I drag my tongue down her slit and sink it deep inside her.

Her hips roll, grinding her pussy harder against my face, and I'm fucking loving every second.

She's so wet, her arousal dripping down my chin as I devour her, pumping my tongue in and out of her heat as she chases her pleasure.

My cock is throbbing, and I can't help but reach down to take it in my right hand, pumping it in time with my tongue. But I stop when I look up to find her unbuttoning the shirt.

"Keep it on," I growl against her flesh.

"So possessive." She chuckles but does as I ask.

The shirt falls open, giving me the perfect view of the underside of her breasts.

"I-I want you to come too," she moans. "Please."

"I will, *zhizn' moya*," I growl as I continue to work my cock.

I glance up to watch her chase her pleasure, those beautiful full breasts bouncing as she grinds against my tongue.

I switch between fucking her with my tongue and running it along her core before moving to suck her clit.

Her breathing is heavy, and her thighs tense on either side of my face.

"Come for me," I order before wrapping my lips around her clit.

"Yes, *yes!*" she cries, her hips bucking as a rush of wetness coats my chin as she rides out her orgasm.

The sweet sounds spilling from her lips are enough to send me over the edge.

My balls tighten, and I furiously pump my cock as I lap up Bianca's arousal until I'm spilling onto my stomach, shuddering with the intensity of my release. "Fuck."

"I-I've never done that," she gasps.

"It's one of my favorite positions." I press soft kisses to her pussy.

She squirms against my touch, but I can't get enough. "Can't you tell?"

She twists to take a look at the mess I've made of myself.

"I can help clean you up if you'd like?" Bianca chuckles.

She's actually trying to kill me.

I lose count of how many times I take Bianca in my bed.

We take it in turns exploring each other's bodies, as if finally admitting that we feel something for one another has given us permission to take our time.

I happily bury my face between her thighs until she's red and swollen, and then she returns the favor, taking me in her mouth for the first time. I don't think I've ever known pleasure like it.

But eventually, I force us into the shower, and then I leave her to spend the rest of the day painting while I head back into the city.

Mikhail and Danil offered to come over and keep Bianca company and for once, I allow it, knowing that the meetings I've scheduled don't include them.

It seems my youngest brothers have taken a shine to my wife, and they're both eager to spend some time with her.

"What have you got planned for the day?" I pull on my jacket as we all stand around in the foyer.

Danil grins. "Bianca's going to paint our portrait."

I frown.

"Fully clothed," she clarifies.

Mikhail and Danil glance at each other, and I can't hide my laugh at the looks on their faces.

"Make sure to hide the one of me," I mutter under my breath as I press a kiss to her forehead before I leave.

Her cheeks flood with color.

"Uh, I'll be right back," she says to my brothers before rushing up the stairs.

They shake their heads, grinning.

"Take good care of her." I clap them on the back before heading out of the house.

Dimitri, Feliks, and our cousin Anton are already waiting for me in the lounge at the penthouse when I arrive thirty minutes later.

It's just past twelve, and the sun is streaming in through the wall of windows, giving us the perfect view of the Manhattan skyline.

Don't get me wrong, I love the family house we have in the suburbs, but I miss the city.

Dimitri smirks. "How are our brothers enjoying babysitting?"

I shoot him a glare as I walk over to the bar cart and pour us each a glass of bourbon.

"She'll give them a run for their money, that's for sure."

"Any word from Emilio?" Feliks asks.

I pick up the four tumblers and set them down on the glass table between the two couches. Taking a seat beside Anton, I lean back into the plush leather, crossing an ankle over a knee.

"Not since the wedding."

Feliks frowns. "Are you worried?"

His dark blonde hair is hidden beneath a backward cap, and he's dressed in gym gear. The guy is a machine, which is exactly why I keep him around. He may be pushing two hundred and fifty pounds, but he's fast on his feet and has a wicked aim.

"Not yet." I take a long swig of my drink. "But we're not here to discuss Emilio. I want to talk about Mario Gilanto."

Dimitri nods. "Still no word on that anonymous tip."

I tighten my hold on my glass, trying to keep my anger under control.

"That's not what I wanted to hear."

Anton leans forward. "I say we strike Gilanto first."

I glance sidelong at my cousin.

He's the same age as Mikhail, and has also inherited the sharp angular features of the Koslovs, though his hair is a lighter brown and his eyes are a deep hazel.

Dimitri looks into his glass. "We think he's trying to get a rise out of us with this email he sent about Ricci."

Anton shrugs. "Perhaps. But wouldn't it be better to strike first, to be the one in control of the attack, rather than waiting around to see if he makes a move?"

I swirl the bourbon in my glass as my eyes go to my brother. "I agree with Anton. We strike first. But this time, we do whatever it takes to take out Mario. Get someone on the inside, find his weak link. There's always one."

Dimitri nods. "I'll get Mikhail on it too."

"Do whatever you have to. Give them whatever they want in exchange. Money, protection, I don't care."

"On it."

"Anton, I want you to have eyes on Gilanto at all times. If he does a shit, I want to know about it. Understand?"

Anton nods.

Feliks sighs. "This is going to be an ugly fight."

I nod. "This life comes with a high price."

20

BIANCA

I didn't think that sex with Alexei could get any better, but I'm more than happy to be proven wrong.

After our conversation where we both admitted our feelings toward one another, not only has the sex become even more intense but so has everything else.

I'm finding myself craving the time spent in my studio with him as he shares stories about him and his brothers while I paint. It feels easy, comfortable.

I'm starting to see a different side of Alexei Koslov, a softer side that I'm not even sure he realized he had.

I appreciate his honesty about his past relationships, or lack thereof.

Part of me is surprised. For someone as devastatingly handsome as he is, he could have any girl he wants. But I can also understand his hesitation about getting close to someone when you live a life like ours.

It was why I had barely dated myself, and why it hurt even more when Jack had betrayed me like he did.

Not only did he break my trust in him, he broke the trust I had with myself. I opened up to him in a way that I never had before, with anyone, and he had to pay the price in the end.

But with Alexei, it's different. He gets it. He gets *me*.

And I like to think that I'm starting to get him.

Perhaps we were a perfect match after all...

He'll be gone a while, and though I never expected it, I'll actually miss him.

ALEXEI COMES HOME AFTER A FEW DAYS IN THE CITY TO find me with my head bent over the toilet throwing up everything that I've managed to keep down over the last few hours.

"Go away," I croak as he forces his way into my bathroom.

"I brought you some water." He leans against the counter.

I lean back against the tub and let my eyes close.

A cool towel dabs at my forehead, and I sigh as Alexei wipes the sweat from my brow.

"Micha told me you've been ill for a few days. I'm sorry I wasn't here sooner."

"It's okay. It's probably for the best if you don't see me like this."

"I want to see you in every possible way, *ptichka*."

I want to appreciate his sweet words, but all I can focus on is the urge to vomit as I swallow the bile that rises in my throat. "Food poisoning sucks."

"I go to the city for a few nights, and you fall to pieces without me."

"Hey, I'm a good cook."

"Clearly. You know I employ a perfectly good cook to make food for you?"

My eyes flutter open, and I wince as my stomach churns.

"Drink some water, *ptichka*."

"I wanted to feel useful." I take the cold glass and slowly sip some of the liquid. "Hopefully, I can sleep this off tonight. It's been over forty-eight hours."

"It might be a bug, but I agree. You need rest." Alexei sets the clean towel on the back of my neck. It feels good. "Do you want me to call a doctor?"

"No, I'm fine. It'll pass soon."

Once I'm certain I won't vomit again, I let Alexei carry me to bed and tuck me in, setting down the water on the bedside table and pressing a soft kiss to my clammy forehead.

He offers to stay, but I know he has work to do back in the city. He's having more and more meetings lately, and I know that this situation with Mario Gilanto is weighing on his shoulders. He looks tired, but he never once complains.

"I'll be back tonight. Sleep well, *zhizn' moya*."

He keeps using these Russian terms.

I know *kisa* means pussycat and *ptichka* means little bird. I hated them at first, but I grew to love them. I have no idea what this new one means, but right now I don't have the strength to ask.

Eventually, I fall back to sleep and wake a few hours later to my phone ringing.

It's hidden amongst the sheets, so it takes me a moment to find it.

Zara's name flashes across the screen. She's been checking in every day since I got my new phone, and it's been so comforting to hear her voice. To have a piece of my old life with me.

I wish I could say the same for my father, who has yet to return any of my calls.

I'm starting to get worried, though I know if I bring it up with Alexei, he'll only say that everything is fine. Perhaps I need to start taking things into my own hands...

I quickly slide my thumb across the screen to answer the call.

"Hey," I croak, my throat dry and scratchy.

"You sound like shit, are you okay?"

"Food poisoning."

"Still? You had that days ago!"

"It won't budge." I reach for the glass of water on my bedside table and take a sip.

Zara is quiet for a moment as I drink until she lets out some kind of strangled cry, making me almost spill my water all down me.

"What is it?"

"Uh, nothing."

"Zara? What's wrong?"

"I-I have to go. Speak soon!"

Zara hangs up the phone, leaving me frowning at the screen.

What the hell was that about?

An hour later, the door to my room swings open to reveal a very flustered Zara in the doorway.

"Oh, my god, Zara!" I sit up in bed.

She's out of breath, strands of her blonde hair sticking to

her face as she darts inside the room and shuts the door behind her.

"What the hell are you doing here? How did you get in the house?"

"I climbed the fence at the back of the house." She gasps for breath.

"You *what?*"

She crosses the room and climbs onto the bed beside me dumping a CVS bag down between us.

"And then the big scary dude downstairs let me in."

"Micha let you in?"

"Yeah. He seemed to know who I was." Zara shrugs. "I guess Alexei put my face on a list of approved visitors. I said I was here to keep you company while you're sick."

"Oh, my god," I groan. "Alexei is going to be so mad."

"Why? I didn't do anything wrong."

"You kind of broke in..."

"*Technically,* Micha let me in. How I got onto the property is a need to know. If he only gave me the code to the front gate, it would have saved me a hell of a lot of trouble."

She looks at her hand. There are bloody grazes on her palms, and the knees of her jeans are scuffed.

"Zara, what was so important that you felt the need to break into my house?"

She wrinkles her nose, avoiding my eyes as she reaches for the CVS bag. "I thought you might need one of these."

She empties the contents onto the bed.

I glance down at the boxes. "Pregnancy tests? Why would I need those? I'm on the pill..."

I *was* on the pill.

But that was before I was whisked away to my new house where everything I consume from food to medication is provided by Alexei. I didn't even think to ask him to get me my birth control...

"Oh no. Oh no, no, *no!*"

"B, it's okay."

"It sure as hell is not okay!" I run my hands through my hair. "I'm such an *idiot*. I didn't even think!"

"Did Alexei not use anything?"

"No. Because I'm an *idiot!*"

"Or you just wanted to hit that bare."

"That is not helping!" I climb out of bed. "I'm so fucked, Zara. I got so caught up in the hot sex and Alexei's stupidly hot body that it never occurred to me that I was no longer taking my pill."

"Let's just take a test and see if we actually have anything to worry about, okay?"

"Zara come on, I've been having unprotected sex for weeks. There's no way any of those sticks are going to come up negative."

"Pee on it, and we'll see." She gathers up the boxes and ushers me into the bathroom. "We might not have anything to worry about, and this might just be food poisoning after all."

I'm shaking so badly I almost pee all over my hand as I reach the stick down between my legs.

Zara unwraps all four tests and makes me use all of them just to be on the safe side.

My cheeks are already damp with tears as we line the sticks up on the side of the bath and take a seat opposite each other on the floor.

Zara reaches for my hand and squeezes it tightly.

"Distract me. I need to think of something other than this. How did you get here?"

"I drove to Forest Hills Park." Zara shrugs. "Alexei

thinks he can put me in the back of a blacked-out car and I won't work out the way to his ridiculous mansion? It's called Google Maps, dickwad."

"He's going to be so mad."

"He can fight me for all I care. There's no way he's going to keep us apart."

"Clearly. Trust you to find a way through Alexei's security."

"He just underestimates what lengths a girl will go to to get to her bestie."

I nod, biting down on my lip to try and stop the tears from falling.

All I can think about is how far Alexei and I have come over the past few days.

He's opened up to me and let me in, and I've loved seeing this other side of him.

Before I got sick, I spent the nights wrapped up in his arms as he made love to me, and I woke up most mornings to him with his face buried between my thighs, devouring my pussy until I was screaming his name.

I was starting to think we could be happy.

"Besides, you got me out of having to go for coffee today with this guy I met at the grocery store. I only said yes because I felt bad. We've run into each other most weeks for the past two months, and he's cute and all, and it's clear it took him a while to muster up the courage to ask me out. So, I said yes, but he hasn't stopped messaging me since. Literally, I must get at least ten messages an hour. You're so lucky that you don't have to worry about any of that. Who knows, you could've found your happily ever after without even searching!"

"Maybe..." I'm barely listening.

The timer on Zara's phone goes off.

"Uh, B? They're ready."

I take a deep breath as I look over at the tests, my stomach churning at the sight of the double lines.

I close my eyes, shaking my head. "I knew it..."

"Is this good or bad?"

"Bad." A whole different kind of nausea hits. "Really bad."

"You don't think Alexei will be happy about the news?"

"He told me the other day that I'm the first person he's let stay over in his bed, and I could tell that freaked him out a little. You think he'll be fine if I tell him I'm pregnant?"

"He seems like a family man..."

"Zara, let's be realistic here. We got married because my father made a deal. He didn't sign up to the whole 'happily ever after, white picket fence' package."

"Okay... Maybe we should wait to confirm with a doctor. Sometimes, these tests can be glitchy, especially if it's early on. Let's not give Alexei a heart attack for no reason."

I know she means well, but I also know this is real.

"And look on the bright side. At least you won't be having this baby out of wedlock. Emilio will be happy."

"Not helping." I stare at the line of positive tests.

How the hell am I going to sort out a doctor's appointment without Alexei knowing?

21

ALEXEI

Bianca is still in bed by the time I get back to Forest Hills later that evening.

It's almost 10p.m., and I've spent the day in back-to-back meetings at one of the clubs my family owns in the city.

My head is pounding, and my temper is on a short fuse.

It seems if you want something done, you're better off doing it yourself.

I lost count of the number of times I reached inside my jacket for my gun, tempted to pull the trigger on the assholes who like to waste my time just to get them to shut the fuck up.

I know even just a glimpse of Bianca will clear my head and bring me back down to earth. I have a tendency to get caught up in business, letting the darker side of my life cloud over the good.

Bianca reminds me that there's good out there, and perhaps I'll show her just how grateful I am…

Dimitri strolls out of the lounge, carrying a glass of scotch as I'm halfway up the stairs.

I frown.

He chuckles. "What have you done to Bianca? I overheard her puking her guts up."

"Food poisoning." I turn to walk back down the stairs. "Is she still sick?"

My chest tightens. I should have stayed with her today.

"Is that what they're calling it now?"

"Calling what?"

"Never mind." Dimitri's smirk tugs at his lips.

I'm growing more frustrated by the second. I wanted to go and check on Bianca as I've hardly seen her the past few days, but it seems business has to come first, *again*.

"Why are you here?" I stalk over to my brother and steal the glass of scotch out of his hand.

"To see my favorite brother, of course."

I down the amber liquid in one long gulp, wincing as the alcohol burns my throat.

"I also thought you'd want to know that there's been a sighting on Ricci."

"Yeah?"

"Anton called as I was on the way here. He's following the SUV as we speak."

"Where?"

"Chinatown."

I pinch the bridge of my nose with my thumb and forefinger as I take a steadying breath.

"How do you want to handle this, Alexei?"

I hand Dimitri the empty glass and check my weapons.

"I need you to stay here with Bianca."

Dimitri opens his mouth, but I shoot him a glare that has him staying silent.

"I need to handle this myself. We might only get one shot with this fucker, and I need to be the one to finish this."

Dimitri runs his free hand through his dark hair. "At least take some backup with you. You don't know what you're about to walk into."

I nod as I re-button my jacket.

My brother reaches into his pocket, pulling out the keys. "Take the hummer. It's freshly stocked."

"Don't let Bianca out of your sight, you hear me?" I pocket the keys.

"I'll watch her like a hawk." For once my brother doesn't fight my instructions which I appreciate. "Give this fucker hell."

I leave Dimitri to head down into the underground garage beneath the house. The door is hidden behind one of the bookshelves in the lounge, and only those with fingerprint access can get in.

Bianca is not one of those people.

As much as I trust her to do as I ask, I have to also be realistic. If I give her access to a garage full of cars, there's no way in hell she wouldn't at least push her luck.

The blacked-out hummer is parked in the far corner next to Mikhail's ridiculous G Wagon that he insisted on buying for his twenty-first birthday.

After unlocking the car, I slide into the driver's seat and power up the engine.

My phone automatically connects to the center screen, and I quickly dial my youngest brother.

He picks up when I'm driving out of the garage and around the side of the house. Club music blasts through my speakers, and I wince at how loud it is.

"Fucking hell, Danil."

"Alexei?" Danil yells through the speakers.

"Where the fuck are you?"

"*Neon.*"

I curse under my breath. Of course, Danil is out clubbing in the city.

"I'll pick you up in thirty minutes."

"Why?"

"We have a fucking job to do, that's why. And bring Mikhail as well. I'm assuming he's with you?"

Danil chuckles. "Yeah, he's here."

"Try to sober up."

I hang up the phone.

Perhaps it would've been better to bring Dimitri along for this job, but I feel guilty for not spending more time with Danil. The most we've hung out was on the anniversary of our parents' death, which wasn't exactly a happy occasion.

After they died, I took on the role of the father figure for my brothers, but particularly for Danil. He was barely sixteen when they died, and I needed to make sure he didn't go off the rails.

Which is hard to do when you've been up around drugs and alcohol.

Danil and Mikhail are waiting for me outside *Neon*, both wearing black shirts and pants. Perfect.

The place is rammed, with a queue around the corner and music blasting so loudly I swear the building shakes from the bass.

I roll down my window as I pull up to the curb. "Get in the car."

Danil rolls his eyes at me as he throws open the car door and climbs into the front seat.

"Is there really a job?"

"Yes. You're not a kid anymore, Danil, you need to step

up and start taking more responsibility when it comes to this family."

"You're finally becoming a man, Danil." Mikhail chuckles from the back seat. "Man, you were so close to getting laid tonight. If only Alexei hadn't cockblocked you."

"Shut up, Mikhail." Danil twists in his seat to glare at our brother in the back seat. "I'm not a fucking virgin."

"The way you were staring at that chick's breasts made it seem like you'd never seen any before."

"I've had plenty of women—"

"Both of you, shut the fuck up. We have more important things to worry about."

I load up my messages on the screen and find Anton's name.

He shared his location, so I import it into my maps before pulling away from the curb. For once, my brothers are quiet as I speed across the city, following the red pin that is telling me Ricci is heading to an old warehouse complex in Chinatown. It's a shady as fuck area, so it tells me everything I need to know about the sort of business Ricci involves himself in.

Because I happen to own one of those nearby warehouses, and I certainly don't use it for storing fucking furniture.

I make sure to switch off the headlights as we approach, the only light guiding us coming from a few rickety old street lights.

I spot Anton's black BMW around the side of one of the warehouses and pull up behind him.

We sit in silence as we watch Anton slip out of his car and come up to my window.

"He's been in there for the past hour." He leans on the

window frame. "I slipped a tracker into his car just to be on the safe side."

I nod. "Is he alone?"

Anton nods.

I nod back. "Good, I've got it from here."

Anton hesitates for a moment but then decides to leave it. He understands that me and my brothers need to be the ones to deal with Ricci.

"Keep me updated." He stalks back to his car.

Adrenaline pumps through my veins as I watch Anton slowly drive away, giving me the perfect view of the warehouse that Ricci is hiding in.

His car is parked out the front, so the moment he appears, I'll be ready.

Twenty minutes later, a figure dressed in all black with a hood pulled low over his head appears, carrying an overstuffed backpack.

Danil leans forward. "He looks shady as fuck."

Ricci opens up the trunk of his car and dumps the backpack inside.

I turn in my seat to face both of my brothers, their faces cast in shadow as they wait for their instructions.

"We need to make this quick, boys." I reach over Danil to open the glove compartment and hand each of them a loaded handgun. "Try not to kill him before we have the chance to get some answers."

Mikhail chuckles.

"But we can wound him, right?"

IT TURNS OUT ONE SWIFT BLOW TO THE HEAD WITH THE base of my handgun is enough to send Ricci to his knees.

Serves the fucker right for having his hood up and his blind spots open.

Mikhail makes quick work of tying up his hands and feet as Danil secures a bag over his head.

It takes all three of us to carry him to the Hummer, where I toss him into the trunk.

We don't have far to drive, but perhaps he'll use that time to think about the benefits of cooperating with us.

I have no conscience when it comes to protecting my family. If I have to take another life in order to protect those I love, then so be it.

My hands are already stained with blood, a little more won't matter.

Mikhail and Danil stay quiet as I maneuver the Hummer through the warehouse complex. They're well aware that those who are brought here never see the light of day again.

I pull the car up to the set of steel rolling shutters.

Many of the windows have been boarded up, and I've had bars placed on all of them for an extra level of protection.

Danil climbs out of the car and jogs over to the shutters, punching in the security code and scanning his fingerprints to unlock them.

Mikhail leans forward in his seat as we wait for the shutters to rise. "Do you think he'll talk?"

"We're about to find out."

I drive the Hummer into the center of the warehouse, wanting to keep it out of sight from anyone who might happen to pass by, and put it in park.

Danil's already working on closing the shutters, and Mikhail climbs out of the backseat and hurries around to the trunk.

I climb out of the Hummer, slamming the door behind me. "Tie him to the chair."

The warehouse is damp and cold, with only a few flickering lights overhead to illuminate the space. But that's how I like it.

It might look abandoned from the outside, but the place is stocked with weapons and underground cells that have proven very useful over the years.

I'd much rather keep my conscience clear and my hands clean, but these fuckers never want to cooperate. So, I have to get *creative*.

Danil drags two rusted folding chairs across the concrete floor, and Mikhail forces Ricci down into one of them.

I roll my shoulders and crack my knuckles as my brothers secure him to the chair, the bag still tied firmly over his head.

Once they're done, Danil looks at me, and I nod once.

Danil smirks as he unties the strings and lifts the bag off Ricci's head.

He squints as his eyes adjust to the low light, his head smeared with blood. He looks to be about Emilio's age, with graying hair and heavy wrinkles around his eyes. But from the breadth of his shoulders, he's packing some muscle.

This should be fun.

"You have some information for me." I pull up the other fold-out chair to sit in front of Ricci, knee to knee.

His eyes are furiously searching around the space, which only makes me grin.

"There's no way out. I made sure of it."

I lean forward and grip the edge of the duct tape covering his mouth, ripping the tape off, taking a bunch of his graying facial hair with it.

Ricci cries out in pain.

"Trust me, that's *nothing* compared to what I'm going to do if you don't cooperate. Now, start talking."

I reach into my ankle holster and pull out a six-inch blade.

His eyes widen as he fights against the restraints.

Mikhail and Danil stand on either side of him, their guns loaded and ready as they watch us silently.

"Do you know where you are, Ricci?" I lean back in my chair, resting my blade on my thigh.

His eyes stay on the blade, but he remains silent.

"I asked you a question."

"N-no." Beads of sweat are starting to drip down his forehead.

"I purchased this warehouse nine years ago. I thought it would be the perfect place to torture the fucker who killed my parents."

Ricci's face pales, and he lowers his eyes—giving me all the confirmation I need.

I remain still. I need answers before I rid the world of this scum. "Would you agree?"

"Y-yes."

I narrow my eyes as I lean forward, resting my forearms on my thighs.

"Good, because according to you, their killer is still running free."

"W-what? I... I don't—"

I glance at Danil who slams the barrel of his gun into the other side of Ricci's head.

The sound of metal crashing against bone echoes around us followed by a deep groan.

Ricci hangs his head, his breath coming in heavy pants.

"The spluttering is starting to piss me off."

I sigh, glancing at Mikhail and nodding. He clicks the safety off his gun.

My eyes set on Ricci again. "You use your right arm to shoot, right?"

Mikhail presses his gun against Ricci's right shoulder.

"No, no. I-I swear." He lifts his head enough to glance at Mikhail.

I hold my hand up, and Mikhail lowers his gun a fraction, his eyes never leaving Ricci's face.

"You swear what, exactly?" I run my forefinger down the face of my blade. The edge is extra sharp, and I will not bleed for this bastard.

"T-that I know n-nothing."

"Wrong answer."

I flick my wrist and catch the edge of the blade along his cheek.

Ricci hisses with pain, but the blood running down his face does little to ease the rage starting to simmer beneath the surface.

"Please. I have no... i-information."

I glance to my brothers who shrug.

We know he's lying, but I have to play this carefully. I need to keep him alive long enough to talk, but it seems he's got his tongue a bit tied.

I'm not about to waste my time waiting for his lips to loosen, I have a wife to get home to.

"You know what? Maybe that bump on your head is making you forget things."

I look at my brothers. "I think a couple of nights of solitary confinement will change his answer."

22

BIANCA

I haven't seen Alexei for more than a few minutes at a time over the past few days. He's been arriving home at all hours of the morning, distracted and tired. And I swear one night, I spotted blood on his white shirt...

But I keep quiet, especially because I'm still throwing up.

The food poisoning excuse won't work forever, and he's bound to notice soon, and I'm not ready to have that conversation.

Not until I'm one hundred percent certain that it's one we need to have.

I sit at my bedroom window, looking out over the drive as Alexei, Mikhail, and Danil climb into the Hummer. I'm well aware that Dimitri is downstairs, no doubt here to keep an eye on me. But I think the vomiting freaks him out, so he stays in the lounge, and I stay here, waiting for the nausea to pass.

The moment Alexei is pulling out of the drive and heading toward the gates at the edge of the property, I pull out my phone to FaceTime Zara.

"How's the baby mama doing?" She grins at me through the screen, her green eyes twinkling with mischief.

"Zara," I groan, rubbing at my temples.

"Sorry." She chuckles. "You know the only way I deal with stuff is through humor. Anyway, what's up?"

"I'm calling in the ultimate best friend favor."

"Hit me."

"I need you to make an appointment with an OBGYN for me."

"That's easy enough." She plops down onto her bed, resting on her front as she props up her phone against her pillows.

"Yeah, it's getting me there that's going to be the problem. Especially when Dimitri is downstairs."

"I'm assuming you have a plan for that?"

I let out a long breath, knowing that Zara is not going to like my idea. "About that..."

"Let me guess. You want me to come over and pretend I'm into him in order to keep him distracted?" Zara screws up her nose in disapproval.

"He's not that bad."

"But I'd rather come with you to the appointment."

"Someone has to stay behind and distract the babysitter. And Dimitri seemed quite taken with you the other day." As much as I don't want to leave Zara alone with Dimitri, I can't think of a better option to ensure he doesn't notice my absence.

"Yeah, I don't think so, but whatever. I'll help you. However, you owe me big time for this."

"Distracting Dimitri is the easy part, it's getting me to the appointment that might be an issue."

"I have an idea." A slow grin spreads across her face.

Dimitri's eyes are locked on me as I stroll into the lounge after showering and getting ready. "Feeling better?"

Zara messaged to say she managed to get me a last-minute appointment with a doctor on the Upper East Side. A Dr.Waite who comes with great recommendations.

"Finally managing to keep a few crackers down, so that's better than nothing."

"Blink twice if you think Alexei's poisoning you." Dimitri chuckles.

He's the picture of ease, leaning back against the couch with an ankle crossed over a knee. He's swapped his usual black pants and white shirt for dark-washed jeans and a pale blue button-down.

I must be staring because he grins. "I'm off duty."

"Ah, so that's your babysitting uniform?" I plop down onto the couch opposite.

"Oh, I think we both know you can take care of yourself."

"Try telling that to your brother." I fold my legs up underneath me.

"He's an overprotective bastard sometimes. He was the same with Mikhail and Danil after our parents died. Well, still is, to an extent."

I try to hide my surprise at the mention of Alexei's parents but it seems Dimitri misses nothing.

"He doesn't talk about them much."

"No."

"He's not much of a talker in general." Dimitri shakes his head. "But you can't deny he cares. I mean, the way he's with you... I've never seen him like that—"

Heavy banging on the front door has us both looking toward the door.

My stomach knots as I glance at Dimitri, trying to read his expression.

"What the fuck..." Dimitri gets to his feet. "Alexei isn't meant to be back yet."

I try to keep my face neutral as I untangle myself from the couch and follow after him.

"Hello?" Zara bangs on the door again.

Dimitri freezes, his broad shoulders tensing. He slowly glances over his shoulder at me, his eyebrows raised.

"Can one of you let me in please?"

I shrug and do my best to feign surprise at the sudden appearance of my best friend.

Dimitri's shoulders shake with silent laughter as he pulls open the front door and steps to the side to let Zara in.

"About time." She flicks her ponytail over her shoulder. She wrinkles her nose as she looks at Dimitri. "Are you always here?"

"Nice to see you again, Zara." He chuckles.

"Mmm, can't say the same."

"I take it Alexei is unaware of our little house guest?" He glances at me.

"I can explain..." I glance at Dimitri.

"Oh, this will be good." Dimitri folds his arms across his broad chest.

"I got an Uber." Zara shrugs.

"You got an Uber?" A deep frown appears between his eyebrows as he takes her in.

There are noticeable scrapes on her hands and the knees of her jeans are scuffed and stained.

She catches him looking and folds her arms across her chest, tucking her messed-up hands beneath her armpits.

The way she's not even fazed by Dimitri's towering build and endless muscles has me biting the inside of my cheek to hide my smile.

She nods. "Yes."

"I didn't see a car come down the drive."

"He dropped me off at the gates."

"I didn't get a notification on the camera."

"It must be broken."

Dimitri's eyes rake over Zara, a smirk tugging at his lips.

"With all this money, you really should invest in better security."

"Duly noted." Dimitri's eyes are still narrowed.

"Are you done with the twenty questions or can I hang out with my friend now?"

"Zara." I reach for her arm. "Why don't we go and make some tea?"

I manage to pull Zara away and drag her into the kitchen where I busy myself with making some tea.

Zara on the other hand goes straight to the fridge and starts pulling out every snack she can find.

"Please, help yourself." Dimitri chuckles, strolling in a few moments later.

I have no doubt in my mind that he sent Alexei a message to let him know about Zara's arrival, and I know I'll need to come up with a good explanation for how she got here, but right now I have bigger things to focus on.

"You're rich as fuck, so I think you can afford to let me have some food." Zara takes a seat at the island, tucking into some crackers and hummus.

I steal one of the crackers, hoping it will help settle my stomach.

"Oh, there are plenty of things I could feed you, *pcholka*."

I almost choke on my cracker, and Zara's jaw is on the floor as she stares at Dimitri.

Zara scoffs. "You're unbelievable, you know that?"

"I've been told that once or twice."

"Do you not have anything better to do than sit with us? Because last time I checked, I didn't come here to hang out with you."

"Ouch." Dimitri puts his hand to his chest.

I look at Dimitri. "Do you mind giving us a minute?"

Zara rolls her eyes at me before popping a hummus-laden chip into her mouth.

"I'm not meant to let you out of my sight."

"I won't tell you if you don't."

Dimitri glances once more at Zara, narrowing his eyes at my friend as she sticks out her tongue.

"I think I'm starting to question your taste in friends, Bianca..." He slides off his stool. "I'll be in the lounge."

Neither Zara nor I speak until Dimitri's footsteps start to fade. My hands are shaking so I wrap them around my mug of tea to try and keep them steady.

"This won't work." Panic is starting to set in. "There's no way he won't find out."

"Shh!" Zara glances over her shoulder. "It's all under control."

"I have no way of paying for it."

"I've got it covered."

"Zara, no. It'll be hundreds of dollars." I run my hands through my hair, trying to ignore my racing thoughts.

"You need the appointment, so it's taken care of. I made it under my name to try and cover our tracks."

"When I tell Alexei, I-I promise..." My voice cracks, and I have to fight past the lump in my throat.

"I know." Zara reaches for my hand. "Let's just cross

that bridge when it comes to it. Now, you should probably get going."

"About that, how the hell do I get out of the house?"

Once Zara has told me in great detail the steps I need to take to get to her car, I take a deep breath and wipe under my eyes. I don't want Dimitri getting even more suspicious.

She squeezes my hand. "Ready?"

I nod, taking her hand as we exit the kitchen and make our way toward the lounge.

"Have you got anything a little stronger to drink?" Zara asks as we cross the threshold into the enormous living room. "Tea just isn't cutting it."

Dimitri looks up from scrolling on his phone, his eyes narrowing as he looks at us.

"You look like the type of guy to have a bottle of scotch older than my grandma just lying around."

I swallow my laugh as Zara drops my hand to make a beeline for the bar cart in the corner of the room.

It's overflowing with bottles of amber-colored liquid and countless crystal glasses that likely cost more than most people's rent.

"Let me do that." Dimitri gets to his feet.

"How gentlemanly."

"I think he just doesn't trust you with the glasses."

Dimitri flashes me a grin.

Zara scowls but steps away to let Dimitri make the drinks. She plops down onto the couch, her eyes never leaving Dimitri as he gets to work pouring three glasses of scotch.

I catch a whiff of the smell, and my stomach churns.

"You know, I've got a really bad headache." I wince as I rub my temple. "I think I might go lie down for a while."

Zara looks my way but doesn't stand. "Oh, really? Are you okay?"

Dimitri pauses what he's doing and looks over his shoulder at me.

I was worried I wouldn't appear convincing, but the smell of the alcohol is doing wonders at inducing my nausea, and a thin sheen of sweat starts to coat my forehead.

"Yeah, I'll be fine. You're welcome to stay."

"You want me to sit here by myself?"

"I can keep you company," Dimitri drawls, grabbing two glasses of scotch and strolling over to the couch.

"Behave," I warn Dimitri who only grins wider as he takes up the spot beside Zara.

"Never." Dimitri chuckles.

Zara dips her chin slightly to let me know that she's okay.

I take that as my cue to leave, knowing that I don't have long to get to the city and back before Dimitri might come to check on me.

Though I'm hoping his keen interest in my friend will keep him occupied long enough not to notice.

I keep my footsteps unhurried until I reach the front door.

There's no easy way of getting out of the house unnoticed. Every door has cameras, and some even have fingerprint access.

I didn't have time to test which ones are Bianca proof, so I'm being bold and choosing to slip out of the front door.

I'm only hoping that once I'm outside the property, I'll be hard to track if I keep to the trees.

Zara's left her car at the far side of the park that backs onto the house, so I only have to scale the fence.

If Zara could do it, so can I.

If all goes to plan, I'll be back in two hours, and no one will be none the wiser.

Unless Alexei decides to check back through the security footage…

Maybe that would be a good time to hit him with the pregnancy news.

I have no choice. I need to see a doctor and confirm my suspicions.

So, ignoring the pounding in my chest and the ringing in my ears, I slip out of the front door and start sprinting for the trees.

The lack of food I've consumed over the past week starts to quickly catch up to me. I'm weak and lightheaded as I run through the trees.

It's midafternoon, and the early May sun is beating down overhead, the trees around me providing little shade.

I'm sweating and exhausted, but eventually, the fence comes into view. It's almost double my height with barbed wire running along the top.

"What the fuck, Zara?"

She warned me about the fence, but I didn't realize it was so high and dangerous.

I look around. "I guess I'm going to have to climb a tree."

I was never an athletic kid, and I haven't changed in the meantime.

My fingernails are bleeding, and my knees are all scratched and bloody as I scale what I thought looked to be the nicest tree. Turns out, it makes no fucking difference. All trees suck, and I wish I could just spend the day hiding under my covers.

What sucks even worse is the drop on the other side. There's no way I can balance on the top of the fence because of the barbed wire. I'm just going to have to take a leap of faith.

"Well, if Alexei won't kill me, this might. So, here goes nothing."

I take a deep breath and push off from the tree.

The ground flies up to meet me, and I let out a pained grunt as I hit the grass.

My knees buckle, and I collapse all of my weight onto my right shoulder, rolling once, twice until I'm flat on my back and staring up at the sky.

A hysterical laugh escapes me as I realize that was actually the easy part.

I KNOW I MUST LOOK LIKE A WRECK AS I SIT IN THE waiting room of the gynecologist.

My jeans have a huge grass stain on the ass, my hands are all torn, and my hair resembles more of a bird's nest than effortless chic.

All the other pregnant women have that glow that everyone talks about.

Will I have that?

As I take in their perfect bumps, my stomach twists.

What if I'm not pregnant?

The pang of disappointment takes me by surprise, but I don't have a chance to dwell on it as the doctor appears and looks right at me.

"Zara Mullens?"

It takes me a second to register that the doctor actually means me.

"Yes." I get to my feet.

"Hi, Miss Mullens, I'm Dr. Waite." He holds out his hand for me to shake.

I cringe as he notices the bloody scrapes on my palms.

But he doesn't comment on them. "Right this way."

He leads me down a narrow corridor and ushers me into an examination room.

"If you'd like to change into this gown and get yourself situated on the chair, we can get started. I'll be back in a few minutes."

I make quick work of changing into the thin paper-like gown.

I feel ridiculous that I got myself into this situation in the first place, but there's nothing I can do about it now.

Dr. Waite appears a few minutes later, a warm smile on his face as he takes a seat beside me.

"So, you're wanting to take a look at your baby today?"

"I... Uh... I wanted to confirm if I am pregnant."

"Right, that's fine. I had you booked in for an ultrasound, but if it's a blood test you need, then I can organize that. The results can sometimes take a few days, and then we can get you booked in for an early ultrasound—"

"Oh, no, I..." I do my best to appear calm, but I can't risk sneaking out again. I need to know *now*. "Sorry, I got mixed up. The ultrasound is fine. I-I'm definitely pregnant."

"Do you know how far along you might be?"

"I'm not sure. Maybe six weeks? I've lost track..."

"Not to worry. I should be able to tell once I get a clear view on the ultrasound. If you wouldn't mind putting your feet in the stirrups, we can get started." He rolls over a cart with a small monitor and pulls on some gloves.

My heartbeat is ringing in my ears, and my eyes start to prick with tears as I lean back.

I wish Alexei was here.

I do my best to stay still as he slowly inserts the ultrasound probe. Dr. Waite's eyebrows are furrowed which is making me nervous.

"Sometimes, it can take a moment for the fetus to appear..." He moves the wand a bit. "Try to relax for me."

I try doing as he says and screw my eyes shut, trying to ignore the weird probe digging around inside me.

"Oh, here you are. Hello, little one."

"Oh, god," I open my eyes to stare at the screen. "Are you serious?"

"Here it is." He points at a blob on the screen. "That's your baby, right there."

There is no more denying it. What am I going to do now?

23

ALEXEI

"This is your final chance, Ricci, because I'm all out of fucks."

"Please."

"I no longer care if you live or die, so it's up to you how you want to leave this world. You can either give me the information I know you have or you can stay here to rot and starve."

"I-I..." Blood spurts from his mouth as he fights against his restraints.

I get in his face. "We know you sent that email."

He reeks of blood and piss. It's fucking pathetic. He's been in this cell for three days and has yet to hand over any information, so my patience has officially run out.

"So, tell me what you know, and I can protect you. Because trust me, Ricci, you want to be on my side. These fuckers think they can mess with me, but they have no idea who they're up against."

He shakes his head, but remains silent.

"Very well. Goodbye." I stand up and get out of his cell, pulling the door behind me.

Before it slams shut, he screams, "Okay."

I smile to myself, but compose myself before going back in.

"What was that?"

Ricci's throat bobs as he looks up at me, his left eye already completely swollen shut from the blow I gave him an hour ago.

"I'll tell you." He winces with every word.

"Let's see if this information is worth your life."

"Ivanov. He's closer to this than you realize."

"What the hell does that mean? My family has nothing to do with the Ivanov bratva."

Ricci's eyes flash with something like amusement, and my blood boils over.

I take out my gun and point it at his crotch. "Speak. Now!"

"There's much you don't know. So much your father failed to tell you."

My chest heaves with every breath, my body a bundle of rage and adrenaline as I try to decipher what the fuck he's talking about.

"I don't appreciate the fucking riddles. You either tell me what you know or I blow your fucking cock out and leave you here to bleed to death!"

"Your father..." Ricci's voice is barely above a whisper now. "Wasn't as faithful as you think."

"What do you mean?"

Ricci looks up at me, and his expression is no longer one of fear, but one of pleasure.

"Let's just say that Alexei Koslov senior didn't keep it in his pants." Ricci chuckles.

My father cheated on my mother?

I barely register the fact that I'm aiming at his face and

pulling the trigger. Not until his head rolls on his shoulders with a bullet wound in the middle of his forehead.

"How dare you speak of my father?" I put another bullet in his chest. "Fuck you."

The fucker asked for it.

I don't make the rules. If he wanted to speak ill of my dead father, then I'm going to make sure his body is unrecognizable by the time I'm done with it.

How dare he try and tarnish the reputation of the most faithful and noble man I've ever known?

I will make him pay for ever speaking such lies.

I punch his face. Again. And again.

I don't stop until my arms are hurting, and I can hardly lift them anymore. Panting, I look at what's left of the man who thought it was okay to insult my father's memory.

Footsteps approach, and I glance over my shoulder to find Mikhail staring at Ricci with a mixture of horror and amazement in his eyes.

"What the hell happened?"

"He proved himself to be full of shit after all." I wipe my face on the back of my sleeve.

I chose the wrong fucking day to wear white.

Mikhail stalks over to Ricci and nudges him with his foot.

"You really wanted to be thorough, huh?" He chuckles. "What'd he tell you?"

"Nothing worth repeating. Clean up the mess and dispose of the body." My voice sounds foreign in my ears.

"On it." Mikhail rolls up his shirt sleeves.

I don't even give Ricci a backward glance as I stalk up the stairs to the main floor of the warehouse where Danil is busy restocking the weapons in the Hummer.

"Heard the shots. Ricci finally give in?" He tosses a few bundles of rope into the trunk.

I say nothing, not wanting to even think about Matteo Ricci again.

I need to get out of this fucking place and clear my head.

Why the hell would he say such a thing about my father?

Unless Gilanto had his claws in Ricci all along, and he wanted me to snap...

It has to be that. There's no other alternative that I can consider.

Danil places a hand on my shoulder. "Alexei? Everything okay?"

I jerk out from under his grip.

"Everything's fine."

My phone vibrates in my pocket, so I pull it out and use it as an excuse to walk away from Danil.

"What the *fuck*."

I blink. This has to be wrong. What the hell is happening right now?

I unlock my phone and dial Dimitri's number.

"*Brat*! I wasn't expecting to hear from you—"

"Where the fuck is Bianca?"

Dimitri is quiet for a moment. "What do you mean?"

"I mean, I just got a notification on my phone saying that she's at some gynecologist clinic on the Upper East Side. Why would she be in the city when I *specifically* told my brother to keep her in the *damn house*?"

"What?"

"Check her fucking room, *now*."

Dimitri huffs on the other end of the line, and I have to

grind my teeth together to stop myself from losing my shit completely.

"You had one fucking job."

"What did you want me to do, sit outside her door every hour of the day?"

"That's exactly what I wanted you to do!"

"You're fucking ridiculous."

"You won't be saying that if Gilanto's got his hands on her." My blood runs cold at the thought. "If anything has happened to her, Dimitri—"

I don't want to finish the thought. I can't.

Dimitri is heaving on the line. "Is this why you came over?"

I blink. "What?"

A muffled female voice says something I can't understand on the other end of the phone.

"Who is that? I swear to god, Dimitri."

"It's Zara."

"Zara? What the *fuck* is Zara doing at the house?"

"She came over."

I almost crush my phone in my hand. As if I didn't already have enough to deal with, Bianca goes and does the one thing I ask her not to do.

Dimitri asks, "Why the fuck is Bianca at a gynecologist?"

"Why do you think?" Zara scoffs.

Dimitri's voice lowers. "Oh *shit*!"

"You have got to be kidding me." I hang up the phone.

My entire body is shaking, and I want nothing more than to slam my fist into the side of Dimitri's face.

He had one fucking job, and he couldn't even do that.

"Danil, I need you and Mikhail to get a ride back to the house with Anton. I have an errand to run."

I try Bianca's cell as I speed through the city, but it rings out every time, making my temper rise even more.

My head is about to explode with everything I need to deal with. But my first priority has to be Bianca.

The fact that she felt the need to hide this from me has my gut twisting.

I thought our relationship was better than that, but perhaps it was all in my head after all.

If she really is pregnant...

My knuckles turn white as I grip the steering wheel and slam my foot down on the accelerator.

I can't have her out alone in the city when she could be carrying my child. A child that would now be considered the heir to the Koslov bratva.

If this got back to Gilanto, I know he wouldn't stop until he put a bullet straight through her womb.

He might even have intercepted her on the way to the doctor.

I know for a fact people like Gilanto have most of the medical professionals in the city by the balls. One phone call, and it could all be over.

It's as if someone else has taken over my body, and I'm looking down on it from above. I don't feel my hands as I swerve the Hummer onto the sidewalk outside the gynecologist's office. I don't feel my feet as I rush up the front steps and barge through the double doors, almost colliding with a heavily pregnant woman.

"Hey!"

I'm already pushing past her toward the reception desk.

"Where is she?" I slam my hands down on the reception desk.

The young girl behind the counter jumps, her hands clutching her chest as she takes me in. "W-who?"

I know I look like hell with my blood-stained clothes, reeking of sweat and piss, but I'm past caring. I need to see Bianca with my own two eyes.

"Bianca," I snap.

"I... Uh, there is no Bianca—"

"Screw this." I push off from the desk, storming toward the examination rooms.

"Sir! Sir, you can't—"

I ignore her as I turn right and head down a narrow corridor.

Most of the doors on either side are open, and I glance in each, my stomach sinking further as they all come up empty.

Please be alive.

There's only one more door at the end of this corridor. If she's not in here, then there's no doubt I'm too late. There's no telling what Gilanto could be doing to her right now.

Sweat breaks out on the back of my neck as I reach for the handle and force open the door.

"Alexei?"

My eyes dart to Bianca lying in the examination chair with her legs up in stirrups. Her bright blue eyes widen as she takes me in.

"Does someone want to tell me what the fuck is going on?" I look to the doctor who is currently moving some probe-like device between her legs.

He looks over his shoulder at me, completely unfazed by my bloody appearance, as if this is nothing out of the ordinary in his line of work.

"I'm sorry, sir, but you can't be in here—"

"It's okay, Dr. Waite." Bianca takes a deep breath, glancing at me. "He's the father."

Oh, fuck.

24

BIANCA

There is nothing but pain and betrayal in Alexei's eyes as he looks at me.

Part of me isn't surprised he found me. What does surprise me is the fact that he's shown up covered in blood and reeking of god-knows-what.

"Alexei..."

As if me speaking his name snaps him out of a trance, he blinks and looks at Dr. Waite.

"She's pregnant?"

My vision starts to blur as I observe the fury on his face. He can barely even stand to look at me.

He doesn't want this.

"She is, yes."

Alexei nods, his eyebrows pulling together in a deep frown.

I hold my breath as he shuts the door behind him.

My fingers itch to reach for him, to feel the warmth of his touch.

"Let me see." He stalks across the room to stand beside Dr. Waite.

Tears trail down my cheeks as Dr. Waite adjusts the probe and brings up the picture on the monitor.

"There's your baby."

A strangled sob escapes my lips as I look from the screen to Alexei's face, at the coldness in his expression.

"How far along?"

"About seven weeks."

Alexei nods.

I want more than anything for him to look at me.

Seven weeks would put the baby's conception at the night in my art studio. The very first time we slept together, and I saw a side to Alexei that I was growing to adore. Perhaps even love…

That side seems so very far away now.

He crosses his arms over his chest. "Are we done here?"

I have to look away, humiliated and hurt by the way he's acting.

Dr. Waite nods and slowly removes the probe.

"Yes. I'll have Rebecca at reception schedule another ultrasound for twelve weeks."

"Fine."

"Alexei—"

He shakes his head. "Get dressed. I'll be outside."

He leaves, closing the door behind him.

The moment the door clicks shut, I can't hold the tears in anymore.

Dr. Waite works quietly to clean me up and then he leaves me to get dressed alone.

My fingers tremble as I pull on my jeans and tank top.

I knew he'd be furious when he eventually found out about me sneaking out. But I had hoped that seeing the baby, *our* baby, would soften the blow, and he'd understand why I did it.

What I was not expecting is this coldness. At worst I thought we would fight and scream and yell until it was out of our system.

But Alexei can barely stand to even look at me, and now I have to go home with him. And know we both know that I'm carrying his child.

There's no way I could sneak past him and make a run for it, and deep down, I don't want to. I *want* to talk about this. I want us to get to a place where we can have a proper discussion about what we're going to do, but it's hard to do that when Alexei is giving me the silent treatment.

Wiping under my eyes and smoothing down my hair, I take a deep steadying breath and open the door to Dr. Waite's office.

Alexei is leaning against the wall opposite, his arms folded across his chest, and his eyes fixed on the floor.

His white shirt is covered in blood, and I spy dark purple bruising along the backs of his knuckles.

"What happened to you?"

He pushes away from the wall. "Let's go."

I hesitate, wanting to push him further, but then he reaches out a hand for me to take. The gesture is enough to shatter the last of the walls around my heart.

"I-I'm sorry."

He takes my hand, pulling me along next to him as we walk down the corridor toward the reception desk.

His fingers are cold and there's nothing tender in the touch.

I try to pull free, but he only tightens his grip.

"Alexei, you're hurting me."

"We're done here."

I don't miss the way the blonde girl shrinks back as Alexei glances in her direction.

This is not the man I know.

This is not the man who built me an art studio and sat with me for hours while I painted.

This is not the man who made love to me in his bed for hours until we both fell asleep, tangled in each other's arms.

This man is nothing but a stranger.

"Alexei..."

He drags me outside to where the hummer is half abandoned on the sidewalk.

"I-I drove Zara's car—"

"I'll deal with that later." He throws open the passenger door, bundling me inside.

I can barely see through the tears as I climb into the seat.

Alexei reaches over and buckles me in, and I catch a waft of his scent.

It's his usual musky smell, but there's a coppery twang to it from the blood that almost makes me gag.

Is this who he's been all along? Have I just been too blind to notice?

I hold my breath as he finishes securing my seatbelt and slams the door shut, making me flinch. Whereas before he would steal a touch, brush his fingers along my thigh or press his lips to my hair, it's as if a switch has turned off and he's nothing but repulsed by me.

It's like a knife to the heart. A hundred times worse after just finding out that I'm carrying his child.

Alexei stalks around the front of the car and climbs into the driver's seat.

I keep my eyes down and my hands in my lap as the engine roars to life.

I wait for the explosion. For the anger and disappointment. For him to tell me how betrayed he feels that I would be so reckless, especially after everything he's done to make sure I'm safe.

But it never comes.

Alexei stays silent.

The only indication he's angry is the way his bruised knuckles turn white as he grips the steering wheel.

We're almost at the house, and I don't want to have this conversation in front of Dimitri or Zara. It has to be now.

"Alexei..." My voice cracks as I twist in my seat. I take in the beautiful lines of his face, his dark hair and hint of stubble that I've grown to crave against my skin. "Say something."

The muscle in his jaw ticks, but he stays silent.

"*Please.*"

He turns down the driveway, the sight of the enormous mansion making my stomach knot.

I can't stay locked up in that house with him, not when he's like this.

"Alexei!" I slam my hand down on the dashboard.

The car grinds to a halt, and Alexei switches off the engine, his eyes still trained forward.

"Tell me what you're thinking, please."

His chest heaves as he takes a breath, and I brace myself for what's about to come.

I'll take whatever he throws at me. I don't care. Anything is better than this silence.

"Go inside." His voice is barely above a whisper.

I almost laugh.

"That's it? You've got nothing else to say to me?"

"Trust me, Bianca. I have plenty to say." His voice is low and cold, and he still won't look me in the eye.

"Then just fucking say it!"

His jaw ticks, and I think for a moment he might actually snap, but he only tightens his grip on the steering wheel.

"Go. Inside. Now."

I stare at him for a second longer. At how far away he is even as he sits right here next to me.

My Alexei is gone. I lost him.

As my heart crumbles, I unbuckle my seatbelt and climb out of the car.

I climb up the front steps and open the front door, my tears blinding me as I try to escape to my bedroom.

"Bianca?"

I glance up and see Dimitri hurrying down the stairs into the foyer, an anxious looking Zara following behind him.

"Dimitri, my office, *now*," Alexei demands from behind me, his voice like ice.

"Bianca?" Dimitri glances between me and Alexei.

"You can catch up later," Alexei snarls. "But first, we need to talk."

Zara opens her mouth to speak up, but I shake my head and glance toward the kitchen. She narrows her eyes at Alexei but darts down the stairs, bypassing Dimitri to follow me. Neither of us speak until the sound of their footsteps disappears upstairs.

Zara holds my hand. "What the hell happened?"

I can't breathe. The weight on my chest is crushing, and bile starts to make its way up my throat.

I dart straight for the sink and hurl up my guts, my stomach wrenching as it brings up the crackers I've managed to keep down over the last few hours.

"B..." Zara rushes to my side. "Are you okay?"

She rubs soothing circles on my back.

"I'm fine." I turn on the tap and splash some cold water on my face.

Closing my eyes for a second, I take a breath.

More than anything, I want to know what Alexei and Dimitri are talking about, what he actually thinks about this baby, but I know if I go storming up there, he'll shut down again.

I hope that Dimitri can get through to him better than I can.

"I don't know how he found out. He called Dimitri out of nowhere and said you were at the gynecologists. How did he know?"

I turn around and lean against the counter, wiping my mouth on the back of my hand. "My phone."

"What?"

"Mikhail put a tracker in my phone and I didn't think to leave it behind. I should've realized." I almost laugh at how ridiculous it all sounds. "I can't even go to the fucking doctor without being followed."

"Bianca, this isn't normal. You can't stay locked up in this house for the rest of your life."

"Try telling that to Alexei." I sigh.

I look sidelong at Zara, and her green eyes shine with tears.

I reach for her hand and squeeze it tightly.

Zara squeezes back. "What are you going to do?"

"I don't know. I-I can't even bear to be around him when he's like this. You should have seen him when I was having the ultrasound, Zara. It was like he was a completely different person. It...it scared me."

"Come home with me, B." Zara pulls on my hand.

"You know I can't do that. Regardless of if he is happy

or not, if I thought he was being overprotective before, it's about to get ten times worse."

We're both silent for a moment. This might be the last time I see Zara for god knows how long.

"How was I so stupid to think that he might be happy about this?"

"Maybe he's just in shock. It's a lot to take in. Not that I'm excusing his behavior, but he might just need Dimitri to talk him down. Becoming a parent is a big deal, and he might just need some time."

"But what about me?" My voice cracks, and I have to blink back the tears that are threatening to spill down my cheeks. "I don't know the first thing about being a mother. Hell, I never even met mine! I needed him today. Not the cold, distant version, but the Alexei that I have grown to... care for. I'm fucking terrified, Zara."

I know it wasn't right doing any of this behind his back. I know I was wrong hiding my pregnancy from him, but I still needed him.

This may be partly my fault, but... I never thought he'd react as he did. That he'd shut me down like that. That I might lose him forever because of this.

I think I love him. I can't lose him now. Not because of this.

But what if I already have?

"I know you are." Lara wraps an arm around my waist. "I wish there was more I could do."

"You've done more than enough. Thank you...for everything."

"That's what best friends are for."

I glance at her and almost crumble at the smile on her face.

She really is like a beacon of light that breaks through my cloud of darkness.

And I don't know how I'm going to get through this without her.

25

ALEXEI

"I asked you to do one fucking thing, Dimitri. *One thing*, and you couldn't even do that right!" I yell the moment Dimitri slams the door to my office behind him.

My entire body is shaking.

Bianca got out. She could have been taken. She could have been snatched from right under my nose, and I could have lost her.

I could have lost my child.

My breath catches in my throat, and my legs almost buckle beneath me.

I stagger over to my desk and brace my hands against it, screwing my eyes shut as images of Bianca lying in my arms as she bleeds out flash in my mind.

"No. No. No. *No*."

"It was an honest fucking mistake, Alexei."

"That could have cost her her *life*!" I roar, whirling around to face my brother. "I told you to watch her! I told you not to let her out of your sight."

"She said she had a fucking headache! What was I supposed to do?"

"Not get fucking distracted by the thought of fucking her friend and follow her upstairs!"

Dimitri scoffs as he stalks over to the drinks cabinet. "Seriously, Alexei, you sound insane. I wasn't going to sit outside her door all day and night. She's a grown ass woman."

"Who has a fucking target on her back."

He shrugs as he reaches for a crystal tumbler, as if Bianca's safety means nothing to him.

The gesture has me seeing red, and I'm pulling out my gun before I have a chance to talk myself down.

Dimitri pours himself a finger width of scotch and downs it in one, slamming the crystal glass back down before turning to face me.

He eyes the gun pointed right at the center of his chest, and a smirk starts to tug at his lips.

"Let's fucking go, *brat*." He reaches into the back of his jeans, pulling his own gun free and pointing it at my chest, clicking the safety off.

We both stand staring at each other, our heavy breathing filling the space between us.

I can barely keep my hands steady. My whole body feels like it's overflowing with rage, and I don't know how to get it out.

"Shoot me, I fucking dare you," Dimitri taunts.

"She could have been taken." My voice feels foreign.

"She wasn't—"

"She could have been!" I click the safety off my gun.

Dimitri doesn't even flinch.

He raises his eyebrows. "I don't think that's what's got you all worked up. So, why don't you tell me what's really bothering you?"

Where do I even start...

"You let Bianca sneak out—"

"What the fuck happened with Ricci?" Dimitri's brown eyes narrow as they flick over my blood-stained clothes. "Because I bet that's what's really got you all riled up. What did he say?"

"He was a waste of my time, that's what."

"He had no useful information? Or did you kill him before he had a chance to talk?"

I have to look away from Dimitri as I try to ignore Ricci's last words.

How could he accuse Papochka of cheating on Mamochka?

"He talked, all right. Nothing but bullshit, so yeah, I killed the fucker."

"Think you did more than that. Mikhail sent me a picture of the body. Looks like he had been put through a meat grinder."

"Since when do you question my methods?"

"Since you don't seem to be fucking thinking straight. So, I'll ask you again, *brat,* what is really bothering you?"

We stare at each other, guns aimed and ready, as I try to work up the courage to speak the words out loud, because once I do they become real.

"Bianca is pregnant." I lower my gun and I sit, head in my hands.

Dimitri's mouth drops open as he lowers his own gun. "She's actually pregnant?"

"Yes, that's why she snuck out. To go and see an OBGYN."

"The doctor confirmed it?"

"Yes."

"And it's yours?"

"Of course, it's fucking mine." Even before the doctor confirmed how far along she is, I knew it was mine.

"This is... Whoa, this is big. I didn't realize you guys were wanting to actually do the whole 'relationship thing'. I mean, it was obvious you were fucking but..." Dimitri shuts up when he sees the look on my face.

Exhaustion plagues me, but I don't have time to give in.

"Trust me, this was not part of the plan." I run my hands through my hair. "None of this was part of the plan."

This is exactly the sort of thing I was afraid of.

I never should have crossed the line with Bianca. I knew better, and I did it anyway, and now the consequences are even greater.

The life of our child is at stake.

"A baby." Dimitri holsters his own gun, moving to take the armchair beside me. "Fuck, this is..."

He leans back in the chair and runs his hands through his hair, his eyes wide.

"As if she didn't already have a target on her back. If this gets out..." I can't finish the thought.

"Alexei, for once can't you take this for what it is?" Dimitri leans forward to rest his forearms on his knees. "It's happy news, *brat*. You're going to be a father!"

I screw my eyes shut as Ricci's words ring in my ears.

"I know nothing about being a father."

"Dad was around for the first two decades of our lives, so you know exactly what it takes. And then when he was gone, you stepped into his role and took care of this family. You took care of Mikhail and Danil. You took care of *me*. He would've been proud."

Would he?

I shake the thought from my mind. This is exactly what

Ricci wanted, to get into my head and have me start to question my family and their loyalty.

"I promised Emilio I would keep Bianca safe, not knock her up and give Gilanto even more ammunition to come after her."

"Gilanto won't find out."

"We can't trust anyone with this information, Dimitri. The fact that some random doctor knows has me on edge. If only she had told me, I could have brought someone in that I trusted."

Dimitri shrugs. "We can pay him off."

"No doubt he will sell the information to the highest bidder."

"Then we just have to make sure that's us. We have the resources to protect her, Alexei."

"What if it's not enough?" The thought has been plaguing my mind since I saw the ultrasound.

She's carrying my child, a child that will be brought into a world filled with nothing but darkness, and I don't know if I'll be enough to protect them.

"What's gotten into you?" Dimitri shakes his head. "This isn't like you at all."

I run my hands over my face and set them before me on the desk, wincing at the sight of the purple bruises on my knuckles.

I didn't miss the flash of fear in Bianca's eyes as I stormed into the doctor's office and she took in my bloody shirt.

She was scared of me.

Good. Perhaps now she'll actually listen to me.

"She could've been taken..."

My chest tightens at the thought of what could've happened. Any one of Gilanto's men could have intercepted her on the way to the doctors, and I wouldn't have been able to get to her in time.

I would have lost her.

I screw my eyes shut as I try to ignore the images that flash through my mind.

It's no longer my father. It's Bianca. Those beautiful blue eyes are vacant as she stares up at me, her blood soaking into my skin as I clutch her to my chest.

"Alexei?" Dimitri's voice pulls me out of my nightmare.

"She has no idea what she's done." I lean forward to rest my head in my hands.

"I don't think she lied on purpose. I think maybe she wanted to wrap her head around the pregnancy first and confirm her suspicions before she spoke to you? I don't blame her, considering how you've acted—"

"How else was I meant to act? She fucking ignored my one request, and now not only has she put her own life in danger but also the life of our baby!"

"You need to talk to her, *brat*. I know you're angry as fuck, but you can't ignore her forever. She's fucking pregnant, Alexei. She needs you now more than ever."

"Which is exactly what Gilanto will think. He'll use this against us, Dimitri. I can't have my wife and child being used as pawns in his sadistic little game."

"Can you for one second not think about Mario fucking Gilanto?" Dimitri slams his hand in the arm of his chair. "Your wife is pregna—"

His phone rings, which I'm grateful for.

I didn't come in here to get lectured by my younger brother.

I know I can't ignore Bianca forever, but I'm too pissed right now to be able to have a constructive conversation with her.

The truth is that I don't trust myself, and I don't want to say or do something that might push her away forever.

I run my hands up and down my thighs, my body a tight ball of nervous energy as Dimitri curses under his breath.

I frown. "What is it?"

Dimitri hesitates, pulling the phone away from his ear, turning off the call.

"Dimitri."

"Anton and I managed to bribe one of Gilanto's men that we intercepted outside Alessandro's to turn his allegiance to us." He rubs his jaw. "A guy named Luca Caruso."

"Caruso? Name doesn't ring a bell."

"For good reason. The guy's a complete ass wipe if you ask me. He folded the moment a couple of hundreds were in his hands, no loyalty to Gilanto whatsoever."

"Which is good for us."

"It is. But you're not going to like what he found out."

I don't miss the pity that flashes in my brother's eyes, and I have a feeling I already know what he's about to say.

"Spit it out, *brat*."

"Gilanto's planning on going after Bianca to get to you. He must know that she's more than just a business deal with Emilio."

"Fuck!" I slam my hand down on the table in front of me, causing my gun to rattle against the glass.

"We don't know that he knows about the baby—"

"It's only a matter of time."

"Should we call Danil and Mikhail? I think we should all sit down and come up with a plan."

"We don't have time for that."

"Then what do you suggest we do?" Dimitri's focus is on me.

"I'm taking her out of the city." I get to my feet. "Pack her a bag, Dimitri. We'll leave in an hour."

"That's ridiculous, Alexei. Bianca is safe here."

I shake my head and shoot him a glare.

I hate the way he's lounging back in the armchair, the picture of ease, as if he didn't just get a call confirming that Gilanto's planning on making a move on my wife.

"Clearly, she isn't. If her friend can get in, and Bianca can get out, any fucker can get in. You, Mikhail and Danil can stay at the penthouse. I want everyone to stay away from this house until the security has been overhauled."

"Alexei—"

"I'm not taking any more chances when it comes to my family, Dimitri. Please, I'm begging you. Just do this one thing for me."

"Fine, I'll make sure Mikhail and Danil stay in the city. Where exactly are you planning on going?"

"Somewhere Gilanto won't think to look."

26

BIANCA

Alexei comes charging down the stairs, freshly showered and changed with a bag in each hand, followed by a grave-looking Dimitri.

I look between them. "Alexei?"

He refuses to speak as he drags me into the garage and loads the bags into the trunk of his Mercedes.

His eyes go to his brother. "You know what to do. Don't let me down again, Dimitri. I need to be able to trust my own family."

My blood boils as neither one of them acknowledges my presence.

He buckles me in, as he always do, but doesn't touch me again. My heart breaks that much more.

As soon as he enters the car, he starts it, and we drive off.

"Where are you taking me?"

He keeps silent and just drives.

Soon, we're flying down the freeway. We've been driving for almost an hour without a word spoken between us.

How did it all go so wrong so quickly?

"Alexei, where are we going?"

"A cabin near Greenwood Lake."

"A cabin?"

"Yes."

"Why?"

Silence. And not the easy kind I used to find with him when I would paint, and he would sit by my side. This silence feels heavy, and with each second that passes it's like another brick added to the wall around Alexei's heart.

He was starting to let me in. We were starting to become something more, something special.

And I had to go and ruin it all.

"You're going to have to forgive me eventually, Alexei. Please." I swallow the lump in my throat.

"I don't have time to think about that right now. I'm too busy trying to keep you and the baby alive."

I blink.

Keep us alive?

"Does Gilanto know about the baby?" I turn in my seat to look at Alexei. "Is that what this is about?"

Alexei says nothing. His throat bobs as he stares ahead at the road, and it's all the confirmation I need.

"What about Zara? She's still at the house! Is Dimitri going to take care of her?"

"Zara is not my priority."

"She's my priority, Alexei!"

I let my best friend be dragged into this world because I was selfish, and it might just cost Zara her life.

"If we're in danger, I need to make sure she's taken care of. I have a right to know what's going on."

"Funny, I could argue the same thing."

My cheeks burn.

I should have told him about the baby the moment I took those tests, but I was terrified of ruining what we had.

I guess it made no difference in the end.

"If my life is in danger, my *baby's* life, I have the right to know why."

"You lost that right the moment you defied my orders and snuck out of the damn house," Alexei snarls. "And it's not just *your* baby, Bianca."

I blink back tears as I turn away from Alexei and stare out the window, watching as the city disappears into our rearview.

He's right.

This is all my fault. And I could have gotten my baby killed. I was stupid, I didn't think.

I just hope this doesn't cost any of our lives.

Before long, we're turning off the interstate and making our way through winding roads, surrounded by nothing but woodland. It's secluded, and under other circumstances, I might have enjoyed the thought of a peaceful stay in a cabin.

Alexei takes a sharp left through an opening in the trees, and my eyes widen as the cabin comes into view.

I had pictured a rickety old log cabin with no electricity or running water, but this place couldn't be further from that.

It has a cozy appearance, with perfectly stacked logs making up the walls and roof, and a large enclosed porch wrapping around the entire property. There's even a rocking chair beside the front door.

But I don't fail to miss the state-of-the-art security cameras on every corner of the property.

If Alexei's brought me here instead of staying at the Forest Hills mansion or even the penthouse in the city, then the security here must be even tighter.

Alexei parks the car alongside the cabin, and we both climb out, the silence still hanging heavy between us as he gets the bags from the trunk.

I follow him up the steps to the front door and wait for him to punch in the code and scan his finger.

He pushes the door open with his foot and carries our things over the threshold, leaving me to trail behind him like a lost puppy.

Lights automatically come on as we enter, illuminating the large living space.

There's a kitchenette to the left and a dining and living area to the right. It's rustic, with mostly wooden furniture and thick rugs covering the floor. A huge fireplace is the main attraction of the room, with two tweed armchairs positioned before it. There's a door just off the small kitchen which I assume leads to the bedrooms and bathroom.

At least I hope there are multiple bedrooms...

I sink down onto the brown leather couch that's immediately to my right, tucking my legs up underneath me as I look around.

Alexei's phone starts ringing, and I wait for him to disappear into one of the rooms, but he does the opposite. He answers the call, muttering under his breath as he starts pacing back and forth in front of me, as if he can't trust me enough to leave me out of his sight.

I keep my eyes on the floor, not knowing what to do with myself.

How long are we expected to stay here?

I need to make sure Zara is taken care of, and I stupidly left my phone back at the house, though I wouldn't be surprised if Alexei smashed the device.

"Aren't you afraid whoever is trying to kill me might trace your call?" I ask when he finally finishes the call.

"I've made sure that can't happen." He perches on the arm of one of the chairs. His eyes never leave his phone and the frown only deepens between his eyebrows.

"So, you didn't get Mikhail to put a tracker in your phone too?"

Alexei's nostrils flare, but he doesn't look up.

"I thought that was part of the deal, or do you get a free pass because you're the head of the family?"

"Bianca..."

I'm done giving him a chance.

"No. Please, tell me how this works. Is it just me that gets the privilege of being tracked?"

"Maybe if you were trustworthy, I wouldn't feel the need to put a damn tracker in your phone." Alexei finally looks up at me.

"For months, I've been nothing but trustworthy, even if I didn't agree with your decisions."

"I beg to fucking differ."

"I left the house one time, Alexei. One fucking time."

"One more than you should have. And you were reckless. Endangering yourself and the baby."

"Doesn't that tell you something?"

"It tells me you can't be trusted."

"Well, it should tell you that I was scared. Worried you would act like *this*." My throat is trying to choke up, but I fight it. Fight the prickling in my eyes. "So yes, I snuck out. But only because I felt like I had no other choice."

Alexei gets to his feet, and I hold my breath for a moment.

Is he about to tell me how wrong I was to think such things? That he's overjoyed by the idea of becoming a father?

Instead, he taps away on his phone and lifts it to his ear once more.

"Please, Alexei. We need to talk about this," I reaching out and take the phone out of Alexei's hand.

"If you know what's good for you, Bianca, you'll give that back."

"I think I've made it abundantly clear that I don't know what's good for me." I turn it off and throw it on the couch.

Alexei glares at me, but I don't back down because I can see behind the mask.

He's just as terrified as I am.

So, I take a step toward him, and then another, and another.

I stop once there's barely any space between us, and he has no choice but to look me in the eye.

Our breathing is ragged, our bodies tense as we silently fight against each other.

I want to break first, to reach out and run my fingers over his chest.

I glance down, and his bruised hands are balled into fists. I pretend he's feeling the same. That he's fighting the urge to reach out and touch me.

"Alexei..."

I look up, and there's nothing but devastation in his beautiful eyes, so I crumble.

I reach out and sink my fingers into his shirt, a strangled sob escaping me as the warmth of his skin seeps through the material. "I'm sorr—"

His lips crash against mine.

His fingers sink into my hair, pulling me closer against him as his tongue forces its way into my mouth.

There's nothing sweet or tender about the kiss, but I don't care. All I care about is that he's here, and his warmth is beneath my fingertips.

I wrap my arms around his neck and rise up onto my tiptoes, pressing myself fully against him.

If this is all he can give me, then I'll take it because it's better than this cold stranger he's becoming.

"I want you," I whisper against his lips. "In whatever way you'll let me have you."

Alexei answers by reaching down to grab the backs of my thighs and lifting me off the ground.

I wrap my legs around his waist as my fingers sink into his hair, angling his head so I can explore his mouth with my tongue.

A deep rumbling sound builds in his throat as he carries us through the door that leads to the only bedroom.

I tighten my legs around his waist, trying desperately to rock against him, but Alexei grips me around the waist and forces me off him.

I lower myself to the ground and try not to show my disappointment when Alexei steps away from me.

"Take off your clothes, Bianca."

My breath hitches as I reach for the hem of my tank top and pull it up over my head, keeping my eyes on Alexei the entire time.

His eyes darken as they dip to my chest, at the noticeable swell of my breasts over the top of my bra.

I'm practically panting with need as I start taking off my pants.

My cheeks heat under the intensity of Alexei's gaze as I slide the denim over my ass and down my thighs.

When I bend down to slip them over my feet, I hear Alexei clear his throat, and I glance down, realizing I'm giving him an incredible view of my breasts.

I kick my jeans aside and straighten, watching Alexei intently as his eyes roam over my body before focusing in on my stomach.

His throat bobs once before his eyes lift to meet mine.

A smile tugs at my lips as I reach behind me and unclasp my bra, letting it fall to the floor.

My breasts are heavy and swollen from pregnancy, and my nipples instantly harden against the slight chill in the air.

"Mmm..." I reach up to cup them. "They're so sensitive." I gasp as I rub my thumbs over the sensitive peaks.

Warmth starts to spread between my thighs, and I rub them together to try and relieve the ache.

"Take off your panties."

My breath catches in my throat as Alexei's eyes flick down to my lace-covered pussy. My clit is already throbbing, and my panties are noticeably damp.

I dip my fingers into the waistband and slowly slide them down my legs, leaving me completely bare before him.

"Did you want me to knock you up, is that it, *zhizn' moya*?"

The nickname on his lips has the last of my restraint snapping.

I didn't realize how starved I had been for his affection, and my body feels like it's on fire as he devours me with his eyes.

"I think you like the idea of carrying my baby." He

makes quick work of the buttons on his shirt. "Now everyone will know who you belong to."

"You don't own me."

"*Kisa*, the moment you signed that marriage certificate, you became mine, and you'd do well not to forget it." He pulls off his shirt, revealing his gloriously tanned chest to me.

The authority in his voice has heat pooling low in my belly.

These pregnancy hormones must be kicking in because I'm practically drooling at the sight of Alexei's muscled abdomen.

"Remind me, then. Show me who I belong to."

Need flashes in Alexei's eyes, and he reaches for his belt buckle.

My eyes fall to his crotch, and I moan at the sight of his hard cock straining against his zipper.

I continue to knead my breasts as I watch Alexei shed the rest of his clothes, my mouth watering at the sight of his cock springing free and already glistening with arousal.

"You belong to me, Bianca." His voice is low and commanding.

I nod, my pussy throbbing with the need to be claimed by him.

"Show me, Alexei."

He closes the distance between us, crashing his lips against mine as he lifts me back onto the bed and settles himself between my thighs.

His cock pushes at my entrance, and Alexei groans as he buries his face in my hair.

"You're soaking, *zhizn' moya*."

"I-it's the hormones." I grind my hips as his cock pushes another inch into me.

I wrap my legs around his waist, digging my heels into his back to force him into me further, but Alexei pushes back.

"Patience, *zhizn' moya.*" He presses a kiss to my collarbone.

I arch into his touch, my nipples pressing into his chest and making me moan with pleasure. "So responsive, *ptichka.*"

"I-I can't help it." My eyelids flutter closed as I try to calm myself down.

"I'm enjoying it." He reaches down to take my right nipple into his mouth.

I cry out at the touch, my fingers sinking into his hair to pull him harder against me.

"Please, Alexei. Fuck me."

Alexei smiles around my nipple before he slams all the way inside me.

"*Yes!*" I cling to him as my pussy stretches around his enormous length.

He pulls himself all the way out and thrusts back into me so hard the bed slams into the wall.

"Oh, fuck." Alexei bites down on my nipple as he sinks his cock into me so deep my eyes roll.

I forgot how big he was, how well he filled me, and I can't get enough.

"More."

Alexei chuckles as he moves to suck my other nipple.

I pull him with my legs, wiggle beneath him to get him to move. "Please, I need *more.*"

"I'm trying to last longer than a few minutes, but you're not making it easy for me, *zhizn' moya.*"

"I don't care,"

"You like it when I come inside you, don't you, Bianca?"

"Mmm..." I roll my hips so that his cock brushes my inner walls.

Alexei shifts to his knees and lifts one of my legs over his shoulder.

"Look at you, *ptichka*, so swollen and beautiful." He glances down to where we're joined.

My cheeks burn as I glance down and his cock's glistening with my arousal.

I can't catch my breath.

The way Alexei's hitting me at this angle sends me crashing over the edge with my release.

I scream out his name, arching back against the pillows as my pussy clenches around his cock, my body convulsing as I ride out my orgasm.

"*Bianca*," Alexei groans.

I grin as he screws his eyes shut for a moment to try and calm himself.

"Come inside me, Alexei." I run my fingertips along the swollen muscles of his biceps.

A thin sheen of sweat covers his chest, and his breathing is coming in heavy pants as he chases his own release.

He quickens his pace, fucking me so hard I know I'll feel him for days.

My body is becoming limp as my orgasm builds deep in my lower belly.

If I thought I felt pleasure before, it's nothing compared to what the pregnancy hormones are doing to my body. I can't get enough of Alexei, and that should scare the hell out of me. But right now, all I care about is making the most of being close to him.

"Come with me, *zhizn' moya*."

His fingers dig into my hips as his thrusts become

sloppy, the sound of his cock sliding in and out of my wetness making us both moan.

"*Alexei*," I moan as one more thrust of his cock sends us both crashing over the edge.

Alexei shudders, my name falling from his lips as he comes.

I watch in awe as his ab muscles clench with each thrust of his cock as he empties himself inside me, my pussy pulsing around his throbbing length as I take every last drop he gives me.

27

ALEXEI

Bianca is naked and asleep in my arms once more. Where she belongs.

I hold myself up on my elbow so I can watch her sleep and listen to the soft sounds of her breathing.

My arm is draped over her waist, and I slowly trace circles with my fingertips over her belly.

Having her pressed against me, feeling each breath she takes, calms my racing thoughts.

She's here, and she's safe.

I know having sex last night wasn't the answer, but being that close to her again made me forget all about the shit show that was the last twenty-four hours.

We'll work through it because it's clear nothing has changed in terms of our feelings for one another.

Bianca stirs, pushing her ass back against me, which has my cock springing into action. She rolls onto her back and looks up at me, her cheeks flooding with color as she realizes I've been watching her.

"Morning." My eyes flick to her mouth.

She sinks her teeth into her lower lip as she reaches her hand up to cup my jaw.

"How long have you been watching me?" Her eyes search my face.

"Not long enough." I dip down to press my lips to hers.

She sighs, parting her lips so I can slide my tongue into her mouth.

"Does this mean you forgive me?" she murmurs against my lips.

I pull back to look at her fully.

"I do forgive you, *zhizn' moya*. But I need you to promise to never keep anything from me ever again."

She nods.

But I need her to understand how serious I am about this. This is something that can make or break us. "I mean it, Bianca. I need you to be open and honest with me at all times."

"Does that go for you too?" She raises her eyebrows.

I let out a long breath. I can't give her the answer she's looking for, but I have to meet her halfway.

"I'll be as honest as I can be, but you need to understand that there are things I might keep from you because telling you could put your life in jeopardy."

Bianca rolls her eyes.

"You sound just like my father."

"Trust me, I don't like keeping things from you."

"That's exactly what he used to say."

"Have you spoken to your father?" I ignore the uneasy feeling in my stomach as I ask about Emilio, knowing full well that Bianca hasn't had any contact with him since the wedding. But she doesn't know I know that.

"Not even once." Bianca shakes her head, her eyes growing sad as she looks up at me. "I mean, we weren't the closest, so I wasn't expecting a daily phone call or anything. But to have heard nothing stings more than I thought it would. I always had this feeling in the back of my mind that he was only ever interested in my life when he wanted something from me."

"What do you mean?"

She shrugs and bites her lip to try and stifle the tears that are pooling in her eyes.

I pull her tighter against me and wait patiently for her to continue.

"When I went to college, we would maybe talk once a fortnight, and even then it was mostly him updating me on the business. He barely asked me about my classes or friends or anything. I didn't think much of it because I was too busy having fun. But when I graduated, he gave me no choice but to come and work for him, being his only child and all. And then every interaction we had was him asking things of me. I never had a say, never had a choice..."

I wince. Maybe I am more like her father than I thought.

"I always knew he was disappointed he didn't have a son, and his absence now just proves it."

"Bianca..."

"I'm honestly surprised you haven't heard from him. Because now you're technically the son he never had."

I have to look away, hoping that she didn't see the guilt in my eyes.

Would it have been better to tell Bianca the truth about her father's silence?

Maybe not. She would have done everything she could to protect him, no matter the cost.

"Don't give up on him, Bianca. You don't know how lucky you are to have a parent in your life at all."

"I know, I'm sorry." She turns to me and snuggles against my chest.

"If he's gone quiet, I'm sure there's a reason for it."

"He's never gone radio silent for this long, I'm just worried something's happened..."

I need to get her thinking about something else because if she looks up at me with those beautiful blue eyes, I'm going to crack. And I can't afford that.

Throwing back the sheet that's barely covering us, I move myself on top of Bianca and settle myself between her thighs.

Her eyes grow wide as she feels how ready I am for her, but first I want to taste her. *Zhizn' moya.* My life.

How she grew to mean so much to me, I don't know, but I will kill this world and the next to keep her safe and in my arms.

"I think we have some more making up to do." I reach down to press a kiss to the spot just between her breasts.

She wiggles beneath me, her fingertips sinking into my hair as I start to trail kisses down her stomach.

"I like your idea of making up." She laughs. "Maybe you go first, and make it all up to me."

I glance up at her, and she grins.

Fuck, she's so beautiful.

"Is that so?" I dig my fingers into her hips as I continue to kiss lower.

"You have a lot of work to do, *husband*—" I run my tongue along her core, and she gasps, arching off the bed.

"What was that, *wife*?" I lick her again.

Bianca only moans, her fingers pulling at my hair as she grinds against me.

I know what she wants, but I'm not going to give it to her just yet.

Instead, I sink my tongue into her pussy, and my cock almost erupts at the sweet taste.

"Fuck, Bianca." I pump my tongue inside her again. "You taste incredible."

"More..."

I smile against her before pressing a soft kiss to her clit.

Her hips buck, and I know it would only take a few flicks of my tongue over the swollen bud for her to come.

My cock throbs at the thought, so desperate to be buried inside her, but I want to taste her pleasure first.

Moving my hands to her ass, I tilt her hips up before wrapping my lips around her clit and sucking hard.

Bianca cries out my name, her thighs tightening around my head as I work her clit faster.

"That's it, *zhizn' moya*, come for me."

With one last lick of her core, Bianca arches off the bed as her orgasm hits.

Her fingers pull at the roots of my hair as she grinds against my mouth as I continue to work her through her pleasure.

When she finally stills, I lift myself up onto my elbows and take a moment to take her in.

Her smooth skin is flushed, and her breasts are rising and falling with each panting breath. Her dark hair is fanned out behind her, and I want nothing more than to run my fingers through the smooth strands.

"Look at you." I bend down to press a kiss to her stomach.

Bianca pushes herself onto her elbows and smiles softly, her eyes glazed with pleasure.

"Shall we take this to the shower?" I get to my feet. Bianca's eyes roam over my bare chest, and I grin as they stray lower.

I glance down at my erection and take my cock in my hand, groaning as I pump it hard.

Bianca climbs out of the bed and stalks toward me, her beautiful breasts swaying with each step.

"There's something I want to do first." She sinks to her knees.

"Bianca," I groan as she reaches for my cock.

"Let me." Her eyes on me as she kneels to undo me.

I move my hands to my sides and watch in awe as she wraps her small hand around my cock and pumps it.

"Fuck, *ptichka*, your fingers barely reach."

Bianca grins up at me under those dark lashes.

"I can't wait for you to fuck my mouth."

A strangled sound escapes my lips as Bianca leans forward and runs her tongue over my head, lapping up the bead of precum.

"Mmm..."

I have to sink my nails into the palm of my hands to keep myself steady as Bianca wraps her lips around the head and sucks.

My legs almost buckle as she starts to take me deeper, her hand still wrapped around the base of my cock, squeezing me hard just the way I like it.

"Oh, fuck."

Bianca's lips curve into a smile around my cock before sucking it once more.

Her tongue licking the underside of my cock has my balls tightening.

"Can you take more, *zhizn' moya*?"

She nods, and I almost erupt as she takes me deeper.

I sink my hands into her hair and slowly start pumping my hips, my eyes rolling as she hollows her cheeks.

Bianca moves her hands to rest on my thighs to steady

herself as I give her another inch, increasing my pace even more.

When my cock hits the back of her throat my restraint seems to snap.

Bianca sinks her nails into my skin as I pump my hips faster, the base of my spine tingling as my release builds.

"Are you going to let me come in your mouth, *ptichka*?"

Bianca looks up at me and nods, her blue eyes watering as I fuck her mouth harder.

"Good girl."

Her mouth feels like heaven, and the thought of spilling down her throat, having her taste me on her tongue for hours has me gritting my teeth as I try to last a little longer.

But as if Bianca can tell I'm holding back, she moves her hand to cup my balls, squeezing them hard as my cock hits the back of her throat.

My release hits me out of nowhere, and my legs threaten to buckle from the pleasure.

"*Bianca*," I groan as my cock spills into her mouth.

She moans as she continues to suck my cock, licking up every last drop that I give her.

When she eventually pulls back, I reach down to wipe away some of my release from the corner of her mouth with my thumb.

"So beautiful," I murmur as I sink my thumb into her mouth and watch her clean it off. I reach out my hand to help Bianca to her feet. "Come here."

"Time for a shower?" Her blue eyes twinkle.

"I think that sounds like a wonderful idea." I chuckle, bending down to grip Bianca by the backs of her thighs and lifting her into my arms.

Bringing Bianca to a secluded cabin in the woods wasn't my worst idea. Considering there's not much to do, we've spent the majority of the past two days fucking on every possible surface. It's as if we've been making up for lost time.

The past few weeks have been draining, and I've hated that I've been away from Bianca for so much of it. Perhaps if I had been around more, she wouldn't have felt the need to hide the pregnancy from me...

The idea of becoming a father still terrifies me, but as Bianca and I talk it through, the way her eyes light up has my anxiety fizzling away.

She seems genuinely excited by the idea of having a baby, and I'm glad that she's finding some happiness among the chaos.

Having some distance from our regular lives and spending some quality time together has been refreshing. It's as if nothing else exists outside of this cabin, and I'm starting to dread the moment when Dimitri calls to let us know the house is ready.

I know Gilanto's threat isn't going to go away on its own, but for a few days, I can pretend that life is normal.

What I can't seem to shake is the knowledge that my father might not have been the man I thought he was.

Part of me doesn't want to find out whether what Ricci said is true and risk tarnishing the memory of my father.

But someone needs to pay for their deaths, and in order to find out who did it, I need to learn the truth.

On our third morning at the cabin, Dimitri finally calls. "Thought you'd want to know that the house is all secure."

"Are you sure? Because we thought that before."

"I watched them put in the new gates and fence surrounding the property, and each of the doors and windows have been bulletproofed. The entrances have new motion sensors and cameras along with retina scanning to open the doors. I could barely get through the front door," he chuckles.

"Good." I glance over to Bianca who's lounging on the sofa. "I don't want anybody getting in or out without me knowing about it."

"See you soon, *brat*."

I pocket my phone and head over to the couch to sit beside Bianca, pulling her into my lap and cradling her against my chest.

"Are we going home?" She sinks her fingers into my shirt.

"Yes, we're going home." I press a kiss to her head.

I just hope home is as secure as Dimitri claims it is. I don't know what will happen if something happens to Bianca or the baby.

28

BIANCA

Alexei put me straight to bed the moment we got back to Forest Hills. The car ride back from Greenwood Lake triggered my nausea, and poor Alexei had to keep pulling over so that I could hurl up my guts every fifteen minutes.

He sets me up in my bed with a cold washcloth over my forehead and a mug of ginger tea to try and settle my stomach.

"I need to go into the city, *zhizn' moya*." He perches on the edge of the bed as he wipes at my forehead.

"Do you really have to?" I pout.

Alexei smiles, reaching down to press a kiss to the tip of my nose.

"You'll be asleep soon, and you won't even know I'm gone."

"Will you be back by the time I wake up?"

"I'll do my best, *solnyshka*." He offers me one last quick kiss before getting to his feet. "I'll see you soon."

It doesn't take long for sleep to pull me under. The last

few days of nonstop sex have finally worn me out, not that I'm complaining.

A few days alone together, away from the stress of real life, is exactly what Alexei and I needed.

The fact that he's on board and even excited about the pregnancy has calmed my nerves, and I keep finding myself resting my hand on my lower abdomen, my heart skipping a beat at the thought of the mini Alexei that's growing inside me.

My phone ringing rouses me from a deep sleep.

I peel my eyes open to find my room in complete darkness, the only light coming from my phone screen on the bedside table. Squinting, I reach for my phone. Zara.

"H-hello?"

"Bianca?"

"Mmm?" I stifle a yawn as I pull my phone away from my ear to see that it's almost one in the morning.

"Bianca? I-I need you to come and help me. *Please,* B. T-there's this guy—" Zara's voice cracks, and I bolt upright in bed at the sound of her muffled sobs on the other end of the phone.

"Zara, what happened?"

"Oh, B. It was horrible."

"What? Zara, what the hell is going on?"

My heart is pounding in my chest as I wait for her to reply. Music is playing in the background but no other sounds come through. "Where are you?"

"I-I'm at *Neon*. Some guy tried to...he tried to—" Her voice cracks again, but I don't need her to finish that sentence for me to work out what's happened.

"Are you somewhere safe?" I climb out of bed and start turning on the lights.

"I'm locked inside one of the stalls in the ladies' room."

Her voice is thick with tears. "Please, B. I need your help. I t-think he's waiting for me."

"Don't worry." I hurry over to my closet. "I'm coming for you. Promise me you'll stay right where you are?"

"I promise."

"Okay, good, I'll see you soon."

I hang up the phone and get to work pulling on a pair of leggings and a sweatshirt.

My hands are shaking as I fumble with the laces of my red Converse, but once I'm dressed I decide to quickly call Alexei. He's already in the city so it's likely he could get to Zara quicker than I could.

"Pick up, pick up," I mutter as the phone rings endlessly. "Fuck."

Perhaps he's with Dimitri. I call him too, but it goes straight to voicemail.

I guess I have to do this alone.

I pace back and forth across the carpet, chewing my bottom lip as I try to come up with a plan.

Alexei would have asked either Micha or Feliks to stay at the house to keep an eye on me, and there's no way in hell they're going to drive me into the city.

"Think, Bianca." I run my fingers through my hair.

I need to get out of the house, and there's only one way that I can think of that might actually work. I dart over to my bedroom door and throw it open before yelling at the top of my lungs.

"Help!" I drop to my knees, clutching my stomach. "Help! It's the baby! Ah—"

I roll onto my side, screwing my eyes shut.

Within seconds, heavy footsteps trample the stairs.

"Bianca?" Micha calls from the floor below.

"Help me."

He rushes up the second flight of stairs and down the corridor, where he halts at the sight of me doubled over in the doorway to my room.

"Shit, Bianca, are you okay?" He drops to his knees beside me.

"Call an ambulance." I reach out to clutch his shirt sleeve. "Something's wrong."

"Everything seems to be fine." The doctor wipes off the excess ultrasound jelly from my abdomen. "But I'd like to keep you overnight for observation just to make sure."

I force myself to look relieved, though I'm nothing but restless as the doctor tidies away the ultrasound equipment. I had hoped they would take me to the ER, and I could slip out, but I had no such luck. It turns out Micha might overtake Alexei in the race for who's the most overprotective when it comes to me.

After blue-lighting us all the way to the nearest hospital, I was rushed up to the maternity unit to be checked out.

"I'm feeling much better."

I glance at the clock on the wall in the examination room and wince.

It's been almost an hour since Zara called me. If I don't get to her soon, who knows what might happen. I doubt one door to a toilet will be enough to stop a guy if he really wants to get his hands on her.

My stomach churns. I'm running out of time.

"Even so, I'd like to keep an eye on you both." The doctor offers me a warm smile.

I wait for him to leave, readying myself to make a run for it the moment the door closes behind him.

But just as I'm about to throw back the blanket covering my legs, Micha opens the door.

"How are you feeling?" He hovers in the doorway. It seems he's taking his role of babysitter very seriously.

"Better." I push myself up onto my elbows. "Do you think you could get me some ginger tea from the cafeteria? I'm feeling a little nauseous."

"Uh..."

"It would really help." I offer him a sweet smile.

"Sure. I'll be right back."

I nod, leaning back against the pillow, closing my eyes for a moment as I wait for him to leave.

The moment the door clicks shut, I throw back the blankets and dart over to the chair in the corner where my clothes have been folded neatly, and my shoes and phone rest on top.

I rip off the hospital gown and pull on my clothes, my heartbeat pounding in my ears as I glance at the clock.

I have maybe ten minutes before Micha comes back, and I need to be on my way to the city by the time he finds me gone.

Once I finish dressing, I hurry over to the door and softly peel it open, peaking my head out to check for any signs of a six-foot-seven, tattooed bodyguard. The halls are fairly quiet as it's about two in the morning, so I sneak out, closing the door as quietly as possible behind me.

I make my way to the elevator at the end of the hall, glancing over my shoulder every few seconds to make sure Micha thought better of leaving me unattended and has come back to check on me.

"Hurry up." I press the elevator button a few more

times, knowing it won't help, but I need to feel like I'm doing something.

The doors ping open, and I step inside, hastily pressing the button for the lobby.

As it starts to go down, I unlock my phone, and a text message from Zara pops up with her location, so I know she's safe for now, but I don't like the idea of her being afraid and alone.

I copy the location into my Uber app and let her know that I'm on my way.

"Can you wait here for ten minutes while I get my friend?" I ask my driver as we pull up outside the club.

The driver nods, and I quickly climb out of the car.

There's still a queue, as some people stumble out of the club.

I force my way into the middle of a group of people who are leaving and sneak through the doors, bypassing the bouncers completely.

I look around for the sign indicating the ladies room.

The bass from the music thumps overhead, and it smells of stale alcohol and sweat, making my stomach churn.

I keep myself pressed against the wall to avoid the crowd as I head to where the ladies room is, praying that whoever took a liking to my friend got bored and left.

The doorway is clear, so I get inside.

"Zara? Zara, it's me."

One of the stalls clicks open, and Zara stumbles into my arms.

"Oh, B. I was so scared." She sobs as I wrap my arms

tightly around her shaking body, holding her tightly as she cries. "H-he just wouldn't leave me alone."

"It's okay." I run my hands up and down her back. "You're safe."

"I'm such a mess."

I smooth her long hair out of her face and wipe under her eyes, offering her a reassuring smile.

"Come on, let's get you out of here." I wrap my arm around her waist. "I've got a car waiting outside."

"I'm so sorry to drag you out here." Zara's still shaken by her close call as we exit *Neon*. "He just wouldn't leave me alone."

"Anytime. I'm just glad you're okay." I walk us toward the waiting Uber.

"Does Alexei know you're here?"

I bite my lip, and Zara's eyes widen. "Bianca, he'll kill you!"

"If he doesn't understand I will do anything to help those I care about, then I don't care what he does. Now, come on, you can come back to the house with me."

I keep a hold of Zara's hand as the Uber starts to take us back out of the city toward Forest Hills. Every time she sniffles, I give it a squeeze to let her know she's not alone.

By now, Alexei must know of my disappearance, but I don't care. There's no way I would have not done everything in my power to make sure my best friend was safe.

"What the hell is this guy doing?" the driver mutters.

I glance out of the back window, and a pair of headlights is coming toward us at breakneck speed.

"Pull over. Let him pass."

"It's probably some drunk asshole." Zara sinks down further into her seat, closing her eyes.

The driver huffs under his breath but indicates into the

next lane, giving whoever this asshole is plenty of room to pass us.

I keep my eyes on the headlights, frowning as it gets closer and closer. "I don't think they're drunk."

Zara sits up and turns in her seat, looking out of the back window. "They're driving way too steadily..."

My heart slams in my chest. "Fuck, they're heading right for us!"

My breath catches as the huge black SUV comes into full view, racing past us at what must be almost triple the speed limit.

The Uber rattles as it passes, barely missing the side of the car.

"Holy shit!" Our driver swerves, which almost sends us crashing into the safety barrier.

"Oh, my god." I clutch my chest.

If they had been so much as an inch to the right, they would have hit us.

"You girls okay?" the driver glances over his shoulder at us.

Zara points straight ahead "Look out!"

The SUV swings around and starts accelerating toward us, their headlights on full beam to blind us.

"Break!" I cry as the driver swerves, but it's too late.

The SUV barrels into the driver's door sending us crashing into the interstate barrier.

Metal crushing metal rings in my ears as I jolt forward, my seatbelt choking me as I slam against it.

Tires screech, and I glance out of my window.

The SUV is backing away, the front of the car mangled but still drivable.

For a moment, time seems to stop, and all I can hear is the sound of my labored breathing.

"Zara?"

"I-I'm okay."

Relief washes over me at the sound of her voice.

I shakily reach for my seatbelt and undo it, wincing at the pain in my neck as I glance sideways at Zara.

There's a large cut on her forehead and blood in her hair but other than that, she looks okay.

She looks around. "W-what about the d-driver?"

I lean forward to find our driver with his head buried in the airbag. His door is completely crushed, and I fear I already know what I'll find when I climb through the center console and press two fingers to his neck.

"I-I can't find a pulse."

"Oh god."

"It's okay. We're going to be okay." I move back to my seat. "W-where's your phone? Call 911."

But Zara's eyes have gone wide as she turns to look at me. "B... Do you smell gas?"

I take a deep breath and almost choke as the smell of fuel hits my nose.

She is taking off her seatbelt and looking around. "We need to get out of the car. *Now*."

"Climb out the back window." My throat feels raw from where the seatbelt cut into it, but at least I'm alive.

There's broken glass everywhere, and my palms are bloody and stinging as I crawl through the back of the car onto the trunk. "We need to get away from the car."

I reach back to pull Zara through.

We stumble away from the wreck, glass crunching beneath our feet.

Every muscle in my body aches and blood drips down my hands, but I don't care.

All I care about is getting both of us as far away from the wreck before it explodes.

A huge *BANG* rings in our ears, and the car goes up in flames.

We dive to the floor, wrapping our arms around our heads.

I think I cry out as a wave of heat cascades over us, but the world around me is a giant ringing in my head as my thoughts go to the driver we left behind.

Zara sobs, wrapping her arms around me. But I can't hear her, I can't hear anything but this loud annoying ring.

I shake my head as Zara's lips move. She is talking.

I shake my head, trying to clear it.

"I can't hear anything," I scream, trying and failing to hear myself. Have I gone deaf?

I can't worry about it now. Reaching out, I hold Zara's hand. "Come on. W-we need to m-move."

My throat is raw, and I have no idea where we are or how to get out of here, but then Zara is sobbing. It starts as if it is at the end of a tunnel, but it gets clearer.

I am not deaf. Relief is momentary.

We were so close to death.

My legs are shaking, and it's taking every ounce of energy I have to climb to my feet.

"We need to call 911." I pull Zara with me.

As we turn, my knees almost buckle at the sight of a man holding a gun pointed straight at my chest, the mangled SUV behind him.

"I'd get into the car if I were you."

29

ALEXEI

"I'm intrigued to know what it is you need me to look into so urgently." Frederik leans back in his armchair.

Handing my private investigator a glass of scotch, I take the seat opposite him.

I chose to have this meeting in the safety of my office at the penthouse rather than at one of my usual haunts in the city. I can't risk this information getting into the wrong hands.

Everyone's loyal until they're offered the right price.

"First of all, I assume I have your utmost discretion. I can't have any of my brothers knowing what I'm about to share with you."

Frederik frowns but nods before taking a sip of his scotch. "Of course." He runs a hand through his hair. "Now I'm even more intrigued."

Downing my drink in one, I let the alcohol burn my throat as I work up the courage to speak the words out loud.

I don't trust many people outside of my family unit, but I trust Frederik.

He's been working with my family for years, but he has been known to do extra work on the side just for me.

I hate the idea of anyone else knowing about my father's alleged adultery, but I don't have the time to look into this myself, so asking Frederik is the next best thing.

"I was given some information that I wanted you to look into. It's about my father."

Frederik raises his eyebrows but nods.

"Go on."

"A man named Matteo Ricci told me that my father might've not been as faithful as we think. We were questioning him regarding Ivanov."

"Ivanov? As in..."

"The Pahkan, yes."

"Fuck." Frederik lets out a long breath as the words ring in the air between us.

My mouth feels dry, and I want nothing more than to down the entire bottle of scotch, but I need to keep a clear head.

"I need to know if there's any truth to it, and how the two are connected."

Frederik downs the rest of his drink. "The Ivanovs are tricky people to look into. It might take some time for me to find any credible sources."

"I want this cleaned up as soon as possible. My father's reputation is on the line, Frederik. Even if this rumor gets out, it could ruin my family."

"I will do everything I can to find out the truth, Alexei. You have my word."

"I expect an update in a few days."

"No problem."

I nod.

My phone rings as I'm showing Frederik out. I pull it out of my pocket.

"Excuse me a minute." I frown, swiping my thumb across the screen. "Micha, this better be important."

"Bianca was taken to the hospital."

My blood runs cold. Bianca? In the hospital?

"Is she okay?" I run my hand through my hair as my mind goes to the worst-case scenario.

It might have taken me a little longer to come around to the idea of becoming a father, but the thought of something happening to my child, to Bianca, makes me sick.

"She was in pain—"

"What kind of pain?"

"She had some cramping, but the doctor checked her out and said everything looks fine, but they want to keep her overnight for observation."

"And you're only calling me *now*?"

"Bianca didn't want me to tell you until we knew for sure what was going on."

"I'm your boss, not her. Put her on the phone now."

I try to take a steadying breath.

Micha had one job, and he let Bianca sweet-talk him into bypassing my instructions.

What if something had gone wrong, and he had failed to tell me? What if something had happened, and I didn't get to her in time?

"Heading back to her room now."

"You're not even with her?"

"She wanted tea—"

"I don't give a *fuck* what she wanted!"

Frederik flinches out of the corner of my eye, but I don't care.

"Let me speak to Bianca."

A door clicks open.

Micha curses.

Something's wrong. "*Micha.*"

"She's not here."

"*Fuck!*" I fight the urge to launch my phone across the room. "I'm going to track her phone."

Hanging up, I notice a missed call from her hours ago.

Fuck!

I pull up the tracking app.

Frederik shifts his weight from one foot to the other. "Is everything okay?"

I don't reply.

My fingers shake as the tracking app opens, and I click on Bianca's cell.

I zoom in on the map.

Her phone is heading toward the interstate leading out of the city.

I try calling her.

Nothing.

"I have to go."

My body doesn't feel like my own as I sit behind the wheel of my Mercedes and race out of the city, Bianca's location loaded up on my navigation system.

Someone took her. Someone took my *solnyshka* and my unborn child right out from under my nose, and I'm not going to stop until the city runs red with the blood of the fuckers who took her.

Micha never should have let her out of his sight. I don't care how badly she begged, he should have known better.

I only hope his mistake doesn't cost Bianca her life.

My knuckles are white as I grip the steering wheel, the adrenaline pumping through my veins making me alert.

When I glance at the navigation screen, I almost run my car off the road.

Her location has stopped moving. She's still on the interstate, but the red pin is stagnant.

"What the fuck?"

I'm only a few miles away, but with each passing second, I start to fear the worst.

There are only two reasons her phone could have stopped moving in the middle of the interstate.

Either it was thrown from the car, or there was an accident.

I swallow the bile that rises in my throat at the thought of the second option.

It can't be.

After everything Bianca and I have been through, I can't let this be the way it ends. There has to be some other explanation because I can't lose her or our child.

As I speed down the near-empty interstate, I notice the smoke first.

My heart stops in my chest.

"Zhizn' moya..."

I push the accelerator to the floor, fighting the urge to vomit as the wreckage comes into view.

The front left side of the car is completely mangled, but the damage is too great for it to have simply come from a collision with the safety barrier.

Someone crashed into them, but whoever the fucker was seems to be long gone.

My car barely stops moving before I'm climbing out of it and running over to the wreckage, broken glass crunching beneath my feet.

"Bianca!"

I peer into the front window and see what's left of the driver—my stomach churning at the smell of the burned flesh.

"Bianca!" I move to look into the backseat, but it's empty. "Fuck!"

I walk around the back of the wreckage and notice spots of blood leading away from the car and a set of tire marks a few meters away.

My legs threaten to give out as I realize what this means.

I'm pulling my phone out of my pocket and dialing Dimitri as I stare down at the spots of blood. *Bianca's* blood.

"What's up, *brat*?"

"Bianca's missing." The words almost have me doubling over and hurling my guts up.

"What?"

"I tracked her phone, but there was an accident." I have to screw my eyes shut and take a steadying breath as I try to think rationally about what to do.

"An accident? What the hell happ Fuck!"

"Dimitri?" My heart hammers in my chest.

"I just got a message from Zara."

"What does it say? Is she with Bianca?"

"Shit."

"Dimitri!"

"It just says '*help*'."

Fuck.

I need to think, but my heart is pounding so hard in my chest I can't take a full breath. Each second that passes is precious time that I can't afford to waste.

"Alexei, what should we do?"

I screw my eyes shut, trying to ignore the panic that's

building inside me. I need to keep a clear head if I have any chance of getting to Bianca in time.

"Get Luc on the phone. Get him to hack into Zara's phone and have him send me her location." It's the only thing I can think of that might actually help.

"Already on it. Do you think they're together?"

"I fucking hope so."

"Alexei, she'll be alright."

"You don't know that." I turn around to face the burned-out wreckage that she came so close to being caught in. "You should see the state of the car she was in."

"Someone ran it off the road?"

"Looks like it. Fuck, if I'm too late..."

"You can't think like that, Alexei. It doesn't help anyone."

"She's carrying my child, Dimitri! *Moy rebenok*. I can't help but think the worst."

"I know."

My phone pings against my ear, and I pull it away.

Luc sent me a new pinned location.

"Dimitri, I'm putting you on speaker."

I click open the message and zoom in on the pin. "Fuck!"

"What is it? Do you know where they are, Alexei?"

All the air seems to leave my lungs as I stare at my phone.

"Gilanto's taken them."

"Fuck. How do you know?"

"Because Zara's phone is at one of Gilanto's properties in Chinatown, and I'm betting Bianca is with her."

My ears are ringing as I think of what might be happening to them right now.

I turn my back on the wreckage and hurry back to my car where I connect Dimitri to the speaker.

"Alexei, this could be a trap. He could be trying to lure you there—"

"I don't give a fuck." I turn on the ignition, putting the car in drive. "I'm not taking any chances, Dimitri, not when it comes to Bianca and my unborn child."

My brother is quiet for a moment, and I take the opportunity to think as the roar of the engine fills my ears.

Gilanto has Bianca and Zara. The one thing I feared the most has come true.

This time, I can't be too late. I won't let that happen. I won't fail them like I failed my parents.

My chest tightens as I try to take a steadying breath.

I can't afford to make any mistakes here. I need to keep my head clear as I try to come up with a plan.

"Where do you want to meet?" Dimitri snaps me back to the present.

"I'm heading straight there. We don't have any time to waste."

"Alexei—"

"Are you in or not, Dimitri?"

"Of course, I'm fucking in." His footsteps in the background are followed by an engine roaring to life. "What about Mikhail and Danil?"

"I want everyone on this. It's likely going to be a fucking bloodbath, so bring as much backup as you can."

"Wait for us there, Alexei, I don't want you getting yourself killed because you're not thinking straight."

"If I have to sacrifice my life to save Bianca's, then so be it. I'll do whatever it takes to make sure she gets out of this alive."

30

BIANCA

My head is pounding, and every muscle in my body aches as I try to stretch out my legs.

The ground is cold and damp beneath me, and my body can't stop shaking from the chill in the air.

What the hell happened?

I peel my eyes open, wincing at the stabbing pain in my head, to find the room cast in darkness.

My heartbeat quickens as I glance around and see nothing but the outline of a door to my right.

"Oh god." A sob tears through me as my right hand moves to my abdomen.

I need to stand up. I need to get the hell out of here.

But as I try to climb to my feet, my teeth gritted with the effort, pain sears through my arm.

I cry out, my legs buckling beneath me.

"No."

I pull against the heavy metal cuff locked around my wrist.

The chain rattles and echoes around the dark room.

But as the cuff grazes the wound on my wrist, I almost black out from the pain.

Panting, I gently feel along my arm and fight back a sob as my fingers come away bloody.

The wound must be a few inches long, and it's still bleeding. It needs to be cleaned and stitched up before I risk getting an infection.

Not that it matters. I don't think I'm going to leave this place alive.

The odds are stacked against me, but I'm going to do everything I can to get the hell out of here. "Think, Bianca."

I need to stop this bleeding, but all I have on me is my sweater, and I'm not sure if it will make the best tourniquet.

I have to at least try.

I shrug my right arm out of my sweater and lift it up over my head, leaving me in nothing but a tank top.

Whimpering as the metal cuff grazes the wound on my arm, I try my best to wrap the arm of my sweater above the wound and tie it in a knot, praying it will be enough to stop the bleeding.

A thin sheen of sweat breaks out over my skin as I take the material in my teeth and pull it tight, doing my best to muffle my sobs as pain shoots up my arm.

I don't want to risk drawing the attention of whoever is keeping me here by crying out in pain, so I grit my teeth as tears stream down my face as I continue to pull the material tighter.

Once I'm certain I can't tie my makeshift tourniquet any tighter, I slump back against the cold brick wall and let my eyes flutter closed for a moment, exhausted from the effort.

My head is foggy, and I can barely make sense of my

thoughts as I try to think back to what happened after the car crash.

I remember pulling Zara out of the car...

Oh, my god.

"Zara?" I whisper. There's no answer, and my heart is threatening to come out of my throat as I realize we could have been separated, or worse... "Zara!"

A soft moan sounds to my left.

I almost sob at the sound. "Are you okay?"

"I-I think so."

"Are you hurt?"

"I-I'm not sure. Everything fucking aches."

"Me too."

The pain in my left arm has reduced to a dull throbbing, and I pray it doesn't become infected.

"Where are we?" Zara groans. "What happened?"

I open my mouth to reply, but heavy footsteps echo from the other side of the door, and my breath catches in my throat. "Stay quiet."

I wince as light pours into the room, my head screaming at me as the door crashes against the wall—the sound ringing in my ears.

I peel my eyes open and look up at the looming figure standing in the doorway.

He's easily as tall as Alexei, and just as broad. As he walks in and light hits him right, I notice his short dark hair and a heavily lined face. His thin mouth is pulled up into a smirk as he looks down at me, and I cower under his gaze.

"Glad to see you're still alive. I would have hated to have gone to all that effort for you to die before we could have some fun."

I take a second to glance around.

It looks like he's brought us to a basement. There are no windows, and the only exit is the door he came through.

I take a peek at my arm, and I'm hit with a wave of nausea as I notice the pool of blood that has stained the concrete beneath me.

I look to my left and fight back a sob at the sight of Zara slumped against the wall.

Blood is caked down her face and neck, and it seems as if she's barely breathing.

"You put up quite a fight."

I glare up at the stranger.

"Who are you?" I'm surprised by the strength in my voice, but it's not only my life at stake here. It's Zara's and my baby's too.

I need to keep him talking for as long as possible. For as long as it takes for Alexei to find me.

"I'm surprised you don't already know the answer to that question, *Bianca*."

Mario Gilanto.

He must be able to read the realization in my eyes.

"I knew you'd work it out."

"What do you want with me?"

"Isn't it obvious? You're the perfect payback, sweetheart."

"I've done nothing to you."

Gilanto only shrugs, shoving his hands in his pockets as he peers down at me with nothing but disgust in his eyes.

"Perhaps not, but your father is the reason my brother is dead. He sold the information to the highest bidder, who turned out to be Alexei Koslov. So no, you may not have hurt me directly, Bianca, but you will be paying for their crimes with your life."

"Killing me won't bring your brother back."

"No, but it does kill two birds with one stone. Not only does your waste-of-space father suffer from your death, but so does your *husband*."

He spits the last word, and I flinch as he stalks closer to me.

I try to scrabble away, but there's nowhere for me to go as the chain attached to my wrist locks out.

My wrist screams as the cuff cuts into the skin, but that only seems to please Gilanto more.

"Alexei will kill you."

"He can try." Gilanto chuckles. "If anything, I'm looking forward to the fight. It's been a long time coming. You see, Alexei Koslov took many things from me, Bianca, and it's about time he paid the price."

"You're no match for him."

"I admire your faith in him. Tell me, Bianca, have you actually come to care for your husband?"

I say nothing, not wanting to give anything away.

"Oh, I know all about your little love affair with the Koslov Pahkan." Gilanto sighs as he crouches down in front of me. "Tell me, are you having a boy or a girl?"

The breath leaves my lungs, and I double over as my stomach heaves.

Gilanto's laughter rings in the air around us as I swallow down the bile rising in my throat.

"You really thought I wouldn't find out?" He reaches out to grab me by the hair before yanking my head back.

I cry out as pain shoots across my scalp, but Gilanto only tightens his grip, getting so close I can smell the stale alcohol on his breath.

"It's about time fuckers like your father stop underestimating me. He really thought he could marry you off and be done with it? Well, it doesn't fucking work like that. Trust me, I don't take your father's betrayal lightly, and he's about to learn that the hard way."

He throws me to the side.

I collapse against the concrete, landing on my injured arm which makes me cry out.

I can't stop the tears that start to stream down my cheeks at the mention of my father.

Has something happened? Is that why he hasn't been returning my calls?

"W-what have you done to him?" My voice is barely above a whisper, and I'm no longer shaking from the cold chill in the air, but from fear.

My father can't be dead.

Alexei promised he would keep him safe. He promised—

"I'll spare you the details." Gilanto chuckles. "It seems you've got quite a weak stomach as it is, what with the pregnancy and all. Speaking of which, how did Alexei take the news?"

I grit my teeth as I glare at Gilanto.

He's only taunting you

"I hope he was delighted by the idea of becoming a father, to have an heir."

"Fuck you."

"I can't wait for him to find you here after I'm done with you. He'll blame himself for your death, of course, and the death of your child. The guilt will eat him alive, and that makes me so...*happy*." He clutches a hand to his heart.

"You're a monster..."

"No more of a monster than your precious Alexei. You'd do well to remember that."

He reaches out to brush the hair from my face.

I cringe at the feeling of his calloused fingers against my skin.

"Oh, we're going to have so much fun together," he purrs.

"W-what are you going to do to me?" Sweat has broken out over my top lip, and I feel dizzy and nauseous from the blood loss.

I need to see a doctor, I need to make sure my baby is okay.

"It's a surprise." He grins. "But don't worry, I'll let your little friend over there live only so she can tell everyone how horrific your death was."

I glance over at Zara.

"Don't worry. I'll still have a little fun with her too."

"Please." I shake my head. "Leave her alone. Please!"

"No, I don't think I will. I'm a sucker for blondes."

"You won't get away with this." I pant, every breath making my chest ache with effort.

Gilanto only smirks at me, his eyes filled with feral delight as they roam over my shivering body.

"I already have, sweetheart, because everyone thinks you're dead," he chuckles as he gets to his feet.

The hair on the back of my neck stands up, and I swallow back the bile in my throat.

"Try not to die before I get to have my fun." He stalks from the room, leaving the door wide open as if to taunt us.

My stomach sinks as I think about Alexei.

Does he know we're missing yet?

My chest feels as if it's being cracked open at the thought of him getting to us too late, at what he might find when he does...

I look over at Zara, and my eyes sting as I watch her chest barely rise with each labored breath.

"You have to stay alive for me, Zara."

I try to fumble closer to her, but the chain attached to my wrist has no give, so I can't even hold my best friend's hand.

Her lips are bloodless, and her skin has turned almost gray.

She's in a bad way, and there's nothing I can do about it.

"Stay alive. You hear me, Zara? Stay alive."

"It'll be okay…" Zara mumbles. "Dimitri…"

"Dimitri? What about Dimitri?"

"Dimitri…help."

"How would he even know we're missing? Zara? *Zara*!"

I scream as Zara slumps further down the wall, her head lolling to the side.

31

ALEXEI

I could be too late.

Bianca could already be dead.

I'm sick to my stomach.

My *solnyshka*.

Zhizn' moya.

I can't lose her, not when we've barely gotten started. There's so much we have left to learn about each other, so much life left to enjoy together.

I won't let Mario Gilanto be the reason my family is torn apart.

My phone rings as I race toward Chinatown, the interstate a blur on either side of me as I push my foot to the floor.

I answer the call. "Anton."

"I'm already here. Dimitri just called and filled me in. I've brought backup."

"What's the status?"

"At least a dozen covering the exits, but they look like they don't know their asses from their elbows, so it should be a swift takeout. I'm betting on the same once we're inside."

"Any sign of Gilanto?" My body shudders at the sound of his name on my lips.

The fact that he managed to get his filthy, murderous hands on my *solnyshka* has me seeing red.

I'll have him begging for death by the time I'm finished with him.

"Not yet, but I doubt he would leave if he's got both the girls inside. He wants you to come to him."

"I know. How far out are the others?"

"Ten minutes. Fifteen tops."

I squeeze my hands into the leather of my steering wheel, my stomach feeling like lead as I look to the clock on my dashboard.

"*Fuck!*"

"I could send some of my men in now, but if Gilanto gets a whiff that you're not here, he might be inclined to send you a message."

"No one enters that property without my say. We can't afford to make any wrong moves. Gilanto is unpredictable."

"*Da, Pahkan.*" Anton hangs up the phone.

My body is running on autopilot as I cross back over into the city.

I barely notice the other cars coming toward me, or the lights as they turn red. All I can picture is my *solnyshka* bleeding out in my arms as she takes her last breath.

Was this how it was always meant to end? With death tapping on my shoulder the moment it could sense I was starting to live again? Ready to crack open my heart once more and leave me to bleed out too?

I glance at my navigation. I'm five minutes away from

the abandoned factory where Gilanto is holding Bianca and Zara prisoner.

I don't care how many people he has guarding the property, I won't hesitate to put a bullet into each and every one of their skulls if I have to. If it means saving Bianca, I will happily let their blood stain my hands.

As I approach the derelict, red-bricked property, I turn down a side alley where I know my brothers and men will be waiting.

I catch Anton's eye as I put the car in park.

He nods once.

They're ready to go.

Reaching across to the glove compartment, I pull out four magazines of bullets and another handgun which I load up.

It's likely I'm going to need them all.

I take a final deep breath as I exit the car and stalk toward my men. My family.

Dimitri's face is like stone.

"Is this everyone?"

My brother nods. "This is everyone."

I balance the gun in my hand, double-checking it as I think through the best course of action.

"Surround the property. Take out whoever you have to in order to get inside."

I look to each of my brothers, and then Anton, Feliks, and the dozen other men they've brought with them.

"Mikhail, Danil, you head around the back. Dimitri and I will take the front along with Feliks and Anton."

My two youngest brothers nod, their eyes filled with determination as they ready their weapons.

It's time to save my wife. "Don't leave anyone alive, and leave Gilanto to me."

"Let's move." Anton crouches low against the brick wall, gun at the ready.

"Ready?" Dimitri moves to stand at my side.

I flex my fingers before clicking the safety off my gun. "Ready."

"See you on the other side, *brat*." A feral grin spreads across his face as he claps a hand on my shoulder.

I take one last steadying breath, letting my eyes close for just a second as Mario Gilanto's face fills my mind.

"Let's go kill this son of a bitch," I snarl before rounding the corner and killing the first man.

Like roaches, Gilanto's men swarm from the shadows the moment the first shot is fired, their guns aimed as we surround the building.

Every time my finger pulls the trigger, and blood is spilled, my mind seems to quieten, my focus honed in on the task at hand.

I just need to get to Bianca.

Dimitri and the others can take care of the rest.

We storm the entrance, leaving a trail of bodies in our wake as we move through to the main factory floor.

It's cold and damp, the only light coming from a few fluorescent bulbs overhead. Old rusted machinery lines the factory floor, giving Gilanto's men plenty of places to hide.

A few of our own go down before we even know they're there.

I dive behind a metal pillar, panting as gunfire followed by shouts of pain echoes all around.

This is going to be quick and dirty.

I take out two more from behind the pillar before I make a run for the main floor, almost colliding with Dimitri.

Shots fire from overhead and I look up to find more men on the balcony above.

"Get down!" I yell, grabbing Dimitri by the back of the shirt and throwing us both to the floor where we take cover beneath an old work table.

"Fuck, they're everywhere," Dimitri wipes his brow with the back of his hand.

"I need to get to Bianca. I think they're below us."

"I'll cover your back."

I nod before getting to my feet and making a run for it.

Danil is to my right. He's fighting a guy almost twice his size.

Danil lands a punch to his jaw, knocking the guy's head to the side. As soon as he steps back to steady himself, I fire.

Danil's already moving before the guy has a chance to hit the floor.

I spot a set of double doors at the far end of the factory floor.

It's the only door that looks like it could take me to Bianca and Zara, so I head toward it.

A shout of pain has me whirling around to find my second youngest brother slumped over by one of the pillars, clutching at his shoulder.

"Mikhail!"

That second of distraction is enough.

An arm slithers around my neck, choking me.

I slam my elbow back into the fucker's stomach before sending my gun upwards to collide with his chin.

He goes down in an instant, groaning.

I put a bullet through his chest before rushing over to Mikhail.

"How bad is it?" I crouch beside him.

He glances up at me, his teeth gritted as blood seeps through his fingers. "I'm good. You need to go."

"You can't die on me." My voice shakes as I look at my little brother. I can't lose him too.

"It'll take more than this to take me down," he grits out. "Now, go. Save Bianca."

I clap my brother on his good shoulder before getting to my feet and sprinting across the factory floor.

Bodies are littered among the rusted machines, and the coppery twang of blood fills the air as I head toward the double doors at the far end of the factory floor.

Once I'm through the doors, I go left and down a flight of rickety iron stairs.

I sprint along a narrow corridor toward a second set of stairs at the far end that will lead to the basement. I take the stairs two at a time.

The sounds of gunshots are getting quieter.

The fight will soon be over.

I'm running out of time.

I creep along the damp corridor, my gun aimed and ready.

A few lights flicker overhead, and my footsteps echo around me.

"Gilanto! Why don't you grow some fucking balls and show your face!"

"I wondered when you were going to show up."

I whirl around.

Mario Gilanto steps out of the shadows, dragging Bianca in front of him, his left arm around her neck.

"It's simple, Alexei," he purrs as he pulls a gun from behind his back, holding it to Bianca's temple. "Put the gun down, or Bianca dies."

My eyes flick to Bianca's, and the air is stolen from my lungs at the terror in her eyes. Beads of sweat cover her forehead and her right arm is half hanging out of her sweater.

She's tied the sleeve around her forearm, the cream material stained red with her blood.

My *solnyshka* is hurt.

I have no choice but to do as he says. I won't risk her life.

Holding up both of my hands, I slowly bend down to place my gun at my feet.

"All of them." Gilanto smirks.

I look up.

The sight of his hands on Bianca makes me want to put a bullet straight between his eyes.

But I can't afford to make any mistakes, not when Bianca's life is on the line.

I reach into my jacket pocket and unholster my spare gun and toss it on the floor.

If it comes down to it, I'll kill the bastard with my bare hands. I'll probably get more satisfaction seeing the life drain from his eyes as I wrap my hands around his neck.

"I'm glad you came, Alexei. It wouldn't be nearly as fun to kill Bianca without an audience."

My lips pull back from my teeth as I glare at him.

"Let her go, Gilanto. We can settle this, just the two of us."

"I don't think so. Not now that I know you actually care for her. I'm very much looking forward to killing your wife and unborn child in front of your eyes, Koslov. Perhaps then you'll learn how it feels to lose something dear to you."

My nostrils flare at the mention of the baby.

"I am intrigued to learn how you found her so fast." Mario tilts his head to the side. "Enlighten me."

"Zara's phone. I tracked it here."

Mario snorts.

"Useless piece of shit she was. I should've tossed her in that burning wreck."

Was?

Did he kill Zara?

"Zara!" Bianca cries.

Time seems to slow as Mario struggles to hold Bianca upright.

Her legs buckle beneath her, her face contorted as she starts to slump to the floor.

I lunge, praying that I can catch her before she hits the floor, but Gilanto clocks my movements.

He thinks I'm reaching for my gun.

My eyes widen as he releases his hold on Bianca and takes aim right at my chest.

A gunshot rings through the air.

"No..." My hand tries to reach for Bianca as I wait for the bullet to find its mark.

But it never comes.

Gilanto's body jerks once before collapsing to the floor, revealing Dimitri behind him.

"Pretty good shot, huh?" Dimitri stalks forward to nudge Gilanto's lifeless body with his foot, but I barely register what he's saying.

I rush to Bianca's side, wrapping my arms around her shaking body and hauling her against my chest.

"*Solnyshku.*"

"Z-Zara," she sobs.

I look up at Dimitri, and his face pales as he reads my expression. Before I have a chance to say anything, he's sprinting away.

"How badly are you hurt, *zhizn' moya*?"

"M-my arm." She moans.

My chest tightens as I look down at the makeshift tourniquet she's made out of her sweater.

She clutches her left arm to her chest, and my eyes fall to the bruising that's starting to appear around her wrist.

Did Gilanto cuff her?

I grind my teeth together as I look at the limp body on the floor, at the blood pooling around his head.

His death was too quick, too easy.

He didn't suffer enough.

"We need to get them to the hospital, Alexei." Dimitri's voice is urgent behind me. "Zara's in pretty bad shape."

I whirl to find my brother's eyes full of fear as he looks down at Zara's limp body in his arms.

Her skin is ashen and covered in sweat, and there's a huge gash on her head that is still oozing blood.

"Zara." Bianca's croaked voice snaps me back to the present.

"Dimitri has her, don't worry." I kiss her forehead. "We need to get you to the hospital, *solnyshka*."

Bianca screws her eyes shut, the last of the color draining from her face. "Please. Don't let Zara die."

"I'm not letting either one of you die. That's a promise."

32

BIANCA

"*Zhizn' moya.*"

I miss Alexei so much I can almost hear him calling me that strange endearment. What does it mean? I still don't know.

Will I ever learn? Will I ever see him again? Ever feel his skin beneath my fingertips or his lips on mine?

The man I was forced to marry is now the man I love.

That thought should scare me before, but not now.

I'm dying in this hole, so I'm allowing myself to fully love him.

Alexei Koslov is my everything.

Lips press to my forehead, and I let out a contented sigh imagining it's Alexei as my eyelids flutter open.

Wow, I must be dead already...

Alexei is leaning over me, his brow furrowed as he searches my face.

"Welcome back." He smiles.

Beeping sounds fill my ears, and I have to blink a few times for my eyes to focus under the harsh fluorescent lights.

I look around.

This is a hospital room.

I look down at my arm and wince at the sight of the bandages on my left forearm and the dark purple bruising around my wrist from the metal cuff.

My joints feel stiff, and my head feels cloudy, but I'm alive.

I'm alive?

My eyes fly to Alexei.

I survived. And he is here with me.

But wait...

"The...baby." My hands move to my abdomen.

"The baby is fine." Alexei places a warm hand on top of mine. "You're both going to be fine."

"W-what about Zara?"

Alexei hesitates, his brown eyes filled with sorrow as he looks at me, but he's not given the chance to explain as the door to my room opens and in walks a young woman wearing pink scrubs.

She offers me a warm smile as she approaches the end of the bed.

"It's good to see you awake, Bianca. I'm Dr. Keller, the OBGYN on call. I just want to do a quick ultrasound."

I nod, eager to see for myself that my baby is okay.

As Dr. Keller sets up the monitor beside the bed, I turn to face Alexei.

"Where is Zara?"

Alexei reaches up to cup my face, his thumb rubbing back and forth across my cheek.

His silence is only making me more nervous. What is he not telling me?

"She's in surgery. She had quite a few internal injuries as well as a broken arm."

"Oh god." My hand flies to my mouth. "I need to see her." I throw back the blanket, but Alexei places a hand on my shoulder, forcing me back against the pillows.

"Bianca. Right now there's nothing you can do for her. Dimitri is there, okay?"

"I can't lose her, Alexei." A sob rips from my chest.

"You won't." He wraps his arms around my shoulders and pulls me against his chest.

Dr. Keller readies the ultrasound probe. "I'm going to need you to please remain calm, Bianca. For the sake of your baby. All the stress is bad for them."

"Can we please let the doctor check on our baby, *zhizn' moya*?"

I pull back to look into Alexei's dark eyes and focus on the sound of his breathing to help try and calm my racing heart.

My baby has already been through so much in the past twenty-four hours, and I don't want to cause it any more stress, but I'm terrified of losing Zara.

Dr. Keller looks at me, probe at the ready. "Are you ready, Bianca?"

Alexei offers me an encouraging smile, and I nod.

"I'm ready."

The moment Dr. Keller points out the tiny blob that is our baby, I can't contain my tears.

My cheeks are damp, and it only worsens when a soft *thump thump* fills the silence.

"Incredible," Alexei whispers.

I look up at him, and his eyes are filled with wonder as he looks at the screen, at the tiny miracle that is half him, half me.

"Everything looks good. But you need to watch your stress levels."

I nod. "I will."

"I'll print this image for you, and I'll be back to check on you in a few hours." Dr. Keller removes the ultrasound probe after pressing a few buttons and hands us the printed image.

Once I'm all cleaned up, Alexei climbs into the bed beside me and pulls me against his chest as we both gaze at the first picture of our baby.

"You're going to be the most amazing mother." He kisses the top of my head. "And I can't wait to be a father."

My heart feels fit to bursting at his words.

"Really?"

"Really. Now try and get some sleep, *zhizn' moya*. Zara should be out of surgery soon."

I don't know how long I sleep for but when I finally open my eyes again, Dimitri and Alexei are talking in hushed tones in the corner.

I try to sit straighter in bed. "Is it Zara?"

Dimitri turns to face me and offers me a weak smile.

"She's out of surgery." He looks exhausted, with dark purple shadows under his eyes and dried blood on his shirt. "She's got a long way to go, but she's stable."

"Oh, thank god." It's like a huge weight lifts from my shoulders, and I'm able to breathe again. "I need to see her."

Alexei glances at Dimitri who shrugs.

"I'll go and find a wheelchair."

I try my best to stay calm as Alexei and Dimitri wheel me to Zara's room.

She's hooked up to multiple machines, and her arm is in

a cast. She looks so small compared to the strong, outspoken girl I know and love.

"We'll be just outside." Alexei parks me beside the bed and presses a kiss to my head.

I keep my eyes on Zara, and the door closing has her eyes fluttering open.

My breath catches as I reach for her hand, squeezing her fingers gently. "You're awake."

Zara offers me a weak smile, her eyes still half closed as she turns to look at me.

"Oh, Zara. I was so worried about you."

"Y-you can't get r-rid of me that e-easily." She squeezes my fingers weakly.

"You can't ever leave me, you hear?"

"Never."

Tears blur my eyes as I cling to my friend.

"I'm s-so sorry, Bianca." A tear spills down the side of her face. "If I hadn't...called you out...that night—"

"They would've found another way to take me." I squeeze her hand tighter. "This isn't your fault. If anything, you were dragged into my mess. I'm the one who needs to apologize."

"It's okay, B. But... What happened? I barely... remember anything."

I look at my best friend, my eyes roaming over the cast on her arm and the stitches on her forehead.

Tears prick my eyes as I realize how close I was to losing her.

"All you need to know is that we're okay now." I hold her hand tight. "Alexei and Dimitri got us out in time."

"W-what about the man who..." Zara's throat bobs, and I give her fingers a squeeze.

"Dimitri took care of him. He's the one who got you out."

I don't fail to notice the slight pink tinge to Zara's cheeks at the mention of Dimitri.

"I think someone might be warming to him after all..." I try to lighten the tone.

Zara huffs, narrowing her eyes at me.

"Hardly. He's...not my...type."

I shrug, but I can't stop the smile that spreads across my face as my hand goes to rest on the slight swell of my belly.

"Alexei wasn't my type, either..."

Dr. Keller keeps me in the hospital for two more days to monitor the baby's heartbeat.

I do my best to keep my stress levels down, though it's hard to do when I'm so worried about Zara.

She's likely to need to stay for a few more weeks as she recovers, and I plan on being by her side as much as I can.

Though according to Alexei, I'm being put on bed rest the moment he takes me back to Forest Hills.

Mikhail is also being kept under observation for a few more days.

I was horrified to learn of his injury, but Alexei assured me that the bullet only grazed his shoulder, and he'll make a full recovery. If anything he's a little disappointed that he didn't have a more dramatic injury, which Alexei says is 'typical Mikhail'.

I'm packing up my things while Alexei signs my discharge papers when a knock sounds at my hospital room door.

"Come in." I fold my pajamas.

Poor Alexei sent Danil to the house to get supplies for me and Zara, and I laughed so hard when he came back with enough clothes to last the year.

The door clicks shut, and I glance up and let out a squeal. "*Papino?*"

"*Bambina.*" He looks thin, and his blue eyes have dark purple shadows beneath them.

"*Papino.*" I rush over to him, throwing my arms around his neck. "I thought you were dead! Gilanto... H-he implied..." I can't even bear to speak the words.

"I'm so sorry, *bambina*," my father whispers as he takes me in his arms and holds me close like he did when I was a child. "I had no choice but to disappear."

"You could've told me." I pull back to look him in the eyes.

"I couldn't risk you knowing, *bambina*. Gilanto is...*was* a dangerous man, and I made an enemy of him the moment I sold information on his family to Alexei. But I had to make sure that you would be taken care of."

My father's eyes shine with tears as he takes my face in his hands. "I hope you can understand that I did it for you, Bianca."

"I never needed protection, *Papino.*"

My dad lets out a breath and drops his hands from my face.

I shake my head. "Especially not when it came at such a price."

"I thought there was no other way. I'm sorry for causing you pain, *bambina*. I will carry the guilt with me for the rest of my life." His shoulders sag.

"I understand." I place a hand on my stomach. "I know now what it feels like to want to do everything in your power to protect your child. So, I forgive you, *Papino*. For all of it."

My father's blue eyes shine with tears as they widen. "*Bambina...?*"

"It all worked out in the end, *Papino*." A smile tugs at my lips. "I hope you'll stick around long enough to meet this *piccolino?*"

"I wouldn't miss it for the world, *bambina*."

"Are you ready to go?" Alexei asks an hour later.

My father stayed with me as I packed up my things, and we spoke about my new life with Alexei.

I told him about the studio he built and the portrait of *Mamma* that I had been working on.

By the time he left, there was a brightness in his eyes that hadn't been there before.

I hope that, despite everything that's happened, my dad and I can work on having a closer relationship, not just for my sake but for my child's too.

I look over to Alexei, and my stomach knots.

He must be able to sense a change as a frown appears between his eyebrows.

"What is it?" He crosses the room and takes my hands in his.

"Can I ask you something?"

"Of course."

"Did you know about my father going into hiding?"

Alexei lets out a long breath, and I watch as his eyes fill with sorrow.

"I did." He bows his head.

"Why didn't you tell me?"

"It wasn't my place."

"Alexei, he's my father!"

"And telling you would have compromised his safety. I made a promise to keep him safe too, Bianca, and this was the only way."

"When will we learn that secrets aren't good for us?"

"I promise from here on out, there will be no more secrets." Alexei brings our entwined fingers up to his lips, pressing a soft kiss to my knuckles. "Now, let's get you home."

"I don't want to leave Zara here alone. What if someone comes after her? What if—"

"Shh..." Alexei wraps his arm around me and cradles me against his chest. "Dimitri has promised to stay with her. So, let me take you home, *solnyshka*, so you can rest."

Alexei grabs my bag off the bed.

"I feel like I've done nothing but rest for days."

"And you will continue to rest for the next few weeks." Alexei presses a kiss to my forehead.

I sleep most of the drive back to Forest Hills, the weight of the last few days finally taking its toll. I wish Zara was leaving with me, but I know she'll be in good hands with Dimitri.

When I finally open my eyes, the sight of the familiar house brings a smile to my lips. "Home sweet home."

Alexei puts the Mercedes in park and comes round to my door, reaching over me to unbuckle my seatbelt.

I go to step out, but he quickly bends down and scoops me into his arms.

"Alexei! You don't have to carry me up to bed!"

"Doctor's orders." Alexei chuckles, bending down to nuzzle my neck.

I wriggle against him, but he only holds me tighter against his chest.

I scoff. "I am more than capable of walking by myself."

"This is one thing I won't negotiate on, *zhizn' moya*." Alexei starts to climb the front steps.

I snuggle into his chest, savoring the warmth of his body against mine as he carries me all the way to my room where he settles me in the bed and climbs in beside me.

"You had me worried there for a while." He pulls me against his chest. "If anything had happened to you... to the baby..."

The breath catches in his throat, and my chest feels as if it's being cracked in two.

"We're safe, Alexei." I reach up to cup his face.

He leans into my touch, his eyes fluttering closed as if to savor my touch.

"You won't ever lose me. I promise."

"That reminds me." He turns his face to press a kiss to my palm. "I have something for you."

I watch with intrigue as Alexei reaches into his jacket pocket and pulls out a ring box.

My eyes go wide as he opens it up to reveal a diamond engagement ring and two matching wedding bands.

"Alexei..." I stare at the rings. "They're beautiful."

"I thought it was about time I put a ring on your finger." He chuckles. "*Zhizn' moya*, would you do me the greatest honor of being my wife, again?"

"Yes!" My hand goes to my mouth as Alexei pulls out my two rings and slides them onto my finger.

"I love you, *zhizn' moya*. More than I ever thought possible. Thank you so much for making me the happiest man alive every single day." He kisses my ring finger as soon as he is done.

"Now, would you like to do the honors?" Alexei holds out the box with his wedding band.

"I love you so much, Alexei." I can barely see through the tears as I take the ring and slide it onto his finger. "When this whole thing started, I was just so mad. At you, at my dad, at the world. Thank you so much for being patient with me and supporting my dreams even when I made your life hell. I'll love you forever."

Not too long ago, I wanted nothing more than to have my old life back. But as I look into Alexei's eyes, I know that a life without him is not one I want to live.

I grin. "Does this mean I can plan a wedding I actually want to be in this time?"

33

BIANCA

Five Months Later

A knock sounds on my bedroom door, and I look up from doing my makeup to find Alexei leaning in the doorway.

My breath catches in my throat as I take him in.

He's all mine.

"Are you ready?" He pushes off the doorframe and crosses the room toward me.

My eyes flick over his body, my hormones going into overdrive as I take in his towering frame.

He's wearing his signature black shirt and pants, with the shirt sleeves rolled to the elbows, exposing those delicious forearms.

"Almost." I wrinkle my nose as I glance down at myself.

"What's the matter?"

"I feel like a beached whale." I run my hands over my enormous bump.

I chose to wear a form-fitting turquoise gown to show off the bump, but now that we're about to leave, all I want to do is hide under a pair of baggy sweats.

"You look..." Alexei puts his hands on my waist, pulling me to him. "Fucking gorgeous."

He leans down to press a kiss to my neck, and I let out a contented sigh, leaning into his touch.

Goosebumps spread across my skin and a whimper escapes me as he pulls away.

"If fifty of our closest friends and family weren't arriving downstairs now for this baby shower, I would be fucking you against the dressing table." His eyes glance down to take in my very full breasts that are almost spilling out of my dress.

Warmth pools in my lower belly as I picture him bending me over the table and fucking me from behind.

"Would anyone really notice if we were a few minutes late..." I run my hands up his chest, sinking my fingers into the soft fabric.

"Zhizn' moya," he chuckles.

I love it when he calls me that. My life. I grin. "What? It's our party, we can be late if we want to."

I reach up on my tiptoes to press a kiss to his jaw. "We can make it quick."

Alexei's fingers dig into my waist, and I squeal as he spins me around.

"I better get to work, then." He fists the silky fabric of my dress and lifts it up over my ass. "Bend over, *solnyshka*."

I bite my lower lip as I move to rest my elbows on my dressing table, pushing my ass up higher in the air.

This is the only way we've been able to have sex since my bump has become so huge, but I don't care.

At this angle, Alexei hits me so deep, and that mixed with the hormones means my orgasms are the most intense I've ever experienced.

Alexei makes quick work of pulling down my panties,

and I'm already moaning with anticipation as he undoes his pants.

By the time his cock teases my entrance, I'm so wet and aching for him that I push back, forcing him to sink into me all the way.

"*Fuck.*" Alexei's hands hang tight to my waist.

I moan so loudly I'm worried all of our guests might hear, but I'm soon forgetting about them when Alexei pulls out and slams back into me.

I press my chest flush against the desk, my aching nipples rubbing against the hard surface with each thrust.

"Feels so good," I groan.

"Do you want more, *solnyshka*?"

"God, *yes.*"

Alexei thrusts into me harder as his fingers reach around to start working my clit.

My body goes limp as my orgasm starts to build with each thrust of his thick cock.

"You're taking me so well, *zhizn' moya.*"

My eyelids flutter closed as he works my clit faster, and I know it won't take much more to send me crashing over the edge.

"Harder," I moan.

Alexei chuckles, but he wraps his free hand around my waist to steady me as he increases his pace.

My legs start to shake as warmth pools in my lower belly, and my thighs become slick with arousal.

"Fuck. I'm coming," Alexei grunts, and with one more thrust, he sends us both crashing over the edge.

"I feel like everyone's going to be able to tell we've just had sex." I sigh as I straighten my dress once we've cleaned up.

Alexei pulls me against him and crashes his lips against mine, letting his tongue trace along my lower lip.

"I like the idea of everyone knowing who you belong to," Alexei murmurs against my lips.

"Stop." I push against his chest. "Otherwise, we're never going to make it to the party."

Alexei smirks and flashes me a wink.

"Let's go and celebrate you." He holds out his hand for me to take.

I cling to Alexei's arm for support as we make our way out of the room.

"Oh my god. I forgot to tell you something."

His eyes fly to mine. "What is it? Are you feeling okay? Is the baby—"

I wave my hand. "No, no. The baby is amazing. It's just... guess who is getting married."

He frowns, shaking his head. "I have no idea. Who?"

"Rosanna."

His frown deepens. "Who the hell is that? Am I supposed to know this Rosanna?"

I hit his arm. "I'd say you more than should. It was her supposed wedding I was planning when I arrived to find out I was getting married instead."

His brows go up, his mouth ajar, then he bursts out laughing. "Does that mean you are planning another wedding?"

"Hell, no."

As we start down the stairs, a huge grin spreads across my face as I take in all of our friends and family who are gathered in the foyer.

Grinning, I spot Mikhail, Danil, and Dimitri.

They really have started to feel like my family over the

past few months, and I'm so grateful that my son is going to grow up with so many people who love him.

My eyes move just past Dimitri, and I let out a squeal as I spot Zara.

"Careful, *solnyshka*." Alexei helps me down the last few steps.

Zara is already forcing her way through the crowd, so the moment my feet are on solid ground, she throws her arms around my neck and holds me tightly, or as tightly as she can considering the size of my bump.

I pull away to put my hands on Zara's shoulders, glancing over her once to make sure she's really okay. "I missed you! I can't believe you made it."

After the attack, she spent weeks in the hospital recovering from her surgery and healing from the internal injuries she'd suffered. It was heartbreaking to see her in so much pain, but I spent every moment I could by her side until she was discharged a few weeks ago.

"Of course I came." Zara laughs. "It's your baby shower!"

"I know, but I didn't want you overexerting yourself."

"I think I'm the one who should be saying that to you, B." Zara chuckles, wrapping an arm around my waist. "Not long to go now."

"Eight weeks." I place a hand on my growing bump.

"It's gone by so fast! I swear that always happens when it's other people's babies. When I'm pregnant, I bet the months are going to feel like years."

"It would be so worth it because our kids could grow up together, so you better get to work." I knock my hip against hers. "I'm sure Dimitri would be more than happy to offer his services."

"Oh my god," Zara groans.

"I'm just saying..."

"I don't think I'm ready to give up champagne just yet. Speaking of which, I need a refill. Go and mingle, we can chat later."

Zara presses a kiss to my cheek, and the moment she steps away, an arm wraps around my waist and a warm body presses against my back.

"Hello, *zhizn' moya*."

My eyes flutter closed for a moment as I let myself become enveloped in Alexei's musky scent.

"Mmm..." I reach behind me to run my hands through Alexei's hair.

His hot breath is in my ear. "You're not ready for round two, are you?"

I wiggle against him and let out a soft gasp as I find him already hard. "Blame it on the pregnancy. It'll be the one thing I miss."

"As much as I would like to whisk you away back upstairs, we should probably go and greet the rest of our guests."

"Only if I can open presents after." I pout, tilting my head back so I can look at Alexei.

Every time I look at him, he takes my breath away. I never thought I could be so lucky, and the fact that we're so close to bringing a child into this world makes my heart want to burst.

We came so close to losing it all, and I will never stop being grateful that everything turned out all right in the end.

Alexei presses a quick kiss to my lips and when I pull away, I spot Dimitri heading our way.

"Fatherhood looks good on you, *brat*." Dimitri claps Alexei on the shoulder. "You're going to be a great dad."

"Thanks, Dimitri."

"But what about you, Dimitri? Do you see yourself with kids one day? This little guy will need some cousins to play with."

Dimitri throws his head back and laughs.

"Let's not get ahead of ourselves. Right now, I'll settle for being the cool uncle."

"You could always be the cool godfather..." I fight a smile as I catch Alexei's eye.

"Seriously?" Dimitri glances between us.

Alexei nods. "It was Bianca's idea."

"I... I would be honored!" A huge smile spreads across his face as he reaches down to hug me. "Whoa, this means a lot."

Tears start to prick at my eyes as Dimitri gives Alexei a hug.

Danil laughs as he approaches our little group. "Uh oh, Bianca's crying already."

"These are happy tears." I wipe at my eyes.

Alexei takes me by the hand. "Why don't we go and mingle some more?"

He leads me away from his brothers before I get even more emotional.

Once everyone's a few glasses of champagne deep into the party, the twinkling of a spoon hitting a glass causes the room to quiet.

"Speech!" Danil and Mikhail call out.

I whirl to find Dimitri standing halfway up the stairs, a glass of champagne in his hand as he grins down at us all.

I groan. "Please tell me he isn't about to do a drunken speech at my baby shower."

Alexei chuckles. "I guess we're about to find out."

"Good evening, everyone!" Dimitri calls out. "I just

wanted to take a moment to congratulate my brother and his wonderful wife on the impending birth of their baby boy. When I look at the both of you, it's hard to deny that you've found the sort of true love we only thought was possible in fairy tales."

Blinking back tears, I glance at Alexei who's smiling down at me with such awe that my chest might explode.

I squeeze his hand tightly before looking back at Dimitri, whose attention is no longer on us, but on Zara.

"If I ever get the chance to experience even a fraction of what you both share, I'll consider myself a lucky man."

I sneak a look over at Zara, but my best friend is wrinkling her nose at Dimitri's words.

"Keep dreaming!" she calls out, and the room erupts into laughter.

Dimitri dips his chin, his shoulders shaking with silent laughter.

I shake my head. "Poor Dimitri."

Alexei grins. "Zara will give him a run for his money, that's for sure."

"They would make such a cute couple, though..."

"Don't meddle." Alexei presses a kiss to my hair.

I go to tilt my head up to capture his lips, but his phone starts vibrating in his pocket.

"Hold that thought." He nudges his nose against mine before reaching into his pocket and pulling out his phone.

As soon as he glances at the screen, his jaw tightens.

This is not good.

34

ALEXEI

I hate to leave Bianca's side, but I can't ignore this call from my private investigator.

Frederik's been looking into my father's alleged adultery for the past few weeks, and I've been anxious to confirm whether what Ricci said is true.

Slipping away from the party, I head upstairs to my office. I can't risk my brothers overhearing this conversation. I still haven't shared the allegations with them, and I don't plan to until I know for sure whether it's true.

"Talk to me, Frederik." I close the door to my office behind me.

"There's no easy way to tell you this, Alexei."

"Just tell me, Frederik. Whatever it is, I can take it."

My chest tightens as Frederik takes a deep breath on the other end of the line.

"Alexei, Ricci was telling the truth. Your father had a secret affair before you were born."

My stomach sinks, and I fight the urge to launch my phone across the room.

"Who with?"

"Igor Ivanov's wife."

"*Fuck.*" I run my free hand through my hair. "Are you certain?"

"Yes."

My stomach drops, and I have to sink down into one of the armchairs before my legs have a chance to give out.

It was all true.

All this time, I had looked to my parents as the perfect example of a marriage. One that I hoped to aspire to have with Bianca.

They were the picture of happiness, or so I thought.

"Is this connected to the Russian properties my father gave to Igor?"

"It's very likely."

I screw my eyes shut as I try to ignore all the thoughts that are forcing their way into my head.

"Okay, thanks for letting me know, Frederik."

Hanging up the phone, I let out a long breath as I glance around the office that once belonged to my father, the man who put family above everything.

"Fuck." I run my hands over my face.

How am I meant to tell my brothers that our father cheated on our mother?

But that is not something that will happen today.

If I'm gone for much longer, Bianca will start to worry where I am, and today is about her, and I'm going to keep it that way.

This news about my father will have to wait.

I head back to the party and plaster a smile on my face as I go in search of Bianca.

She's hovering near the food table, picking at a plate of fruit.

The way her eyes light up when she sees me almost sends me to my knees.

How did I get so lucky?

"Is everything okay, Alexei?"

I reach up to tuck her hair behind her ear and bend down to press my lips to hers.

"With you by my side, things couldn't be more perfect."

At least something in my life is right. If only the rest of it ran as smoothly...

EPILOGUE
ALEXEI

Bianca is glowing. "I can't believe he's finally here. He's perfect."

I press a kiss to her hair and smile down at the sleeping baby in her arms.

"You did amazing, *zhizn' moya*."

She turns to look up at me, her blue eyes shining.

My finger caresses her cheek. "Are you happy?"

"So happy I feel like I could explode." She chuckles.

My eyes start to sting with tears as I watch my newborn son sleeping peacefully in my wife's arms.

I never knew I could love like this. I knew becoming a father would change me, but I had been so focused on the negative. That I would fail him in every possible way, that I wouldn't be able to protect him from the world.

But as I look at Bianca, knowing she's by my side through this journey, she gives me the confidence that I can do this, and do this well.

"Who would've thought a year ago that we would be here today." I chuckle as I stroke the dark tufty hair on my son's head.

Bianca laughs. "Definitely, not me."

"You didn't picture it the moment you chased me into that elevator?" I smirk.

Bianca scoffs, swatting at my chest. "I did not chase you down."

"If you say so..."

"Did you picture it?" She looks up at me under her dark lashes.

I cup her face, running my thumb over her bottom lip as I gaze at her.

"The moment we exchanged vows, I knew that this was going to be so much more than a business deal. You were everything I didn't realize I had been looking for, Bianca."

"Alexei..." Her voice cracks.

"I knew I was going to have my work cut out." I chuckle. "But there was never a moment where I thought it wouldn't be worth it."

She laughs though her eyes shine with tears. "Look at you getting all soppy."

"I love you, Bianca. More than I ever thought possible." I bend down to kiss away the tears that have spilled down her cheeks. "Thank you for bringing such light into my darkness, *solnyshka*."

Bianca reaches her hand to cup the back of my neck and presses her lips to mine.

Dimitri knocks on the door. "Can we come in now?"

I chuckle against Bianca's lips as Danil and Mikhail mutter in the background.

"Are you ready for visitors?" I search Bianca's face to make sure she's okay. "I can tell them to go away."

"It's fine." She smiles. "I'm excited for this little guy to meet the family."

I give Bianca one last peck on the mouth before sliding

off the bed and striding across the room to let my brothers in.

"About time." Dimitri scoffs, barging past me to go to Bianca's side. "Congrats, Bianca," He kisses the top of her head.

"Do I not get congratulations?" I close the door behind Mikhail and Danil who are hovering.

"Fuck no, you literally did none of the work. This is all Bianca's work."

"True." I laugh as I head back over to the bed and perch on the end, looking at Bianca. "Do you want to tell them his name?"

She smiles before glancing at each of my brothers.

"Everyone, this is Leonid Emilio Koslov. Baby Leo, meet your uncles." She strokes his cheek.

"We're going to give him a very thorough education when the time comes." Dimitri grins at Bianca.

I shake my head. "God help this child."

Bianca catches my eye and grins. "Now you just need to hurry up and give him some cousins. Otherwise poor Leo here is going to get lonely in such a big house."

I swallow my laughter as Dimitri's face pales.

I chuckle. "You're going to give Dimitri a heart attack."

"I just delivered a baby. Let me have some fun."

I glance over my shoulder at my two youngest brothers who are still hovering by the door.

Mikhail looks like he wants to be anywhere else, but Danil is looking at Leo with nothing but wonder in his eyes.

I smile and nod at him. "You can hold him, you know?"

"Really?" Danil looks at Bianca.

"Of course!"

"Let me." I scoop up Leo and carry him over to Danil who takes him into his arms. "You're a natural, Danil."

My youngest brother shrugs, a faint blush coloring his cheeks.

I shake my head. "I remember when you were that small."

"Really?"

Dimitri laughs. "You looked like an alien."

Danil glares at him. "Fuck off."

I shake my head. "You looked a lot like Leo, actually. Lots of hair and a wrinkly forehead."

Dimitri laughs, clapping me on the shoulder. "Sorry, *brat*, but I think he looks just like Bianca."

Mikhail peers over Danil's shoulder to get a closer look at the baby. "Just as well."

Bianca scoffs. "Are you saying I have a wrinkly forehead?"

"Uh..." Dimitri looks to me for help, but I shrug.

"I'm not getting involved in this."

Mikhail looks at me. "He's definitely got the Koslov chin. You can't deny who fathered him."

Danil sighs. "Poor kid, having to grow up to look like Alexei."

I shake my head, smiling. "You're all assholes."

Mikhail shrugs. "Just speaking the truth, *brat*. Just because you have a son now doesn't give you a get out of jail free card when it comes to piss-taking."

Dimitri laughs. "If anything, it's going to get worse."

Mikhail smirks. "So much worse. Now, come on, let me hold my nephew."

As I help maneuver Leo from Danil's arms to Mikhail's, sniffling comes from behind us.

I turn around to find Bianca wiping her eyes.

"What's wrong?" I come to perch on the bed beside her.

She shakes her head and offers me a watery smile.

"It's just..." She gazes at Leo who's now being held like a football by Mikhail. "I've always wanted a big family, and now I have one."

I laugh. "Trust me, you won't be saying that when these idiots are over every damn day. You'll never have another moment of peace."

"I don't want a quiet house. So, I want you all to know that just because Alexei and I have chosen to reside there most of the time, the mansion is still very much your home too, so stay as long as you want. But if you're there, you help change diapers."

"Yeah, no. I'm out." Mikhail hands me back the baby.

I laugh. "Well, that's one way of getting rid of them."

Dimitri smiles. "We should leave you to rest. Congrats again."

Once everyone has gone, I hand Leo back to Bianca and shuffle in closer so that I can pull her against my chest.

As I stroke her hair, I watch Leo sleep, and my heart feels like it's fit to burst.

"Thank you for being mine," I whisper against Bianca's hair. "You make me the happiest man alive, and I want you to know that even if the vows we exchanged were spoken under 'unusual' circumstances, I meant every single one of them. I will love you, cherish you, take care of you, and our son, for as long as we both shall life and not even death will tear us apart."

She looks up at me and smiles, a tear sliding down her face.

"Though we are lacking the witnesses here, I too vow to love you, cherish you, take care of you and our son, for as long as we both shall live. I love you so much, Alexei Koslov."

"I love you too, *zhizn' moya*. My life."

Printed in Dunstable, United Kingdom